BEYOND The CROOKED LIMB

May God bless you all of your days.

MLputnam

"In the beginning God created the heaven and the earth.
And the earth was without form, and void; and
darkness was upon the face of the deep. And the Spirit
of God moved upon the face of the waters."
(Genesis 1: 1-2 KJV)

BEYOND
The
CROOKED LIMB

A novel by

Marsha Bingham Putnam

Beyond the Crooked Limb

Published by Bingham Putnam Publishing
Copyright © 2004 by Marsha Putnam
International Standard Book Number: 0-9760504-0-4

Overseer, the Lord who is all bountiful and all sufficient

Advisor and general support, William J. Putnam

Cover design and creation, Angela Marcine Putnam

Photography, Max L. Hoskins II

marshaputnam.com design and creation,
Vincent Wallace Putnam

Editorial work Martha & Vincent Putnam

For information:

Bingham Putnam Publishing, 326 Newport Drive # 1710, Naples, Florida 34114

Dedicated to Mom and Dad:

*Lynn Bingham and Marcine Mead Bingham
who taught me to love God and who gave me an
appreciation for the beauty of
His created world.*

With deepest appreciation to:

The Lord for giving me the vision and ability to create this work

My husband, Bill, for his love, wisdom and encouragement

My children, Max, Vincent, Angela & daughter-in-law, Martha
for their support and time.

Written for:

My grandchildren, Lilly and Grace

My family and friends and all readers everywhere

Beyond the Crooked Limb — a gripping tale set in the Florida Everglades — has both action and fantasy. The characters drew me into the story and made me feel like a member of the family. It was an entertaining distraction from my hectic schedule.
- **Mr. Art Allen, CEO Allen Systems Group, Inc., Naples Florida**

Marsha Putnam's dialogue puts you right in the middle of an exciting world she has created. Her knowledge of Florida, the ability to spin an engrossing tale, and characters we care about make *Beyond the Crooked Limb* worth reading.
- **Carmen Leal, author of six books including *The Twenty-Third Psalm for Caregivers***

Beyond the Crooked Limb is a fanciful and entertaining story of people interacting with wildlife in South Florida. Because communication barriers are broken, they are able to come to each other's aid and help preserve the natural environment. A wonderful tale, especially for the area's residents to share with their grandchildren.
- **Deborah Jansen, Wildlife Biologist.**

No wimping out in this adventure. *Beyond the Crooked Limb*, you were there!
- **Pastor Don and Mrs. Toni Tomei, Restoration Church, Naples, Florida**

The book, *Beyond the Crooked Limb*, is an exciting and interesting fantasy-adventure story that takes you deep into the Florida Everglades, and gives you a special look at the endangered species that live there. I especially enjoyed reading *Beyond the Crooked Limb* because I am from Florida. Also, it was very captivating to read. From the very beginning it catches your attention, and holds it there.

- Heather Zimmerman, age 17, senior of Estero High School, Estero, FL.

We were very please to present *Beyond the Crooked Limb* in serialized form to the readers of *The Marco Islander*. Marsha Putnam's story about family, faith and Florida's environment touched a chord with our readers, who let us know they were eagerly looking forward to new chapters each week.

- Kim Folstad, Editor, *The Marco Islander*

The author's immigration and writing style were enjoyable and refreshing. The story line and description of the Florida Everglades and wildlife were remarkable and realistic. *Beyond the Crooked Limb* is an interesting story for ages from junior high through adult.

- Louise Hodson, Retired Elementary Teacher
- Robert Hodson, Retired High School Principal

The Lord says, "Stand by the roads and watch. Ask for the ancient paths; learn of the good way and walk in it. Then you will find rest for your souls."

(Jeremiah 6:16 paraphrased)

Inspired by Ernest Henry,

A great blue heron

South Florida

Lake Okeechoee

Naples

75

Fort Lauderdale

Big Cypress National Preserve

Grand Island

Ten Thousand Islands

Everglades City

41

Miami

Banyan City

Chokoloskee Bay

Everglades National Park

997

Gulf of Mexico

Flamingo

Hwy 1

Key West

CHAPTER 1

Tom turned his old blue pickup onto the highway and headed north. The lights of Flamingo twinkled behind him; ahead stretched Everglades National Park and the whole of Florida.

A big man with long arms, Tom cranked the driver-side window down then reached across to the passenger side and did the same. Cool air burst into the cab, swooshed across his brown face and tousled his straight black hair.

He steered with his knee and poured coffee from a Thermos into a chipped mug with a faded sheriff's star on the side. Pungent steam rose from the coffee to condense on the inside of his bug-splattered windshield.

On the outside of the window morning dawned across the Everglades. A yellow-orange sun blazed into the eastern sky and rose over the River of Grass. This 50-mile-wide shallow river of fresh water and saw grass yawned and stretched as wood storks set out from twiggy nests to soar above its waking vista.

Below them an alligator's snout, flanked by hooded eyes, emerged from a freshwater pond. The gator's greenish-brown orbs studied a great blue heron that stood belly deep in golden saw grass. The heron clutched a snake
in its beak; the snake, attempting to wind its body around the heron's neck, writhed and fought for its life.

The glory of creation shouted from both sky and earth, yet Tom, his smoky gray eyes filled with anger and bitterness, missed it. He clenched the steering wheel fiercely. What did those rotten sleazebags want with his daughter, and why hadn't they contacted someone, anyone, with their demands? Surely there were phones, smoke signals or something — even in the bush country of Africa. Tom refused to believe the embassy's story about the Mara River and the sleeping crocodiles — well-fed crocodiles as the ambassador's aid had put it — on its banks.

"If they touch a hair, one hair, on her head," Tom yelled to the River of Grass. "Someone is going to pay. Boiling them in oil is too good for them."

Tom snapped on the radio and the words of *Amazing Grace* drifted from the speakers. He snapped it off and slouched in his seat. He attended church when he was a kid, even remembered the Sunday he'd made an altar call. His faith moved mountains back then. But now, now what remained couldn't dismantle an anthill. What happened? Time passed; he drifted from belief, to laws and religion, then to disillusionment. But his defining moment had been the news from Africa.

"Africa!" Tom said, pounding the steering wheel. "Africa happened."

Fury once again raged inside Tom, and his foot pressed heavier on the gas pedal. Old Blue's oversized tires whined against smooth blacktop. His wide-brimmed raffia hat slid forward on the dash. Road signs, warning of an upcoming turn, flew by unnoticed. Then Tom entered the crossroads. Halfway through it, familiarity with his surroundings jolted him into awareness.

More from instinct than conscious effort he jerked the steering wheel left, but due to speed and sharpness of the turn, Newton's first law of motion took control. The back tires, fighting to go straight, failed to follow the front tires around the corner, and the truck began a sideways skid toward a water-filled canal.

Dislodged by the abrupt change of direction, Tom's raffia palm hat skimmed across the dash and sailed out the passenger-side window. Once out the window, a stiff wind filled the crown and, pushing it up then letting it fall, caused it to flutter like a kite on a spring day.

Tom steered into the skid, he pumped the breaks, he stared into the rearview mirror. The hat was a gift from his daughter; he wasn't about to lose sight of it.

His concentration remained divided and not until he saw the rim of the hat touch down in a clump of swampy grass did he return his full attention to the road ahead.

That's when he saw it. A great bird stood directly in the path of his speeding truck. Its luminous white wings spread wide and its eyes blazed with light like flames of fire. Tom went from pumping the brake pedal with one foot to tromping on it with both feet. The pickup fishtailed. Its left front tire lifted from the pavement. The truck tipped sideways, and Tom saw his reflection in the freshwater canal looming on his right.

"Confound it! I'm going to get wet."

■ ■ ■

He didn't remember bringing the pickup out of the roll. He didn't remember maneuvering it around the bird. He didn't remember parking the pickup on the side of the road. Yet that's where it stood — three feet off the blacktop in fender-high brown grass. Tom unclenched his white knuckles from the steering wheel and climbed from the truck's cab.

The realization of how close he'd come to being fish food made Tom's knees buckled as he stepped from the truck. In the process of killing himself he most likely would have run down the great white bird as well.

The large bird stood with its back to Tom. Its outstretched wings curled protectively over something in the middle of the road. Tom thought the bird looked like a great white heron — a bird at one time thought to be extinct.

Tom did not, at that moment, focus on why he and his pickup were not submerged upside down, in five feet of water. Nor did he fuss about the sun that beat without mercy on his uncovered head. Curiosity had him in its grip. Tom needed to see what the great white bird was doing, what its wings shielded, and the eyes. He wanted to see those flaming eyes again.

He walked a half-circle around the bird. On the front side of it Tom saw a 20-inch turtle plodding across the road; the turtle was moving slow as dawn on the heels of a sleepless night. Tom kept his distance from the heron like bird and from its sword-shaped beak but he looked directly into its eyes — blazing like fire.

A sudden sense of vulnerability caused Tom to look away and hurry past the odd pair. He walked back to find his hat.

Animal crossing guards, birds with flaming eyes, rolling pickups that don't roll. What was going on? Had he taken a turn to the wrong side of normal?

Tom searched the ground until he spotted the crown of his raffia hat, sinking into reddish-brown swamp water. He picked it up and shook it hard in an attempt to dry the hat as well as knock sense into the situation, but it didn't. The intricately woven palm, with its brown leather band, dripped a steady stream as he carried it up the road.

By this time, the turtle and bird were in the grass alongside the blacktop. Tom walked past them. "IT'S NOT NORMAL!" he shouted as if words and volume could be a catalyst to shame the odd couple into more typical behavior.

Back in Old Blue, Tom dropped his hat onto the seat and steered the pickup north toward U.S. 41.

Since his daughter's disappearance Tom had been on leave from the sheriff's department. During his 25 years of active duty, however, he'd seen strange things; some might even be considered bizarre. This had them all beat.

His training taught him to observe what was and to analyze what should be. Animal crossings were common in this area but a great white heron helping a turtle across the road? That sounded like the beginning of a bad joke. A bird like that would rather eat a turtle than escort it out of harm's way.

The incident was crazy enough just as it stood, but there was something about those flaming eyes. The sight of them branded Tom's memory. When he stared into their depths, he felt naked, exposed, like they knew of his anger, felt his pain.

And no shadow. A bird that size should have thrown a noticeable shadow.

"No!" Tom tried to dismiss it all. "The bird was just curious about the turtle. The sun gave its eyes their brilliant appearance. Because I was, as my grandson might say, weirded out, I read more into the incident than it deserved.

Shock, shock's the reason I don't remember pulling the pickup out of a roll and to the side of the road. And I'm not telling anybody about any of this. They'll think I'm nuts."

The landscape changed as Tom entered the Big Cypress National Preserve. Spanish moss swept downward from bald cypress trees; bright red bromeliads spiked out from the branch forks of stately slash pines. A canal of clear, fresh water meandered alongside the road.

Tom's windows were closed and the air-conditioner on high by the time he turned south onto Highway 29 and headed toward Everglades City, gateway to the Ten Thousand Islands. (The Ten Thousand Islands are mostly located within the boundaries of Everglades National Park and are sprinkled along its western shore in the Gulf of Mexico's salty-water.)

Tom's heart ached when he looked at his hat, drooping pathetically beside him. Jade gave me that hat, he thought.

How could this terrible thing have happened? How could his only daughter and her husband disappear without a trace — abducted while on a photo shoot in Kenya's, Masai Mara Game Reserve?

He didn't allow himself to believe any of it at first, but the embassy's report was persuasive. The abandoned Jeep, crushed grass smeared with human blood — the blood type of Alan, his son-in-law. Jade's sweater caked with mud and lying under the Jeep. A red and yellow flowered sleeve torn from Jade's dress and trampled in the broken, bloody grass.

The Kenyan police, and later the FBI, traced tire tracks for miles across Africa's grassland. After finding the truck, stuck and deserted, they followed four sets of boot prints, and one more delicate pair of shoe prints, through mud and grass until their quarry entered heavy brush.

Footprints became harder to find, so the trackers searched for other signs. They began to rely on threads, clinging to half-broken branches. The yellow and red strands from Jade's dashiki dress led them to the rain-swollen banks of the Mara River, where dozens of crocodiles dozed lazily on the far side. There on the river's muddy shore all trace of Jade, Alan and their abductors disappeared. Five sets of footprints went into the fast-moving water, but no trace of them leaving the river was found on either of its slippery banks.

A horn blared. Tom's eyes darted from the hat to the road. With one swift motion he yanked the steering wheel to the right and waved apologetically to an oncoming car.

Tom continued south on Highway 29 toward Everglades City. He wondered why Max wanted him to stop by his place. The old man's request sounded more urgent than just loneliness. Max was a peculiar old duffer. He and Tom had been friends for more years than Tom could remember.

The blue pickup passed through Everglades City. Tom steered it right and crossed over a bridge. He then bumped down a dirt road for half a mile and pulled off the road onto a narrow sandy driveway.

An old Florida style house, surrounded by areca palms and banana trees, slouched at the back of a clearing. Peeling paint and a sagging roof testified to the house's state of disrepair. It appeared to Tom that little had been done to maintain or improve it since the day it was built — except maybe the addition of an indoor bathroom. This lack of attention was hard for Tom to understand since Max, over his lifetime, had most likely squirreled away a sizable amount of money.

Tom climbed out of his pickup and grabbed his hat. He slapped it on his head; the raffia palm brim went limp across his face. The flaming eyes of the great white bird once more burned across Tom's mind as he strode across the clearing toward the house.

Max stood on a landing at the top of his porch steps. His hands, twisted by time and arthritis, held a white butcher-paper package. He alternately waved it in welcome and fretfully clasped it, as if to wring the life from it. The old man's swarthy face appeared strained as he watched Tom climb the splintery front steps. Arthritic fingers gripped Tom's hands in welcome.

Max squeaked open a sagging screen door that led onto a covered porch. The screened lanai was furnished with chairs and table. A sideboard stood against the wall adjoining the house and on the sideboard sat a pot of steaming coffee.

"Glad you come. Got something to tell you," Max said, handing over the white package. He pointed Tom to a straight-back chair.

Tom watched his host's slow, deliberate movements. Max poured strong-smelling coffee into antique china cups, reminiscent of happier, less lonely days. Frayed lace curtains on an inside window and a black-and-white photo of a young couple holding hands on the beach were the only other reminders of Max's wife, Molly, dead now some 10 years.

Tom accepted a china cup cradled in a matching saucer. Max, hobbling on one leg, carried the second cup to a wooden rocker and sat down.

Max's slippered feet arched and flattened as he rocked in his favorite chair. He wore a flannel robe made soft by much use. As the chair moved back and forth, the robe's sleeves rubbed across the chair arms and involuntarily liberated splinters of cracked paint. The white slivers flashed as they danced freely through sunbeams onto well-worn floorboards; the floorboards creaked and squeaked in rhythm to the rocker.

Max exhaled the ragged breath of an old man and sipped his coffee. By the time the pinched expression on his weatherworn face relaxed, Tom was getting restless.

Tom looked at the white package in his hands. The words "Gator Jerky" were scrawled across it. He gulped his coffee. It was strong as expected; but not expected, it was burning hot! Tom sucked air and fanned his mouth. He was certain blisters were forming on its roof and probably on his tongue as well.

Apparently lost in thought, Max didn't react to Tom's discomfort. He persisted with sipping his coffee and pushing the rocker back and forth.

Tom's restlessness increased, but he knew from experience not to rush Max. He looked around the porch. He stared at his hands, put his elbows on his knees and studied his feet. He tenderly inspected the roof of his mouth with his tongue. His hat drooped on the floor next to the chair; the smell of soggy palm drifted upward. Tom picked up the hat and tossed it around, willing the airflow to dry it.

Max showed no notice of Tom's impatience. He finished his coffee and gently placed cup and saucer on a nearby table. With twisted fingers he picked up a gold cross that gleamed as it caught the mid-morning sun. He fingered it reverently then hugged it to his chest. He stared out the window into the distance. When he finally broke the silence, his voice cracked with emotion.

"I found another panther carcass yesterday; skinned slick as snot. Same poachers as before, I'd guess. Them low-down snakes. I called the law, but things ain't as good around here as when you was sheriff. Seeing that critter, lying with its gut ripped open by vultures and with flies and maggots crawling all over, made me sick to my stomach. Them varmints! All they wanted was the hide. Can't believe there's a market for panther hides these days."

"There's a good market; that's why they do it. Skins go high as fifty-grand in the Arabic counties where the glut of oil makes even that seem inexpensive," Tom said.

"Well the whole thing makes me sick. Ain't them poachers been learned that God gave us the job to care for His creation?" Angry lines crept across Max's forehead.

"In the old days Indians and settlers needed hides to clothe their children and wild meat to feed their families. Things were different then. With panthers as scarce as they are now days," Tom said. "Not much excuse for it."

"Greed, that's why they do it," Max said, his rocker fiercely flying back and forth. "Being top dog ain't no excuse for greed and don't excuse freeloading neither. Earth's caretakers, that's what we are." Max's agitated rocking eased a bit. "It's our job to tend the earth and those what live in it and I'm here to tell you some of us is doing a mighty pitiful job."

The creak of the floorboards under the rocker's weight seemed to grow louder as an uneasy quiet loomed. Tom watched Max's face slowly transformed from tight and angry to thoughtful and sad.

"Any word about your daughter and son-in-law? Real nasty business, that," Max finally said.

Tom braced his elbows on his knees and looked at his feet. "No, not a blasted thing. Sometimes I think I can't live with it another minute, but then there's the grandkids. I love those two little rascals. They're taking it hard." He looked up to search Max's face. "Why does God let things like this happen?"

"I ain't got it all figured out yet," Max said, kneading his arthritic hands. Just when I expect I do, some mess like this happens. There's lots of wisdom in this here book though," he said, tapping a well-worn leather Bible that rested on the table next to him. "Got me through when Molly died. Thought I couldn't go on, but I did.

"Isaiah 40's my favorite. It speaks to how the Lord gathers us in His arms, like a shepherd carrying His lamb, and holds us close to His heart. That's where you is now, being carried close to the Lord's heart. When we're hurting bad, He does that for us. Can't explain it but I know it to be true." Max leaned back in his rocker and closed his eyes.

"Nope, ain't got God all figured out yet. Most likely won't neither, not on this side of heaven. I know He's good and He's in charge and somehow, when all's said and done, He brings blessing out of our mess. No matter how things look to be stacked, God don't ever let us down." Max stretched out his legs and relaxed. His crippled frailness conquered by the certainty that everything he said was true.

Tom yearned to believe Max. He longed to have God stop the pain of loss that clutched at his heart. His intellect, however, reminded him that Job trusted God, and look where it got him. Instinctively Tom folded both arms across his chest and logic took control of his thoughts. God may have created us and even sent His Son to save us, but now? Where is he now?

The mind is a complex instrument. While Tom's logic argued against Max's words, another piece of his brain recalled the great white bird with its burning eyes and its snow-white wings spread protectively over the plodding turtle. It brought to mind Tom's pickup, one minute skidding with its front tire off the blacktop and the next parked safely on the side of the road.

Tom's gaze moved across the porch and into the sky — its blueness marred only by a scattering of white, wispy clouds. He wished he could find faith like Max's. He thought he believed once, but when hard times came, his faith dried up like a Florida swamp during the dry season. Tom cleared his throat and changed the subject.

"What's this I hear about you wanting to sell that beach lot you own? Be a shame if it fell into the wrong hands. The curve of the land protects the beach against wind and high surf there. It's a favorite place for loggerhead turtles to lay their eggs."

"Yeah, had a railroad easement and some deed restrictions that give it special trouble but you needn't worry. I done sold it to an outfit called Turtles and Me Educational Foundation. Red-haired fellow were here and wrote up the paperwork. I had Jeb Smith look at them papers. He said they was right as rain, so I signed them and put the money in the bank. Paid five grand for that land 30 years ago; they give me two million. I suspect it were worth three, but they agreed to leave it be; make a reserve out of it for school kids to learn about sea turtles and such."

"Jeb Smith must be close to ninety by now. I didn't know he was still practicing law," Tom said.

"He ain't, just done me a favor."

"You know, Max, the railroad easement and special deed restrictions on that lot might make it impossible for anyone to build, unless they build directly on the beach. Doing that would destroy the turtle nesting grounds. I don't remember the particulars but seems to me..."

"It's not your worry," Max said. "I told you, Jeb took care of all that."

"OK," was all Tom said.

Max continued to rock but soon the forward, backward motion of the chair slowed. His wrinkled eyelids blinked heavily and his chin sagged to rest on his robe. The rocker stopped. The floorboards were silent. Tom's presence again seemed forgotten.

Tom had never heard of a Turtles and Me Educational Foundation and he wasn't satisfied that "Old Jeb" took care of anything. He stared for some time at the gold cross, gripped tightly in Max's gnarled fingers.

The china clinked as Tom set cup and saucer on the table. He picked up his hat and pushed it down on his head.

God's relationship to man. Marx called it the "opiate of the masses." Caesar thought it a "fool's game." Yet throughout history, millions have called it "the greatest story ever told."

Tom squeaked opened the screen door. He glanced back to watch Max's sleeping figure as it huddled in the rocking chair. Sun glinted off the gold cross. Tom thought about the great white bird and about the pickup that should have rolled, but didn't. He pushed the hat brim away from his face. "The greatest story ever told?" Maybe, but it took more faith than Tom could muster to believe it.

Florida Panther

Florida Panther

Florida Panther

CHAPTER 2

Joe saw them yesterday and hoped they would come back. With legs straddling a lofty cypress branch and gaunt body molded into the tree's curved trunk, he patted his sparse mustache and waited. An hour passed. The late-morning sun glared hot on his bare neck and shoulders. Sweat dripped down his face and underarms.

He shifted his weight to escape a sharp protrusion of bark then shifted again in an attempt to find a more comfortable position. This twisting and turning eventually broke loose a small limb that toppled downward. Joe watched the stick as it fell into rusty brown water that surrounded the cypress where he sat. The water swallowed the stick and as it did, two greenish-brown eyes popped to the surface.

Somewhere Joe heard that alligators eat only once a week, but what if this one ate on Sundays? His legs tightened around the branch and he forced his gaze from the water to a nearby stand of trees.

A hint of movement followed by the rustle of dry grass caught Joe's attention. He braced his rifle against the trunk and, peering through cypress branches, scoped the area.

Beyond the receding swamp water, in the shadow of a tall slash pine, two Florida panthers moved in single file. Placing one padded foot in front of the other, they threaded their way through the trees. Their eyes, ears and noses were alert to danger.

Joe's greed-glazed eyes watched through clumps of sweaty blond hair. He wetted a finger and stuck it in the air; he was up wind. His thin face twisted into a half smile. "That's them," he breathed. "The ones I saw yesterday. Prime, really prime, and a matched pair. Abdul, my Saudi buddy, will give me fifty grand a piece for those buggers."

Unaware they were being stalked, the golden-brown panthers sought refuge from the unrelenting sun in a stand of trees. Their muscular frames appeared relaxed as they laid down and stretched out, but their black-tipped tails flicked from side to side and their black-tipped ears stood at attention.

Joe fingered his rifle then brought the weapon to an upright position. He wrapped the barrel in his shirt to muffle the sound and forced on a silencer. Sheer determination kept his hands steady. Shoot, reload, shoot again, the whole plan needed clockwork precision. Joe braced the gun's stock against his cheek. With luck, he'd get them both.

Joe aligned the crosshairs midpoint between the male cat's black-tipped ears. His finger pressed on the trigger then quickly let go. "What the heck?" He mouthed as a large bird floated onto a tree branch and blocked his view of the panthers. White as sugar, the bird balanced on the small limb then stretched its wings — a span that appeared to Joe to be over seven feet.

"Curse it," Joe said under his breath.

Joe speculated the bird was a great white heron, a species not commonly found this far north of the Keys, but Joe didn't spend time congratulating himself on the rare sighting. Instead, he glared at the bird; he swore silently at it and cursed his bad luck. What was the witless thing up to? And why, today of all days, had it shown up here?

A mosquito buzzed Joe's head. He puffed stale breath toward the insect to keep it from landing. Impatient for the bird to move, he fidgeted, shifting from side to side. Finally in exasperation he decided that he might get off three shots before the panthers bolted and were completely out of range.

He raised his rifle. The great white bird stood fast. Silhouetted, its beak looked like a sword. Its head turned and flaming eyes look intently into Joe's. They searched him with such intensity that, try as he might, Joe could do nothing but stare back. As he did his conscience stirred.

From a suppress brain wrinkle in the crevices of his mind, his mother's voice drifted forward, "You've been caught poaching twice before. Three times and they'll lock you up for more years than I got left. What happened to you? You use to be such a nice, quiet boy."

"Ma, they're prime. I got a contract with this Saudi guy; see. He'll pay me fifty-K, for each of them. My land payment's due. Them payments is eating me alive. I need a partner, one with money, loads of it. Abdul Bahar Habib is an oil sheik. He's got lots of cash, but he wants hides. It's more than the money. It's good will. I need this guy. Ghost Orchid Hotel is going to be a beauty and right on the beach. You'll like it Ma. You can visit as much as you like but I gotta have them hides," he argued to the voice in his head.

It wasn't so easily stilled. "They're God's creatures; leave them be. They're endangered you know."

"They're in danger all right." Joe closed his ears to mother and conscience. His old schoolmates labeled him a "loser." His dad called him a "good-for-nothing," but he'd be the richest man in town soon. That'd show them. Show them all. He'd buy his ma a gold necklace. She'd like that.

Joe pulled out a third shell and braced himself against the tree. Rifle leveled and with finger resting on the trigger, he aimed at the bird's chest. He could shoot high and scare the bird. No, it caused him to lose precious time and he didn't take kindly to the delay.

The great bird stared at Joe. Joe, not able to look into its eyes, aimed at its snowy white breast. He tightened his grip on the trigger and started to squeeze. His mother's protests pounded on the inside of his head. He grit his teeth. He squeezed harder.

As he did, gray clouds were hurled away from the sun. Blinding rays shot toward a mirror mounted crookedly on a blue pickup. Light flashed, piercing an impenetrable forest. The explosion of its brightness caught Joe in the eyes. Joe flinched. The rifle fired.

Dust rose up as the bullet plowed into dry ground. Branches moved and twigs snapped. The panthers disappeared into the brush.

"BLAST IT!" Joe slammed the tree with his rifle butt.

The white bird continued to stare.

"You dimwitted fool! Look what you made me do. I lost them, you idiot!

"Why you still here, anyway?" He asked the bird. "Get outta here before I shoot you. Them panthers are the ones with sense. They hightailed it and you, you're left wondering whether to pick your beak or fly." Joe waved the bird away and when it didn't budge he shouted, "BEAT IT, BIRD BRAIN!" The bird folded its wings but continued to look directly at Joe. Joe shook his head in disgust then looked away, to search the nearby road. He wanted to know what caused the flash that blinded his shot.

Hearing the distant pop of a backfiring truck and seeing a glimmer of blue through the trees, Joe slammed his fist against the tree trunk. "DRAT! Been a couple of years but I'd know that old truck anywhere. Is everybody against me today? What is that nosy sheriff doing out here? It's Sunday. Why doesn't he stay home and tune up that piece of junk he calls a pickup?"

Old Blue backfired again, shooting fiery debris onto the dirt road. It was the hottest, driest spring in Tom's memory. The fire danger was high, so driving a truck that was suddenly flinging sparks out its backend was not a good idea.

Tom had left Max's house and driven to a restaurant in Everglades City. Halfway through his turkey sandwich and ice tea something inside of him grew restless. By the time he finished his cherry pie the restlessness intensified into alarm. As a result Tom was now headed back toward the Big Cypress National Preserve.

His stomach was full, the weather was steamy and it was Sunday afternoon. All Tom wanted to do was go home and take a nap. Instead he was headed in the opposite direction, all because of a gut feeling.

Tom, after years of law enforcement training, developed the ability to sense trouble before it happened. Some talent, he thought sarcastically, it couldn't even save my own daughter. He'd been uneasy about Jade and Alan's trip to Africa, but Jade dismissed his objections as those of an overprotective father.

Well I'm here now, he thought as he stopped the pickup. With binoculars in hand he scanned the cypress forest. A pin-dot of

27

white in a distant tree caught his attention. He adjusted the binoculars and searched the trees until his eyes rested on a giant cypress with a white bird sitting on one branch. It appeared to be a great white heron. Strange.... He'd seen maybe half a dozen in his lifetime and now two in one day?

Creatures of mangrove keys and open mud flats, great white herons don't usually hang out in cypress trees. Tom continued his perusal of the area but nothing else seemed out of order. A bird big enough to be spotted from such a distance aroused his curiosity. He wanted a closer look.

The great white bird continued to balance on the limb and Joe's cold blue eyes shot daggers of hate toward it. "HEY featherbrain," he said. "Don't you know them cats are gone? What do you think you are anyway, some stupid guardian angel? That's a joke. Them cats would rather eat your mangy body than hide behind it. That'd be heaven's mercy all right, to be killed by the ones you saved.

"It don't matter. They'll be back and I'll be waiting."

He dropped his gangly, 5-foot-10-inch body from the massive cypress tree and, daring any alligator to come within range of his steel-toed boots, kicked his way through the receding swamp. Once back on the road, Joe ran 15 yards to his red pickup. He yanked open its door, wrapped the rifle in a blanket, shoved it under a tarp in the back and leaped into the truck. The engine roared and Joe drove toward home — dust spewing out behind him.

Tom's eyes darted from one side of the dirt road to the other. What was he looking for? Would he know it when he saw it? A familiar red pickup turned onto the road ahead and Tom snapped on his siren.

"What're you doing out here?" Tom asked, scanning the interior of Joe's pickup.

Sheriff Tom was taller than Joe remembered. He heard once that Tom's grandparents came from Cuba and were distant descendants of the Calusa Indians, probably the reason he was so big. Looking into the suntanned face, he noticed Tom's square jaw, set in determination, and his smoky gray eyes that held no friendly welcome.

Joe gathered his courage. "I live out here."

"You know what I mean," Tom fired back. "Out here, in the reserve, in the heat of the day." He saw Joe's eyes flutter a glance at the back of his truck. "What's under the tarp?"

Joe hated the fear that rose to his throat. "Fishing poles." He worried his answer was too quick. His hand rose to his lip; he nervously petted his mustache. The smell of sweat, dripping down his underarms, rose to assault his nose. He swallowed, "What right you got to pull me over? I'm just minding my own business, taking a Sunday drive, marveling at the wonders of nature," he faltered.

Tom didn't answer but studied Joe's eyes. Prison had changed him. He looked older and harder, thinner too.

"Look, I gotta go. Got company coming."

"What company would that be?" Tom asked, his eyes skimming the bed of Joe's pickup.

"No one you'd know."

Tom's response was a cold stare.

"You got no call for holding me, I'm leaving."

"I'd like to see what's under that tarp."

"You got a warrant?" Joe asked.

"All I need is just cause. What if I said you were speeding, exhibiting suspicious behavior?"

"I wasn't speeding and if going for a Sunday drive is suspicious behavior, the jails would be fluffing over with cotton balls."

"Cotton balls?"

"You know them white-haired people."

"In the first place it's disrespectful to call elderly people anything but sir or madam, but if you're going to be sarcastic, at least get it right. The slang term is Q-tips, not cotton balls."

Joe noticed gray fringes along Tom's temples and silver flecks hiding in his thick black hair. The gray hair wasn't noticeable two years ago when the two of them played checkers — Tom on the outside of the bars and Joe on the inside awaiting arraignment on a poaching conviction.

The years haven't been kind to the old sheriff. He's turning into a cotton ball, Joe thought smugly, and the thought gave him courage. "Yeah, well maybe I'm starting my own slang," he said to Tom. "The point is, you stopped me for no good reason, and I don't have time for you to mess with me."

Joe didn't know Tom was on leave from the sheriff's department, but Tom knew he was out of line stopping Joe. His gut told him Joe was up to no good. He had no legal right to search the red truck, but he also knew that law sometimes gets in the way of justice. The inner struggle continued even after Tom said, "Stay out of trouble or I'll get that warrant. Now get out of my sight."

Joe touched his forehead in a two-fingered salute, put his truck in gear and drove away.

Tom watched the red pickup disappear. The truck tires threw up yellow dust that filled Tom's nostrils and burned his eyes. "Joe, out here marveling at the wonders of nature? Now why don't I believe that?" he mumbled, mopping his face with an almost clean white handkerchief.

At one time, back when Joe was at the county jail, Tom checked into Joe's background to see if he could figure out why the young man had such a chip on his shoulder. Despite his sometimes-bad grammar, Joe graduated high school with a C average, even got an A in French his senior year. His dad was a drinker, spent time in the slammer more than once for beating up on his wife and kids. The report said Joe struck out on his own, right after high school.

Tom, perturbed by his inability to fix the world's problems and by the dust, the heat and his unquenched thirst, searched the horizon for some sign of the white bird. Seeing nothing but black thunderheads piled up in the eastern sky, he turned to go.

Better hurry, he thought. His wife and grandkids wanted him home for supper. Tomorrow Mariana was flying to Washington, D.C., with her best friend. After six months they were finally closing up Jade and Alan's house and shipping the kids' remaining stuff to Florida. When she offered to go to D.C. without him, Tom didn't object. Mariana's faith was sustaining her far better than his lack of it was sustaining him. He hoped she could handle it. He knew he couldn't.

Tom walked toward his truck. A bolt of lightning shattered the sky; he turned as splinters of light race toward the ground.

The brilliance faded and Tom took one last look around. From high in a cypress tree the great white bird watched him, and when the big man swung his binoculars around, their eyes locked. Tom, mesmerized by eyes that appeared to burn into the depths of the universe, stared back.

He watched the great white bird spread its wings and soared south toward the Everglades. It flew above the cypress forest — no shadow darkened the treetops as its great wings glided between sun and cypress. Tom speculated after the large bird until, devoured by distance and darkening sky, it became a speck on the horizon.

The landscape looked thirsty — parched grass, brown leaves hanging off brittle limbs, dust devils dancing down the road. Tom climbed into the pickup and reached for his canteen. "We sure could use some rain," he told another lightning strike as it fingered across the sky with thunder booming at its heels.

The pickup door closed; Tom rolled down the window. He leaned back and gulped a drink. The water flowed cold down his throat.

I wonder? He thought as he turned the key in the ignition. Had to be the same bird.

Great White Heron

Great White Heron

Great White Heron

33

CHAPTER 3

He told her about the great white bird, though he said he wouldn't tell a soul. It was OK to tell her; she was a part of him. In fact, sometimes, she was the best part of him.

Almost three months had come and gone since she closed up the D.C. house, but the pain came in fresh waves every day. Mariana's green eyes studied the stark white canvas; a silver-gold curl fell across her forehead. Her agile fingers moved the brush from pallet to picture, dabbing on more white. She didn't understand artists who, right away, started mucking up a new canvas; it wasn't her style. Change came hard for her. She'd waited six months before closing up Jade and Alan's Washington, D.C., house, and almost another two before totally unpacking the red and blue trunks filled with the twins' belongings.

She didn't like change but she wasn't normally a procrastinator. This situation, however, seem utterly hopeless at times, and even her strong faith didn't remove the pain it caused. Yet, in the midst of her anguish over Jade and Alan's disappearance, she still trusted that wherever her daughter and son-in-law were, they were in the hands of the Almighty.

In Mariana's mind this unwavering belief didn't make her a faith giant. To her it was reality — God is faithful. He takes care of His children. Her paintbrush moved with rhythm, down to dip the paint, up to dab the picture.

She came from sturdy missionary stock — dip, dab, dip, dab. She knew wisdom and spiritual growth often come from hardship — white on white, dab, swirl, swirl — but this was too hard. Her only daughter, her Jade. And Alan, funny, strong Alan. The children. How were she and Tom ever going to take care of them? To be what Jade and Alan were to them. She looked at the empty blue and red trunks stacked in the corner.

"Oh, Jesus, I need your help," she cried silently. Tears streamed down her cheeks; she shook her head. This was silly. The picture couldn't be totally white. On the other hand, maybe it could. She'd call it *Shades of Sameness*. Pinching more white from the tube, Mariana glanced outside the lanai. Areca palms rustled in the wind like waltzing green taffeta. Golden sunbeams drifted warmly onto her easel. God hadn't created the world all white; neither was it shades of sameness. Her grief didn't change that.

Mariana forced herself to squeeze red, yellow, blue, brown and green onto her color board. She stared at the glob of red and thought of blood smeared across African grass. Shadows of palm fronds flitted in and out of the yellow paint; she remembered Jade's dashiki dress. Blue paint flowed around the brown to invade the green and Mariana's mind was in Africa on the banks of the crocodile- infested Mara River.

"Let them escape; please let them find their way home," she prayed for the thousandth time. Her tentative dabs changed to forceful strokes. Smells of oily pigment swirled; her brush moved as if in time to a symphony. She swept the paintbrush up and down to outline a pair of widespread wings. Mountains and valleys, highs and lows, life wasn't one without the other.

Determination swelled up within her. It glittered from her every pore like the paint, glistening wet, on her canvas. She filled a paintbrush, poised it at the bottom of the canvas, then resembling a conductor rising to the peak of a Tchaikovsky overture, she swept the brush high and to the side. In fairy tales they lived happily ever after. Why, oh why couldn't she?

The rift in her concentration came with a melody that danced out from the house. The song soared and faded as its source skipped and danced around the lanai until at last the singing stopped and her granddaughter spoke.

"You know the Sunday School teacher, the one named Miss O'Keefe? She spelled my name with two m's again, and I told her that's not the way my mom intended it to be spelled. Gram, did you hear me? That teacher spelled my name Summer; you know, like the season. Don't they know I'm a kid not a season?

"Gram, did you hear me? What are you doing?" Sumer stopped in front of Mariana's easel.

"Painting," Mariana said, placing an arm across the girl's shoulders. "I'll bet you set Miss O'Keefe straight."

Sumer hugged her grandmother's waist. "It's almost all white. What's it supposed to be?"

"Oh it's a bird your grandpa knows." Mariana pushed a silver-blonde curl back from her forehead and flexed the fingers on her right hand.

"Gram, you can't know a bird."

Sunlight melted like gold into the girl's light brown hair as her deep gray eyes searched the picture. "Mom said I can't fly like one either. I tried once, fell off the shed and broke my arm."

"Yes, I remember," Mariana said, and she did remember. Late, after supper a couple of years back, the telephone had rung. Mariana answered it and Jade on the other end sobbed into the receiver. Jade rambled something about Sumer, a fall ... no, a headlong dive from the shed and a broken neck that turned out to be, thank God, only a broken shoulder. Then another sob and, "Oh, Mom I was so scared."

"Gram," Sumer shifted at her side. Mariana looked down at the lovely young girl. "I got a story that'll make your gut smile," she said.

"I don't think you're allowed to use words like gut."

"Yeah, Dad don't like it. When he worked in D.C. for the government, he told me I should act more proper," Sumer said, batting her eyelashes and sipping a pretend teacup with curled pinkie. Suddenly she dropped the pretend cup and turned sober.

"When are they coming back, Gram? When are Mom and Dad coming home?"

"In God's good time; in God's good time. Tell me your story; I think my gut could use a smile."

Sumer studied her grandmother for several seconds then, as clouds pass across the sun and race away, her eyes grew bright and out chattered her story.

"Samuel thinks he's way cool now, but before he worried about being cool, he liked to chase birds, mostly pigeons 'cause they're so fat. Well, one day he saw a bunch of pigeons on the White House lawn and he took off after them. He ran and hollered until every last one of them flew. He continued to run underneath them and before long he came back to where me and Dad were standing. Dripping down his face was a runny glob of white bird poop. The pigeons pooped on his head! Can you believe it?"

Sumer melted into a fit of giggles. "I laughed and laughed 'til Dad said I should be more ladylike. We were with Senator Gall and he's kinda stuffy," Sumer said, giving Mariana a knowing look.

Mariana noticed more and more lately the way Sumer swooped from child to young woman and back to child, from laughter to devastation and back to laughter again. One minute she was sitting cross-legged on the floor, playing with her dolls, laughing; the next she threw them aside, declaring they were for babies, and ran in tears to her bedroom."

"What make's you say Grandpa knows this bird? I don't think you can really know a bird," Sumer said.

Thump, thump, squ-e-a-k. Two wet sneakers dropped to the concrete. The screen door opened. Samuel came through the door and padded across the lanai in stocking feet.

"Grandpa's on a first name basis with lots of birds, specially the ones that eat his strawberries," he said. He resembled his twin in coloring only — keen gray eyes peering out under strands of golden brown hair.

The smell of damp hair and garden dirt hung like nature's perfume around him. A stripe of water-soaked mud ran from his back, over his shoulder and down the front of his white dress shirt.

Samuel continued, "Let's see there is Lousy Pot Licker and one he's named ..."

"That's not exactly what I meant," Grandma Mariana interrupted. "You probably shouldn't be repeating the names your grandpa calls those birds. Some of them are not very nice."

She looked at Samuel. "How'd you get so dirty? You've been back from church less than half an hour."

"Grandpa needed the hose drug around back. He's planting stuff."

"You'd better put on a clean shirt."

"No need to now; I ain't going anywhere."

Samuel pulled at his shirt and, licking his index finger, attempted to remove the mud. Sumer rolled her eyes at her brother. "Dad don't let us use the word ain't."

"I like the word ain't; besides it's doesn't, not don't," her brother corrected. She stuck out her tongue at Samuel then shifted the conversation back to Grandma Mariana.

"You were telling me about Grandpa and this white bird knowing each other?"

"Your grandfather and Old Max have seen a very special bird several times in the past few months. They say it looks like a great white heron. Max saw the bird while he was fishing; he said it saved some manatees. I'm sure you've heard the story; Max has such a vivid imagination."

Mariana stared at her canvas. "Max named the bird Yatzu, Hebrew for..." She scratched her head as if that helped her to remember. "'One Sent Out,' I think. I decided the bird was worthy of a painting."

"No we haven't," Samuel said.

"Haven't what?"

"We haven't heard the story."

"With all the stories Grandpa Tom tells you kids, how'd he miss that one?"

"Why don't you tell it to us while we eat lunch?" Samuel hinted, moving his eyebrows up and down in a comic display.

Mariana laughed and ruffled her grandson's hair. "Your grandfather is a better storyteller than I am."

"And lunch? What about lunch?"

"Give me a minute, then I'll see what I can find."

Sumer walked to the screen door, opened it and yelled into the yard, "Grandpa, hey, Grandpa, where are you?"

"What is it?" The muffled response came from somewhere outside.

"Come in and tell us a story. Gram said you should."

There was a surge of movement in the bushes next to a banyan tree, then a great hunk of a man appeared and sauntered toward the house.

"Oh she did, did she?" The deep voice held a chuckle.

After pausing to rinse the dirt from his hands and shoes, Grandpa Tom pushed open the screen door. With a flip of the wrist, he sent his dilapidated straw hat sailing through the air to land on its peg.

A short time later, smelling faintly of soap and water, Tom, with one large hand wrapped around an icy glass of lemonade, stood between his grandkids. Samuel, with one elbow deep in a bag of potato chips, kept a watchful eye on Sumer, whose left arm snaked behind Grandpa Tom and reached toward the crackling red and yellow bag.

Mariana's paintbrush moved swiftly over the canvas. Pink and gold clouds haloed the sun as it hung on the horizon like an orange ball. Shimmers of fading light reflected off dark water enclosed by cattails and long grass. Above the water, a great white bird hovered, with wings set, ready to land.

"So tell us about this Yatzu dude," Samuel said.

Tom shot Mariana a look that said, "You weren't suppose to tell!"

"The one Max told you about two weeks ago when you went back out to his place to look at that contract," Mariana said.

Sumer and Samuel missed the look that passed between their grandparents because the twins were wrestling on the floor — each struggling to gain custody of the half-eaten bag of chips.

Samuel jumped up, and by standing on his toes, was able to hold the bag out of reach. Sumer jumped for the bag, screaming, "Give me some or I'll tell."

As Samuel waved the crackling red and yellow bag through the air, it was suddenly pulled up and away from his hands. He shot a look upward into a face that sympathized with boyhood fun yet understood the need for discipline.

"Drat!" Caught in the act, what else could he say but, "Ah, Grandpa, we're only messing around."

"I believe it's time to feed these two," Tom told Mariana. "And, while Gram is fixing lunch, I remember, as I walked down the hall earlier, seeing two unmade beds surrounded by untidy rooms."

"A guy could starve to death around here," Samuel muttered as he and Sumer slumped toward their rooms."

"I hate the word 'untidy,'" Sumer added. "Why didn't he just say our rooms look like trash heaps with a case of three-day mold? At least that would be descriptive."

Mariana quickly cleaned her brushes. Can't seem to find any peace and quiet to paint these days, she thought, but aloud she said, "Lunch will be ready in a few minutes."

Tom sat down in a large wicker chair and sighed heavily. He tried to relax, but his mind was never still long. He thought about the strawberries he planted that morning. He hoped it would rain. He thought about the twins and what a huge responsibility it was to raise them. He hoped he and Mariana were up to it. He thought about Max and the beachfront lot he sold. When Tom visited Max at his old Florida homestead a couple of months back, Max told him he wasn't to worry about the contract with the Turtles and Me Educational Foundation — an organization that neither Tom, nor anyone of his acquaintance, had ever heard.

Max said his 90-year-old attorney took care of everything, but Tom had received a call from Max two weeks ago, and as a result Tom made another trip to the house that slouched among banana trees and areca palms. Tom climbed the splintery front porch steps and Max squeaked open his screen door and handed Tom a six-page contract. It was the sales contract for the beachfront lot that Max sold to the Turtles and Me Educational Foundation.

Tom studied the contract. Max rocked in his rocker.

"I'm a-feared that I were wrong. Old Jeb don't appear to have taken care of everything. He paid me no mind when I told him to write down that no one were to build on the beach side of them grass-covered dunes," Max said.

Tom worried that Max was right. The deed contained a railroad easement that ran on the east side of the lot. Deed restrictions forbade building within 200 feet on either side of the easement. These limitations rendered the lot unusable for any large building project unless the buildings were constructed directly on the beach itself.

"Where's your phone?" Tom asked Max.

"North wall in there," Max said, pointing Tom to the kitchen. Tom phoned old Jeb, Max's 90-year-old attorney. Jeb assured Tom there was no need to spell it all out, because environmental law prevented building on the beach side of the grass dunes. Max took the phone from Tom's hand. "Good thing I sold it for a turtle sanctuary, since you is getting senile and can't follow directions no more," he told Jeb.

"Don't get your knickers in a knot. I told you there's no need to write it all down 'cause it's covered by law," Jeb rebutted.

"It better be!" Max said and hung up the phone. "I think it's time I got me a new lawyer. Old Jeb is past his prime."

Tom watched Max hang up the phone. Max's fingers were twisted with arthritis; he had a bum leg and his back hunched to the side. "I think maybe we all are," Tom smiled. "I'll see what I can find out."

Max sat back down in his favorite chair and began to move back and forth. As the floorboards squeaked and creaked to the rhythm of his rocker, Max had become chatty.

"Lunch is ready," Mariana called.

Tom unwound his tall frame from the chair and walked to the kitchen. Mariana didn't like to cook, but when she set her mind to it, she did a fine job. Tom's stomach growled in anticipation.

Sumer and Samuel ate like they'd been starved for a week. When Sumer had stuffed the last bite of chocolate cake into her mouth, she remembered that Tom was to tell her and Samuel Old Max's story about the great white bird.

41

Mariana went back to her painting. Sumer and Samuel flopped onto floor pillows. Tom returned to his comfortable chair and, propping his bare-feet on a cushioned ottoman, closed his eyes. A breeze drifted onto the lanai and across his face. With it came the faint smell of salt water. He breathed slow and deep. The pages of his memory fluttered backward a bit, until they stopped on Saturday two weeks back.

Tom was known for his storytelling, and he wanted to set the mood. In his mind he could hear Max's rocker creak and squeak across the porch floorboards. He remembered thunder rumbling in the background and smelled the wet grass. He heard the rhythm of the old man's voice. He saw a crow, ink black against green palm fronds, in a tree next to the house. The bird echoed the old man's crackling voice — sometimes high with excitement, sometimes low with sadness.

"I dropped my dinghy in one a them bays northwest of the Glades on the edge of the Islands. It turned out to be a regretful morning for fishing — I caught some little bitty ones but throwed them all back. Spent most of my morning getting the line back from them grabby mangroves.

"Just as the sun climbed straight up in the sky, I anchored that old dinghy a mine between two fair-sized islands and leaned back with a ham sandwich and soda pop. I hadn't more than taken my last bite and I heared a w-h-o- o-f, then another w-h-o-o-f a bit closer and another, a bit farther away. I set myself up straight and took a look around.

"Sure enough, I spotted the nose of one of them manatees as it come outta the water, blowed its nose and sunk back down. There must of been six or seven of them. I watched to see if they was any calves. Then just for fun I started timing one to see how long it stayed under. The sun was warm as melted butter and a bit a wind blew off the water, rocking me like a baby. Waves hardly big enough to notice slapped against the dinghy. I were having trouble keeping my blinkers open. Finally they slammed shut.

"Sometime later I woke to the whine of one of them blasted speedboats off in the distance. I got good ears, I heared it 'fore I saw it. Well, I opened one eye just a peek and watched the boat as it shot around the point of one of them big mangrove islands. It looked like a giant cigar. It were still off a ways but coming fast and headed my way.

"With binoculars I could see three of them men on deck, the captain and two others. Two was arguing. One grabbed himself a handful of the other's shirt and pushed him real hard. The second guy stumbled back, lost his balance and fell against the captain. The cap let go of the wheel for a sec and the boat spun quick-like to the right. In less than a shake, the cap brought it back around.

"I wished it would of kept spinning — them darn fools was acting dizzy in the head, might as well be so. The bow of that daggone boat was headed directly for the half- dozen manatees. The men in the boat was so busy fussing at one another, I don't reckon they even seen them sea cows. I tooted my horn then hollered and yelled. Thought I'd zip over and cut them off, so I pulled at the starter cord then cussed at the motor, but it were no use. It didn't catch.

"I watched the other boat as it came closer and closer; the captain didn't throttle back and he didn't change direction. The boat was coming at them tees full speed. I began again; I blasted the horn. I bellowed at them 'till I had a coughing fit; I whipped my arms through the air 'till both good and bad was crippled with cramps. Nothing I did got them darn fools' attention. I sat down breathing hard and feeling mighty wretched.

"This whole time I were asking the Almighty for help. Then I pulled off my cap, sat down and got real serious with the Lord. The thought of that cigar boat colliding with them manatees at that speed, well it made me sick. It filled this old nose of mine with a bad smell 'till I thought I'd puke. Then sudden-like, the sky dimmed. Air cooled down considerable. I slapped my cap atop this old head and gandered about.

"That's when I seen it. A large white cloud, hanging to the east. It looked like a balled-up fist, and I'm here to tell you; it drifted toward me with misty fingers uncurling from it, and them a-spreading out across the water. Right from the middle of that dad-burned fist came a white bird, big as life.

"This bird took its direction, seems like, from one of them foggy fingers, and it beelined straight for that cigar boat. Snow-white wings, 7-feet across if they was an inch, flew over top a me. I looked up and seen its eyes. They burned like fire that went clean through to the belly of me— knowed all there was to know in a blink.

"Its beak shined like a sword what's been spit polished. That captain, dimwitted as he seemed, could no way miss the blazing eyes and the daggerlike beak. As the great white bird came close, he started hollering and flailing his arms like a rag doll in a windstorm. He flopped them this way then that, trying to shoo the bird away, but it just kept on. Well, that captain must of decided it were no use to tangle with the 7-foot wingspan, the burning eyes and the sword like beak, 'cause he yanked the wheel hard to the right.

"That hunk of cigar-shaped fiberglass turned 90 degrees and forced itself right onto a sandbar. The boat pretty near tipped over as it dug a plow- line through the sand. It were like a game of chicken and them dummies lost big time. Once they knew they was grounded, them three cursed up a gray cloud and shook their fists at that bird. The great white bird turned south and headed toward the Everglades.

"Them three boaters, with hats and arms swinging at the swarms of bugs, ratcheted their cuss cloud up to black when they found out they was to be mosquito bait for the rest of the day.

"Manatees, I love them but, well, they don't seem to notice much. They continued to eat and w-h-o-o-f. I doubt they even took a clue how close they come to being manatee soup. I worked my motor 'til it caught then I turned from them three sorry-acting chaps and spun my dinghy toward home. Left them out there for the bugs to gnaw on.

"A little respect that's what they needed. I figured God's creatures should do the teaching."

"Is that story true?" Samuel asked when Tom was finished.

"Max says it is," Tom said once more closing his eyes. "Said the bird looked like a great white heron. Named it Yatzu. Hebrew for 'One Sent Out'."

"Why'd Gram say you knew this Yatzu?" Samuel asked with his head cocked to one side, studying Tom.

Tom looked at Mariana who appeared to be completely engrossed in her painting. "I asked your grandmother not to say anything about my involvement with that heron-like bird but I guess she forgot."

Sumer and Samuel watched Tom expectantly.

"I feel like a fool telling it."

Sumer and Samuel didn't blink. Tom shrugged, "OK, but it stays just between us, right?" The last part of the sentence rose in volume to include Mariana.

"Sure," the twins echoed.

"Sorry and right," Mariana said, proving that, as Tom expected, she was listening all along.

Tom related the story about the close call with Old Blue, the bird with the 7-foot wingspan, and the slow-walking turtle. Then he told them about the great white bird staring at him from a cypress tree and the meeting with Joe.

"How do you know it was the same great white bird all three times?" Sumer asked.

How had Old Max put it? "Its eyes burned like fire that seen clean through to the belly of me — knowed all there was to know in a blink."

"The eyes, I knew it because of the eyes. They have a fiery appearance, and when it looks at you ... Ah, never mind."

"No, what?"

"When they look at you, they seem to see inside your soul — like it knows your guilt and it knows your pain. Doesn't throw a shadow either."

"Doesn't throw a shadow?"

"The bird didn't have a shadow. It was sunny, and no shadow."

"You think it's an angel?" Sumer asked.

"No!" Samuel scoffed."

"Flaming eyes, sword like beak, knows your heart, sounds more like..." mused Mariana.

"What's the deal with the name Yatzu?" Sumer asked.

"Max gave it that name. Means 'One Sent Out,' like I told you. The cloud, the misty finger, the light-filled eyes maybe Yatzu is the perfect name for it after all," Tom said. His mind drifted from the lanai, from Mariana's painting, from the kids and his stories.

If God really did help people in times of trouble, what about Jade? Tom's soul moaned with grief. He closed his eyes and allowed himself to remember his daughter, to smell her orange blossom perfume, to hear her sandals slap against the tile floor, to see her slender suntanned arms encircled with three bracelets of gold, sparkling up and down her arm. It seemed a lot longer than a year since her last visit to Florida, when she gave him the raffia hat.

"Dad, will you open your gift now?" Jade had asked. I bought it in the Straw Market in St. Augustine. It's made of raffia palm that comes from Madagascar. Isn't it just the greatest?"

Tom took an intricately woven Panama-style hat from the box. It was tan with a 1-inch chocolate-brown leather band wrapped at the base of the crown. It smelled of grass fields and cattle on a hot summer day.

"Now Mariana, did you put her up to this? You know very well, I like my old straw just fine. It's broken in, not all stiff and new."

"What's the matter, Dad? Don't you like it?"

"Sure, it's a beauty and I really do need one for Sunday best."

"No, I bought it for everyday. Mom said your straw hat is dirty and has a big hole in it. She says she's embarrassed to be seen with you in it."

"O-h... Well, sure... Guess I didn't look at it hard enough the first time. Now I can see; it'll make a fine everyday hat," Tom said and gave Mariana a hard look.

"Come on kids. It's time to go to Everglades City," Jade called. "I signed the twins and me up for a boat ride into the Ten

Thousand Islands this afternoon; and if we don't hurry, we'll miss it.

"By the way," Jade continued as she followed the twins to the car. "Alan and I confirmed our trip to Africa next fall. The kids will stay with Aunt Ruth since we'll be gone the whole month of October. They can't miss that much school. I'll fill you in on the details later. See you this evening."

"Jade, wait! Let's talk about it now." Tom demanded. "Why do you have to go to Africa? With all the terrorist activity, travel outside the country is dangerous. And what about Ebola outbreaks in Africa?"

"We'll be traveling in the Masai Mara Game Reserve in Kenya. The latest Ebola outbreak is in Uganda, several hundred miles away. Senator Gall and his wife are going. Alan said this trip could make a difference to the security of our nation."

"What'd he mean by that?" Mariana asked. "I thought he had a grant to do a documentary on Africa's endangered animals."

"Jade, I don't want you going if there's a political agenda for this trip. Think about your children and their future," Tom said.

"I am thinking about the children and their future. We need to be going or we'll miss the boat. Love you both." Jade blew a kiss carried on the wind by orange blossom perfume and the melodic chime of three gold bracelets jingling on her arm.

The twins waved and Tom and Mariana watched until the car was just a pin-dot on the horizon.

"How can she do this to me? First she married that politician — which didn't turn out too bad. But then she moved to Washington, D.C., and got pregnant against the doctor's orders — 'course that turned out pretty great. But now, NOW she wants to pick herself up and go to Africa. Doesn't she have any consideration for her poor old father's heart? You've spoiled her that's what you've done. She's always gotten everything she ever wanted."

"Why is everything my fault? You did your share of spoiling too, you know," Mariana rebutted.

Tom refused to drop it. "And the two of you conniving to make me get rid of my old straw hat. Low down trick that's what I'd call it. I may have to wear this fancy raffia- palm-whatever so I don't hurt her feelings, but I'm not going to like it, and I'm not throwing my old hat away either!"

Indignantly, he had pushed the new hat on his head and stomped out of the house, slamming the screen door for emphasis. Why had he been so angry when his beautiful daughter gave him that wonderful hat?

"What is it Grandpa?" Sumer's alarmed face was inches from Tom's. He clutched his chest. His mind fuzzily drifted from the past back to the lanai, to Mariana painting, to the story he'd been telling the twins. He tried to focus on Sumer's face. Pain exploded from the left side of his chest and raged down his arm like a forest fire. Sweat dripped from his face.

"GRAM! Something's wrong with Grandpa," Sumer screamed. One look at Tom and Mariana sent Sumer and Samuel scrambling for the aspirin bottle, while she grabbed the phone and dialed 911.

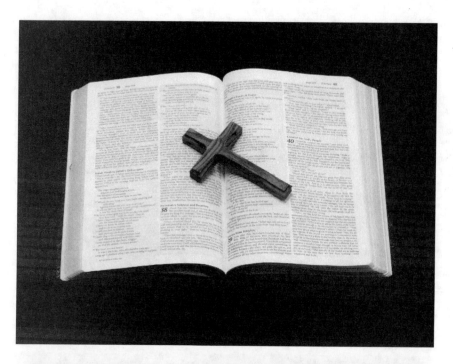

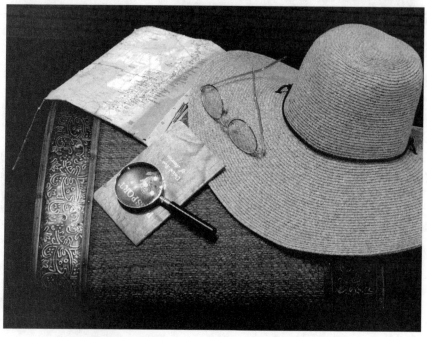

CHAPTER 4

Tom opened his eyes and saw Old Max looking down at him. "Are we dead?" he asked.

"Weren't last time I checked," Max said, allowing a crooked smile to brighten his wrinkled face. He was wearing the gold cross Tom remembered from the house in Everglades City. A worn Bible was tucked under his arm.

"Gave us a scare, you did."

"A heart attack?" Tom asked, his eyes exploring the hospital room with wires, IV bag and monitors surrounding him.

"Mild one is what the Doc said. You was talking in your sleep. Mumbled something about Jade and how you wasn't wanting to go on living without her. You know what I think?"

"No, and I'm not sure I want to," Tom said, trying to read a card wedged in the 'Y' of a stick protruding from a potted flower that rested on a table next to his bed.

"I think you're giving up, and you're work ain't done yet."

Tom rolled toward the window, away from Max, but as he did, he crimped a wire and a monitor blared loudly. The floor nurse rushed into the room, adjusted the wires and told Tom to lie still. Tom frowned, "I'm in no mood for a lecture."

"This ain't no lecture. Just felt the need to impart some wisdom," Max said, studying Tom. "I learned it the hard way; ain't no use you doing the same."

"I can't very well run away. If you're going to say your piece, get on with it."

Max gingerly lowered himself into a chair next to Tom's bed. "Remember Job, one of them characters in the good book?" He asked, removing the well-worn book from under his arm and sliding his thumb down the index tabs. "Remember all the fussing Job done at God, wishing he hadn't been born and all? Do you recall what God told him? I'll just read it if you'll give me a sec."

"Don't read it. Just give me the highlights," Tom said, waving his hand impatiently."

"Why you in such a hurry? You going someplace?" Max chuckled. Tom gave him a sour look.

"OK," Max stopped thumbing through the golden-edged pages. "Well, let's see." He knit his eyebrows together in concentration. "Job was fussing about his situation, and it were indeed grim. Children were dead; friends were a nagging him, and him with sores all over his body. Even so, God asks Job, who Job thinks he is that he should try to instruct or advise God. God tells Job he's puny against Almighty God and has no credentials to pester God about how He does His business. God is mighty. Man is not."

Max looked at the book in his hands and reverently rubbed an arthritic finger across the ancient brown leather. When he spoke, Tom could barely hear him. "You got a good woman and you got two grandkids to raise. Let God handle His business and you get on with the work He give you to do. Trust Him for a bit. Give Him a chance to answer all them prayers you been throwing His way." When he finished Max looked up from the cracked leather book to search Tom's face.

Weariness spilled from Tom's eyes and into his voice. "You think I've been acting like I believe God doesn't know what He's doing? Like He's failed me?"

"Well, if the shoe fits, maybe you ought to try it on," Max said. He stood up stiffly and hobbled to the window. Thunderheads were mounded in the western sky and only a fringe of sunlight was edged out around them.

"How can I believe God cares about me and my family, that He's in control? My daughter and son-in-law are gone ... maybe even dead!" Tom choked back tears.

"That's a tough one, all right. But the answer I hold to is that God's smarter than the likes of us. He don't answer to you and me." Max turned from his view of the threatening clouds to look at Tom.

"Job all over again, huh?" Tom said, shutting his eyes.

"Seems like it."

"How'd you get so smart, Max?"

"I is older than you. It comes with lots of getting knocked down and looking to Jesus to raise me back up," Max moved close and put his hand on Tom's shoulder. "I know it's hard to think about, but if that beautiful daughter of yours and her husband was to leave this world? Would they be any less in the hands of the Lord?"

"No, but I couldn't bare it," Tom said. Tears flooded from under his closed eyelids and run down his cheeks."

Yes you could; Jesus'd give you strength. He done it for me when Molly died." Max squeezed Tom's shoulder.

"Besides," Max continued, "we got ourselves another problem, one where you and me can do some good. I did me some checking and that Turtles and Me Educational Foundation, the one I sold my beach property to, turns out they unloaded that land a week later to a developer."

Tom, felt the warmth of the old man's hand on his shoulder. "Hand me a tissue, will you?"

"You heared me?" Max asked as he walked with difficulty across the room to a box of tissues and handed one to Tom.

Tom blew his nose loudly and wiped his eyes roughly.

"Yes, I heard you. I rather suspected they were up to no good. In fact, I am surprised they even exist."

"Yeah, well I messed up." Max again looked out the window, his back to Tom. "I suspect the Lord'll be calling on me to fix it. I'm old and I'm crippled. I'm gonna need your help. Buck up man. Start living for the work God's called us to do."

"What makes you think he's called me to do anything about your screw-up?"

"I already telled you! I'm old and I'm crippled. I need your help."

"I'm not giving up on Jade and Alan."

"I ain't asking you to. Just stop stewing and give the Lord a chance."

"Maybe you're right. Not sure there's anything I can do about it at this point anyway."

"You got one of these?" Max asked, thumping his Bible. "It's your best sword against them dark moments."

"Yes, I have one. Maybe I need to start opening the cover a little more often."

■ ■ ■

Monday morning four weeks later, Tom was at home dozing in the bedroom. The phone rang; Mariana answered on the first ring, "He's sleeping right now. Why are you calling, Senator? Do you have news?" Her anxious voice prompted Tom's bolt from the bed.

"Give me that," he said, running down the hall.

"Senator Gall. He says there's nothing new. Just wants to talk to us," Mariana gave Tom a reproachful look as she handed over the phone.

"This is Tom. What can I do for you, Senator?"

"Sorry to hear about your heart attack. I really hate to bother you, but can we meet? I could be at your place, say tomorrow."

"What's this all about?" Tom asked, pacing up and down the kitchen floor. "If you have news let's hear it."

"It's just a hunch. I don't want to talk about it over the phone."

"Tomorrow's fine." Tom turned a dinette chair to face the phone and sat down heavily. "Need a ride from the airport?"

"I'll rent a car; I have other business to address after I leave your place."

"What time will you be here?"

"Ask him for lunch," Mariana said, hovering over Tom."

"I'll see you tomorrow," Senator Gall said and hung up.

"What was that all about?" Mariana stood over Tom, concern etched across her face.

"You heard most of it. Says he has a hunch. Doesn't want to talk over the phone. He'll be here tomorrow morning, 10:30. Gave

54

me a start. I'm going back to bed," Tom said as he stood up and moved slowly down the hallway.

"You shouldn't be running like that. You OK?" Mariana called after him.

"Yeah, just peachy!"

Manatee

Manatee

CHAPTER 5

Sumer sat up in bed and opened her deep gray eyes. She pushed light brown hair behind one ear and, half asleep, attempted to focus around the shoulder length strand that clung to the other side of her face.

What woke me? Sounds of running water and muffled singing came from the adjoining bathroom. Ah, Samuel was up.

Falling back, she stretched and yawned then curled up under her favorite quilt. A breeze, blowing through an open window, danced her yellow curtains up and down. Outside, pink and apricot clouds shimmered above an orange-red sun that slowly emerged from the Gulf of Mexico. The blades of a ceiling fan hummed slowly in a clockwise direction.

Suspended halfway between wakefulness and sleep, Sumer was momentarily content. Grandpa Tom, home from the hospital for a month now, was gaining strength each day and she just dreamed the most wonderful dream.

In the dream her mom and dad stood next to a one-lane dirt road; behind them emerged thatched-roofed huts of an African village. Jade, dressed in a yellow and red African dashiki, tried without success to tame strands of pale brown hair that blew in the wind like long threads of silk. Alan, suntanned and tall, stood with his arm wrapped protectively around Jade's shoulder. The dream engulfed Sumer's senses. She smelled orange blossom perfume; she heard the jingle of gold bracelets moving up and down her mother's arm.

Sumer, feeling safe and content, stretched out under the covers. But as dark smoke drifts silently yet deadly through a keyhole, the black Cadillac drifted unwelcome into her memory. It emerged over the hill toward their old home in Virginia and started up the driveway. The midday sun glinted off its inky surface.

It had been a perfect Indian summer day and she hoped they wouldn't come. She wanted Senator and Missy Gall to forget, but when she saw the car she knew they hadn't. She knew her mom and dad were leaving with the Galls. It was all planned; they were going to Africa. Her dad had been awarded grant money to make a documentary film on the endangered wildlife of Africa. Senator and Missy Gall were going along on the trip.

Suitcases were thrown into the car's massive trunk; Jade and Alan smothered Sumer and Samuel in hugs. Then, seeing the tears on Sumer's cheeks, Jade said, "Don't worry we'll be back soon." Sumer waved until the black Cadillac disappeared on the far side of the third hill.

The last week of their month-long safari, the phone rang at midnight. Aunt Ruth answered and was told that Jade and Alan had been attacked and kidnapped while traveling through Africa's bush country. No one knew why the two of them were alone, so far from camp.

Sumer at first was sure Senator Gall was wrong and that the whole thing was a giant mistake. As the details of the abduction bore down on her, however, she threw herself onto the couch and sobbed inconsolably.

Samuel sank to the floor, curled his body into a tight ball and rocked back and forth. A waterfall of tears poured down his face. "Why didn't God protect them?" He asked over and over again.

Aunt Ruth, the type that needed to stay busy in times of crisis, grabbed a bucket and mop to scrub the floor. "Keep praying," she told Samuel as she flung soap and water across the tile. "We don't know that He didn't." The floor finished, Aunt Ruth fidgeted then took down a bowl and dumped flour and yeast together. After heating the milk, she added butter, eggs and salt, she stirred and kneaded until she had a dough ball that was smooth. The next morning the floor gleamed and the smell of cinnamon rolls filled the kitchen, but Aunt Ruth, exhausted from no sleep, still faced the dreadful job of breaking the news to Tom and Mariana.

Over the next few weeks, adult conversation stopped abruptly whenever Sumer and Samuel entered a room. The twins fought back by listening through heat vents and at doorways. They heard disjointed conversations about the attackers being poachers, but

Senator Gall once mentioned he suspected Alan might have left camp to meet with a group of anti-terrorists. Official Washington was silent. The FBI launched an investigation.

Days turned into weeks and weeks into months; no ransom note came and no terrorist group took credit for the attack. All leads turned cold as the north side of an ice floe.

Yet seared into Sumer's memory were her mother's words, "Don't worry, we'll be back soon."

The twins moved to Florida to live with their grandparents and in the beginning, nights were the worst for Sumer. She frequently padded back and forth across her bedroom floor long after the house was dark. She stared out her bedroom window into the moonlit back yard and often saw Grandpa Tom's silhouette kneeling in the shadow of a giant magnolia. Snippets of his prayers drifted to her on the ebb and flow of the nighttime breeze. Sometimes she could hear him plainly as he cried into the star filled sky, "Why God? WHY?"

Months later, Sumer still had an ache deep in her gut that refused to go away. It subsided when she kept her mind busy, but renewed its assault whenever her thoughts were quiet. She stubbornly refused to give up hope. Her mother's voice echoed from every recess in her brain, "Don't worry, we'll be back soon." Yet in unguarded moments Sumer wondered if she'd ever feel whole again.

The shower water turned off and Samuel's muffled singing faded into a low hum. Sumer's curtains again caught her attention as they bounced in the wind, and the sun now peeked through large tree branches to shine in her window. She threw back the covers, stepped out of bed and walked across the room. Elbows braced on the cool windowsill, oval face resting in her palms, she breathed in the early morning fragrance of orange trees and salt water. A wind chime jangled somewhere in the distance.

Sumer picked up a picture that was taken of her grandparents, Samuel and herself. Most people thought the twins didn't look much alike except for their coloring. Sumer's facial features were similar to Mariana's — high cheekbones, large eyes, small nose and mouth. Samuel was a good mix between his dad and grandpa. Both twins, however, had golden brown hair like their mother and a lighter version of Grandpa Tom's smoky gray eyes. Grandma Mariana's smaller stature, golden-silver curls and green eyes stood out in contrast.

Sumer put the picture back and turned toward the window to look for a red cardinal that whistled, "Cheer-whoit; cheer- whoit-whoit; cheer-whoit- whoit-whoit." She caught glimpses of the scarlet bird as it played hide and seek in a massive banyan tree with stringy roots dangling from its branches toward the ground. Further out on the lawn, a canopy of lacy green leaves and bright orange flowers formed the top of a royal Poinciana tree. A triangle of 4-year-old navel orange trees stood to the right of her window. In the center of the yard, a majestic southern magnolia tree towered, guarding Grandma Mariana's rose garden.

Immersed in the beauty that surrounded her, Sumer sensed the Lord's presence. Warm and loving, it buoyed her like floating atop warm ocean water on a summer day.

The dream seemed real; the colors were vivid. Sumer wondered if the dream was God's way of telling her that her mom and dad were okay.

■ ■ ■

Samuel's sharp thump, thump, thump on the bedroom door startled Sumer. As a result her reply was harsher than intended, "Don't be so loud! You'll wake Grandpa!"

"Well, are you going to sleep all day? I'm bored. Let's go do something," Samuel said. Silence was the only answer.

"Sumer, are you ignoring me?"

"No, I'm thinking."

"Well?" He was getting impatient.

" OK," she agreed. "Meet me under Old Smoky in 10 minutes. We'll take the canoe and look for Mindy."

"Hurry!" With shoes in hand, Samuel left the house and sprinted across the lawn to a large banyan tree that, last summer, had been struck by lightning. He was soon climbing from one branch to another, headed for the top.

Sumer pulled on denim shorts and a white tee shirt then sat down to buckle her sandals. As she did, her eyes lingered on a large painting that hung above her bed — colors of an evening sun mirrored in shallow water; a pond surrounded by swamp grass and cattails and a great white bird with iridescent wings set to land. Gram painted that picture on a Sunday, the same day Sumer and Samuel first heard about Yatzu; the same day Grandpa Tom had his heart attack. Sumer loved that painting and usually it gave her great comfort.

Today looking at it brought back the memories and with them came pain and fear. Once upon a time, she thought, my life was happy and carefree, but that seems like another life. One where families lived happily ever after and parents protected their children from the dark. That life now seems a lie. Grandpa is sick and Mom and Dad are gone. Grayness threatened to pull her down.

"NO! Not today!" She forced back the dark thoughts.

"Grandpa is home from the hospital. Mom and Dad will be found any day now, and through it all, God never leaves or forsakes." She buckled her shoe, snatched a wide-brimmed hat and owl-shaped sunglasses. She dashed off the porch and ran toward the bay.

■ ■ ■

Samuel looked small perched at the top of Old Smoky. Actually, he was tall for his age. His dark complexion made him less susceptible to sunburn. A thoughtful, square jaw gave him the appearance of stubbornness, and his gray eyes and light brown hair mirrored Sumer's.

Samuel braced his back against the tree's trunk. Holding binoculars steadily to his eyes, he searched Chokoloskee Bay for Mindy.

Mindy, along with five or six other manatees, frequently fed in the bay near Banyan City where the twins and their grandparents lived. Banyan City, a small town located on an island, was surrounded by Chokoloskee Bay and the Gulf of Mexico. This island was located inside the boundaries of Everglades National Park and was one of the larger of the Ten Thousand Islands.

Today, even with the help of his lofty perch and binoculars, Samuel was unable to find a single manatee. "Great! No manatees and my best friends have abandoned me. Now what?"

Samuel gave in to a somber mood. He already missed his buddies and they had only been gone one day. The two friends were traveling up north with their families for two months. This left Samuel to fend for himself during summer break.

"I guess I do have Sumer to hang out with," he admitted. Sometimes it was handy having a twin. The fact that she was a dedicated tomboy suited him just fine.

A screen door slammed. Samuel jerked out of his reverie. He saw Sumer dash out of the house, jump off the porch and run hard toward the water. "I'll beat you to the canoe!" she shouted at Samuel.

Scrambling from his perch, Samuel sprinted across the lawn toward the water. He mentally kicked himself for staying in the tree so long. He and Sumer had a deal. First person to the canoe sat up front; the other one paddled. When Grandpa Tom was feeling better, Samuel needed to ask him about buying a second paddle.

His sister had a significant head start, but Samuel ran hard to catch up. He pushed alongside and, grabbing her wide-brimmed straw hat, threw it high over his head. The hat caught the wind and soared through the air. Samuel sprinted a few more yards. Confidant Sumer would go back to pick up her hat, he slowed his pace and swaggered toward the canoe.

Sumer watched the wide brim of her hat float across the blueness of the morning sky. She lost speed momentarily, but quickly regained her focus and recovered her rhythm. Arms and legs pumping hard, she mustered enough speed to catch up to her brother.

If he had not been congratulating himself so loudly he might have heard her coming. Two hands planted in the middle of his back. Two hands, propelled by 80 pounds of forward motion, shoved him hard.

Caught off guard, Samuel lost his balance. His arms flung forward and his legs tangled together as he took a nosedive onto the sand. He lay there, stretched out on his stomach, and glared at Sumer. She, on the other hand, catching her breath and feigning nonchalance, climbed into the canoe.

Samuel stood up and inspected his stinging knees. Damp sand clung to his shorts and shirt. Maybe I should go back to the house and leave Sumer to spend the day by herself, he thought. Anger at his friends resurfaced. How dare they abandon him for a summer up north? He brushed his knees and knocked sand from his clothes. I'll be bored stiff if I spend the day hanging around the house. I can work in the yard. That ought to be a real blast, he thought with sarcasm.

As he saw it, he had two choices. Swallow his hurt pride, ignore his scuffed knees and go with his sister or get even with her for something he'd actually started by spending the day in the doldrums — boredom, pride; pride, boredom. The decision was not easy for a 12- almost 13- year- old boy. Finally, with as much dignity as he could muster, Samuel walked to the boat and stepped inside.

The twins sat in the canoe and looked at each other. "Is that sand in your hair?" Sumer asked, a smile twitching at both corners of her mouth.

"Yeah, thanks," Samuel countered. "Your glasses are crooked." He looked at the straw hat, abandoned on the lawn. "Did you drop your hat?" He grinned.

"Me! Drop my hat! I don't think so. You're the one who threw it. You get it!"

"You get the hat. I'll paddle first, no complaints," Samuel compromised.

Sumer didn't want to argue anymore and she hated to paddle, so she clambered out of the boat and ran in the direction of the straw hat. As her index and middle fingers grasped its rim, something white fluttered into her peripheral vision. She looked up to meet the flaming eyes of a large white bird with tall yellow legs and sword like yellow bill.

"Sumer, let's go!" Samuel shouted. The bird flared and Sumer ran back to the boat.

"Did you see that?" She squealed.

"See what?"

"The great white heron?"

"You're nuts! Great whites don't come this far north of the Keys. Must've been an egret."

"It had yellow legs; egrets have black. It was bigger than an egret, and the eyes burned bright like a star."

"What are you babbling about?" Samuel asked.

"The heron, the great white heron."

"It wasn't a heron. I've never seen one around here; so forget it and give us a shove."

Sumer took off her sandals and threw them into the boat. Cool waves lapped around her ankles as she stepped into the water. She pushed until the water was knee-deep then belly-flopped into the canoe.

Samuel skillfully maneuvered the canoe away from shore and into Chokoloskee Bay. He dipped the canoe paddle, pulling it through velvety smooth, sun-sparkled water, and relaxed as his attention was drawn to nature at its best — the bright smell of salty sea air, the sound of a osprey's urgent cry, the sight of an eagle soaring through infinite blueness. Samuel pointed skyward, motioning for Sumer to look.

She positioned her face toward the gliding eagle but behind her apparent watchful gray eyes her mind raced. It was a great white heron; at least it looked like one. Sumer thought about Grandpa Tom's description of the great white bird he and Max had seen. Was the bird she just saw the same one?

Sumer's mind twisted and turned down a trail of unanswered questions while Samuel's drifted at peace with his surroundings. Yet both sat in the same canoe. A canoe that followed a trail forged hours before by an odd, if not bizarre, twosome — a 50-year-old loggerhead turtle and an injured brown pelican. Two species in danger of extinction.

■ ■ ■

Tom lay in bed next to Mariana. Comforted by her quiet breathing, he thought about Senator Gall and what possible reason there was for him to fly all the way from Washington, D.C., to Southwest Florida.

The screen door slammed. Must be the kids, he thought.

After pulling on shirt and shorts, he went to investigate. Padding in bare feet through the kitchen, he looked out the window and saw Sumer running hard toward the water. As Samuel caught her he heaved her hat skyward. Tom started toward the door but stopped when Sumer knocked Samuel cart-over-teakettle into the sand. Before he could decide whether or not to interfere, they were both in the canoe headed toward the north end of the bay.

"Kids!" Tom chuckled to himself.

Sumer and Samuel often rose early to go canoeing. They liked to swim with the manatees and dolphins that frequented the north end of Chokoloskee Bay. And as long as they were together, Tom didn't worry much. He knew by lunchtime they'd be back, clamoring for food.

Actually he was glad the twins were out of the house for the morning. He didn't want them around until after he discovered the reason for Senator Gall's visit. If the Senator had good news he'd have told Tom and Mariana on the phone. It was either bad news or no news, which to Tom amounted to basically the same thing.

Loggerhead Turtle

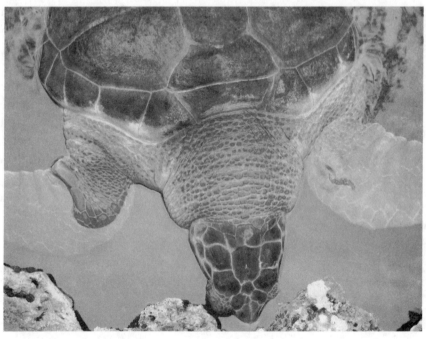

DO NOT DISTURB SEA TURTLES OR THEIR NESTS!

Between May 01 and October 31: The Marco Island Beach is an important nesting area for the endangered Loggerhead Sea Turtle.

Sea turtles need a beach free of barriers that would prevent nesting and hatching. ALL BEACH FURNITURE, EQUIPMENT, AND GARBAGE SHOULD BE REMOVED FROM THE BEACH EVERY NIGHT.

To report disoriented, injured, or dead sea turtles, please contact the Sea Turtle Stranding Network at **1-888-404-FWCC**

City of Marco Island Sea Turtle Protection Ord. 01-35

Loggerhead Turtle Nest

CHAPTER 6

Trina was miles from shore in the Gulf of Mexico. She swam just under the surface of the water. The dark reddish-brown color of her head and upper shell hid her from sharks that swam above, while the color of her light-yellow flippers and lower shell camouflaged her body from predators beneath. Her disproportionately large head won her the title of loggerhead.

Trina pulled her paddle-shaped flippers rhythmically through the salty water; their dip-drag-lift, dip-drag-lift, dip-drag-lift motion seemed to repeat, "a few-more-miles, a few-more-miles, a few-more- miles." A secluded beach on Grand Island, largest of the Ten Thousand Islands, was the loggerhead's destination.

One year earlier, she arrived at the midnight hour; a full moon shimmered off the water. Trina had labored to drag her 200-pound body onto the dry sand of Grand Island, only to find the nighttime quiet shattered and the apparently deserted beach suddenly come alive. A robust woman with curly red hair and two children scampered from the shadows in hot pursuit of tiny creatures that dashed across the wet sand. The children squealed with delight and the woman puffed from exertion as they attempted to herd a swarm of early turtle hatchlings into the ocean.

The three stopped long enough to stare at Trina but were soon compelled to resume their running, dodging and shooing. Trina waited until the last unruly hatchling was noisily escorted into the surf and the humans had departed back into the night. When quiet once more reigned, the loggerhead dug a hole in the sand and laid her eggs.

This year it was late afternoon when she approached Grand Island. As the loggerhead neared the beach, the 50-year-old turtle's wrinkled head and neck broke the water's surface. She looked, closed her eyes, opened them and looked again. Instead of the lonely, peaceful beach she expected, the loggerhead saw a tall concrete pillar spiking into the sky. Other pillars were being pounded and steel cross beams were piled high on the ground. In and around the concrete and steel, noisy construction machinery spewed smoke into the air.

The machinery's oversized tires ripped craters into the sand. Next to one such depression, a half-dozen people kneeled. They sifted the sand with their fingers and carefully removed small white turtle eggs.

Construction workers with angry faces loomed over the egg gatherers. "Hurry up!" they yelled. "We've got work to do!"

Most confusing was the location of this new building compared to the ones that sparkled in the sun behind the grass-covered sand dunes. Why wasn't this one back there with the rest of them? Fear encouraged Trina to turn back to the sea, yet instinct drew her to the only place she had ever laid her eggs. She began the laborious job of dragging her large saucer-shaped body onto the sand until a bulldozer headed toward her.

She felt the heat of the machine's exhaust and the thunder of vibrating earth. Fear overcame her bodily urgings to lay eggs and she pushed herself backward, scooting into the water.

Overhead a large white bird hovered, then swooped down to land between bulldozer and turtle. It watched as the loggerhead paddled safely into deep water and sank out of sight. The magnificent snow-white bird then turned its eyes, like flames of fire, on the machine and its driver.

Brown Pelican

Brown Pelican

Brown Pelican

CHAPTER 7

A large dump truck bore down on Trina. The loggerhead dug faster and faster, widening the hole in the sand. The faster she dug the faster the truck approached. The huge vehicle was almost upon her. She saw the driver's face. He laughed, deliberately aiming for her. His foot pushed hard on the gas pedal. Trina turned toward the safety of the ocean but her legs froze. The truck was inches away! It was going to crush her!

Trina woke with a start; her large body still rested on the ocean floor. She shook off the dream and headed for the surface. Her head poked cautiously above the water, but to her dismay, the construction project had not been a dream. The concrete pilings still towered against the sky, but the machinery now stood quiet and the humans were gone.

The loggerhead swam to shore. She had broken through a thin but tough eggshell to see her first glimpse of the world from this beach 50 years ago, and now instinct drew her back year after year. Performing the ritual of digging a hole and depositing in it was futile this year. The eggs would be crushed before they could hatch.

Trina flopped down on the beach in despair. Her solitude was once again brought to an end. This time neither a woman with curly red hair nor noisy construction machinery invaded her space. Instead it was the great white bird with eyes like flames of fire. The large bird flew silently overhead and landed a few feet away. Its long yellow legs sloshed through shallow water along the beach. Though its sword like beak gleamed with light from the sinking sun, its majestic form did not create a shadow on the water.

The loggerhead sprawled in despair on the wet sand and watched the great white bird with uneasiness. The bird navigated slowly along the shoreline until it reached the shade of nearby mangroves. The sun set and darkness settled in for the night. The moon moved in and out of gathering clouds. Sometimes it illuminated beach and water; sometimes it hid its light behind giant thunderheads.

During one dark period of the moon, Trina's solitude was again disturbed, this time by the sound of shuffling footsteps. The loggerhead turned around and stared into the night. Her stare was met with silence. Some moments later she heard it again, drag shuffle-shuffle, drag shuffle-shuffle. Silence. Drag shuffle-shuffle, drag shuffle-shuffle. Silence. As the drag shuffle-shuffles grew louder, a bolt of lightning lit up the sky and Trina saw a large, squatty bird, dragging its left wing and shuffling its webbed feet across the sand. The brown pelican, seeing the loggerhead, emitted a long series of croaks and squawks that echoed down the beach.

Lightning flashed, thunder exploded. The great white bird emerged from under the overhanging mangrove branches. Making use of its 7-foot wingspan, it sailed through tumultuous skies to hover closely above turtle and pelican.

The rain started slowly, like a sprinkling can watering a garden, then intensified into a steady sheet of water reaching from sky to earth. The water flooded over and around the loggerhead. It drenched the brown pelican. Then the dark clouds, the lightning and rumbling thunder moved south, toward the Everglades and the Ten Thousand Islands. The rain on Grand Island's beach slowed to a drizzle, then stopped. The pelican shook himself and sent another series of croaks and squawks in the direction of the loggerhead.

Trina, annoyed by the disturbance, listened to the bird. At first it was only clamor, but slowly it became more; Trina sensed the bird's distress. The loggerhead's eyes skittered nervously across the panorama of her surroundings. What was going on?

Her attention skimmed past but immediately returned to the great white bird. Its long legs once again sloshed through shallow water under the dark foliage of entwined mangrove trees. Its flame-filled eyes burned with passion. Another series of croaks and squawks caused the loggerhead to turn her head toward the brown pelican. No interpreter was needed. The squatty bird croaked and Trina began to understand the sounds.

"Bad form busting in on your holiday like this, old girl, but I've met with a bit of an accident," the brown pelican squawked as it shuffled closer. "Name's Nigel. Minding my own business, I was, cruising along the water's edge. Didn't see the daft thing, flew right into it, that tall concrete spike I mean. What daft critter would be about putting such rubbish so close to the water? It looms in the dark with no notice at all of its presence. My wing feels blooming awful; I should think I broke it!" With that, the pelican moaned and plopped down onto the sand.

Trina turned to glare at the great white bird. She was a loner and didn't want to get involved with some frumpy pelican. Loggerheads take care of themselves and expect everything else to do the same. They don't even stay around to raise their own hatchlings; they leave that to God and nature. She didn't want to be drawn into this pelican's problems. But for some unexplainable reason she was. She even felt a twinge of pity for the injured bird.

The great white bird's flaming eyes continued to looked directly into hers. Somehow that feather-covered torch was behind all this, Trina just knew it. Compulsion to answer filled the turtle, and finally she gave in to its urging. A low groan rose and fell inside her throat.

"I think it painfully obvious that humans put that building there. You have humans where you come from, I assume? Seems that these particular ones could be beat out by a peanut in a contest for common sense."

"I was hatched in England, I was. Lived most recently in Australia, but ... long story. Mind peeking at my wing, old girl, see if it's busted? Hurts like the deuces, it does!"

The loggerhead scooted backward toward the Gulf. Maybe this beach was not, after all, the only one where she could lay her eggs. "Old girl yourself!" She mumbled as her hind legs reached toward the warm seawater. "Fifty in turtle years is not considered old; 200, maybe, but not 50."

Trina, her large body buoyed by the salt water, took a last look at the pelican. He did look pitiful. While free-floating in the water, the loggerhead studied the great white bird. Oh condemnation! She thought. I do, after all, have a common bond with the squatty pelican. We are both victims of that absurd construction project. She swam to the beach and again dragged her saucer-shaped shell onto dry sand. New to this Florence Nightingale act, she wasn't sure what she could do to help, but she motioned to the pelican.

Nigel managed a pigeon-toed, drag-waddle-waddle to where Trina stood. He was a stocky bird, brown body, white head crowned with yellow. His long white neck exhibited a deep cinnamon stripe down the nape and was attached to his pointed bill by a leathery pouch.

"Here, old girl, help me brace this daft appendage next to my breast. Then it might not be so blasted painful," pleaded Nigel.

"Old girl! Old girl? I'll have you know I'm not old," huffed Trina. Nurse Nancy she was not, but as she grudgingly examined the pelican's wing, her attitude softened. "Perhaps you're right; it could be broken." Then, gently maneuvering the wing with her lips and teeth, she managed to pleat it close to his body.

"Good form, old ... I mean, mate. Good form. By the by, you never mentioned what it is you're about, here on the beach, in the shank of the night? You'd have to be daft as a brush to make a nest and lay eggs next to that confounded blighter."

Wrinkling her face even more than usual, Trina returned her attention to the looming concrete and piles of steel. "Well, I'm not daft, as you so kindly put it, and I'm not planning to lay my eggs next to this mess. It's not an option. But I do need another one. Now don't bother me; I need to think." Without further comment, she closed her eyes and laid her leathery head and neck down on the sand.

With nothing else to do, Nigel settled down next to the turtle. While resting his head and bill on Trina's shell, he noticed a large white bird. It moved away from the black shadows of the mangrove branches only to return to them. The pelican studied the white bird's eyes. They blazed, piercing the night. The light grew fuzzy as fatigue drifted over the pelican and the injured bird slept.

A full moon broke through the scattered clouds and Trina's head popped off the ground. She looked around. She saw Nigel using her shell for a pillow. She saw the concrete pillar casting an eerie shadow on the beach and she saw the great white bird now wading in the surf. Its eyes, bright like fire, seemed to beckon to her as it rose from the water and flew south over the mangrove islands. Trina remembered visiting a unique lagoon that was hidden deep in the Ten Thousand Islands. She watched the great white bird as it became smaller and smaller in the distant sky.

"Come along, we're going to Kingdom Cove, and if we start now we might make it by morning," the turtle groaned.

Nigel did not know what Kingdom Cove was, where it was located or what possible good it would do to go there. But not knowing what else to do, he followed Trina into the water. With a broken wing he was unable to fly, and even paddling as fast as his webbed feet could move, the pelican was soon left far behind.

Trina considered leaving him to fend for himself, but she decided instead to go back and try pushing him. The pelican wasn't crazy about traveling alone in unfamiliar territory, but being goosed by a turtle's nose was not to his liking either.

Trina finally agreed to let him ride on her shell. After several dunkings and many remarks such as, "bad show, old girl" and "I say, this isn't working a whit," Nigel finally mastered the art of gripping the wet shell. With Trina swimming just above the water's surface and the pelican hanging on for all he was worth, the unlikely twosome swam through the Gulf into a large bay. From one end of the night to the other, they wove their way through the Ten Thousand Islands, using the stars to guide them and the full moon to light their way.

A bright orange sun was just peeking above the Gulf waters when the strange duo rounded the northern tip of a large mangrove island. "I say, old girl, is this it? The sun is showing its barmy face, we should be there by now," Nigel croaked.

"I told you not to call me old girl! I'm a mere teenager in turtle years."

"Sorry, mate. I have a fierce cramp in my leg; mind if I hop off for a spell?"

"Suit yourself. This mangrove island does look familiar. I think I'll check around and see if I can find the hidden channel. It's been a long time since I've been to the lagoon. You stay put; I'll be back before you can shake a lamb's ear."

"A lamb's ear? I recall it being a rabbit's ear," Nigel croaked.

"Stay put! I'll be back shortly," Trina grunted, shaking her head in irritation.

Ignoring Trina's order to stay put, Nigel swam toward a nearby beach. He paddled slowly, debating with himself whether it was most likely a rabbit's ear and not, after all, a lamb's ear as Trina had indicated.

"I suppose rabbits, though not plentiful, are more likely than lambs to be found on an island. I should think, however, that a bunny would take offense at one mussing with its auditory apparatus. Lambs, if one could be gained, are more gentle creatures and mightn't fuss about a tug on the ear. Come to think of it, I'm not sure, not sure at all, whether it would be more seemly to shake a rabbit's ear or a lamb's. ..."

"Lambs, rabbits, rabbits, lambs. Why does it matter?" Trina called back to the pelican. Worn out by his incessant clatter, the loggerhead dived underwater to search the island's perimeter. Halfway around she found a large crooked limb, hanging into the water. After investigation, Trina discovered that beyond the crooked limb was a narrow channel — a channel that twisted and turned its way into the island's interior. She raised her head above the surface of the water intending to call out to Nigel, but was distracted instead by the sight of the great white bird, standing on a branch near the channel's entrance.

The majestic bird didn't appear to notice Trina, but looked intently beyond the crooked limb. It's the same one from last night, Trina thought. Is it following us or are we following it? "I've found it!" she finally called to Nigel.

Apparently done with his discourse on ear tugging, Nigel performed a pigeon-toed jig on one leg while stretching and shaking the other leg. "I am delighted with the news; I can't recall when I have been this exhaustificated, and my leg still has a beastly cramp in it."

Exhaustificated? Trina wondered as she swam over to Nigel. Seeing the pelican's gyrations, she shook her head in disgust. He was such a nuisance. She'd love to leave him behind and go on alone, but remembering his broken wing, she felt pity for the bird. An in an annoying way, he was somewhat endearing. "Come on Nigel; let's get started. I'll swim slow so you can keep up."

Loggerhead turtle, with the brown pelican trailing behind, ducked under the crooked limb and entered the obscure waterway. Dodging one branch after another, they slowly twisted and turned down the dimly lit channel. After a half-hour of fighting through insects and tangled vegetation, Nigel complained, "I certainly can't imagine anything worthwhile being at the end of this bug-infested unpleasantness."

"Life is but a hazardous climb to the heights of glory. The harder the journey the greater the reward," Trina said.

"If that's true, then this lagoon must be a blooming beaut," Nigel responded.

CHAPTER 8

Senator Gall drove up in a white convertible. Tom and Mariana had not seen him in over a year. Time has not been kind to the senator, Tom thought, as the balding 6-foot-2 man emerged from his rental car and walked stiffly to the front door.

Settling down in an overstuffed chair with a glass of cold lemonade, Senator Mike Gall cleared his throat. "I'm not sure how to say this."

"Just get to it," Tom said.

Mariana shot him a look.

The Senator fumbled with his tie, then loosened it and pulled it over his head. "I had a dream. No...I have a recurring dream. In it Alan is standing and begging me to come over to Africa and help him."

Mike Gall looked at Tom then Mariana uncertain he should continue. "I believe God sometimes talks to people in dreams. I think He is talking to me through this dream. I wanted you both to know."

"Oh," Mariana said.

Tom sat in silence, his eyes staring a whole through the Senator's head. "Have you lost all of your marbles as well as some of your hair?" He finally said.

"Tom!" Mariana said. "Let him finish."

"I suffered though the dream every night for a week. Every time I closed my eyes, there it was. Vivid. Bright colors. Always the same, Alan standing and begging me to come help him. I couldn't get it out of my head. I had to do something." Mike Gall picked up his glass and His hand shook as he tilted the rim and took a long, slow drink.

"After browbeating friends and anyone who owes me a favor, I convinced a couple of agents on assignment in Kenya, to poke around, see if they can find some answers. This is not to be taken lightly. They could get in trouble or even be in danger. Nobody, not the U.S. government nor Kenya, has sanctioned any farther investigation. Normal channels are closed. The FBI's evidence pointed to ... the Mara River at flood stage, strong currents, crocodiles. I don't need to spell it out.

"That's why Samuel and Sumer received all the life insurance money and you, as their guardians, were given the authority to manage their trust.

"I suspect there was more to the government grant that Alan received. More than the making of a documentary film about Africa's endangered animals." The senator stared at his shaking hand. "Alan said something about an informant that could give the FBI information concerning terrorist camps in Africa."

"What?" Tom asked. "What did he say?"

"Not much. I'm sure he told me more than he intended. He immediately changed the subject, refused to discuss it further." The senator stood to pace in front of a large window that faced into the back yard. "I've mulled over our conversation a hundred times, and I think he planned to meet with this informant while in the Mara Reserve."

"I don't believe Alan would intentionally place Jade in a situation of such danger," Mariana said, indignation straightening her spine.

Senator Gall walked back to the chair and sat down heavily. "I'm sure he intended that she should stay behind and bring help if he failed to return."

"Jade would have insisted on going along," said Tom.

"Not to be disrespectful, but your daughter did have a stubborn streak, and she hated to be kept out of the action."

"Why didn't you know about this at the time?" Tom's voice was hard with accusation.

"Even though Alan was assigned to help me most of the time, he did special projects for others in the department. It may have been top secret." Mike looked down at his hands then up to search Tom and Mariana's faces. He saw Tom's square jaw set in anger and his dark gray eyes filled with jagged pain. On the other end of the couch Mariana sat; her eyes brimmed over with sadness, but behind the sadness was hope that refused to die.

"Did Jade ever mention anything about Alan's plans to meet with someone while in Africa?" Mike asked.

"Just that Alan told her this trip could make a difference to the security of the nation," Tom said, squinting his eyes at Mike Gall.

"She did tell us that! I remember now. She said it the day she and the kids went on that Everglades boat ride. We asked her what he meant and she didn't answer." Mariana sat on the far side of the couch and twisted the corner of her apron.

"We should have pried harder," Tom mumbled, leaning back against the couch and closing his eyes.

"I suspect there was a meeting and Jade insisted on going along. They may have been set up from the beginning, or a traitor infiltrated our organization and they were betrayed. Either way, they and their captors headed directly — no wrong turns or side trips — toward the Mara River. This tells me their captors were familiar with the area and must have known the river was at flood stage and teeming with crocodiles. I am convinced they did not wade into that river to their peril."

"You think they had a boat tied off, waiting for them?" Tom asked. He rose from the couch and walked to the window where he stood, staring into the yard.

"A boat, a raft, a helicopter. Something..."

"Was there room for a helicopter to land?"

"I don't know, but I think something had to have been waiting for them. Nothing else makes sense.

"Alan was like a brother to me. I should have suspected he was up to something and put a stop to it!" Mike Gall buried his head in his hands.

Mariana rose from the couch and walked to the senator's chair. Her warm touch patted comfort into his shoulder. "Thank you for coming. I feel it too, a sense, deep inside my heart, that they're still alive. Can Tom and I do anything?" she asked hopefully. "Should we go to Africa and look for them ourselves?"

Mike's head shot up. "No! We can't tip our hand. That's why I didn't tell you all this on the phone. Someone in the organization may be a double agent. If Jade and Alan's captors think we have given up, they may let down their guard and make a mistake. Bill and Ed may learn something. We have the hardest job. Stay put and act normal."

"And what, in the middle of all this mess, can be considered normal? You're putting your faith in a dream that was most likely caused by bad pizza," Tom said, giving Mike a sour look.

"I'm not putting my faith in the dream, but I am putting it in the one who, I believe, sent it. Joseph with his many-colored coat dreamed his brothers would one-day bow down to him. I'm sure he suffered doubt many times. He was sold into slavery and put into prison, but when the time was right, as second in command in Egypt, he was in a position to save his whole family from the famine in Israel. The apostle Peter talks in the book of Acts about how, in the last days, old men will dream dreams — and right now I feel very old.

"I waited a long time before coming to you. I didn't want to disrupt your lives, but the dream kept coming back."

"God is faithful," Mariana said as she sat down again on the edge of the couch and smoothed the twisted corner of her painter's apron.

"When I heard about Tom's heart attack I decided to make this trip. I hope I did the right thing."

"Act normal, dreams, bah," Tom said and turned his scowling face to look out the window once more.

Mariana gave the back of Tom's head a sharp look. "I for one am glad you came. I'm glad someone else is convinced that there is still hope. " She got up from the couch and once more gave Senator Gall a pat on the shoulder. She smiled a reassuring smile. "You are welcome to come back, anytime.

"Now let's have lunch. Tom, have you seen the children this morning? They should be clamoring for food by now."

"I saw them take off in the canoe this morning. They'll be back."

Everglades River of Grass

CHAPTER 9

Samuel, enjoying the warm sunny day, and Sumer, lost in her thoughts, continued to travel by canoe through Chokoloskee Bay. Their search for Mindy and the other manatees had been futile even though they visited most of the sea cow's favorite feeding spots.

Paralleling the shore, 50 yards out, the twins' canoe glided past Mr. Greentree's store. Greentree's, a red, square structure with its porch facing out to sea, served as Banyan City's grocery store and post office. In the 1800s, however, it had been a bustling trading post. Samuel could visualize dusty, bearded trappers and dark-haired Indians going up and down the stairs of the stilted, wooden building to trade their furs and hides. He was sure that Indians in their canoes and trappers with their muskets had set out on many life-threatening adventures from right there at Greentree's Store.

"Mindy, Mother Manatee and the others usually hang out in this area. They like the water that runs into the Gulf from springs on these islands," Sumer said, interrupting his reverie. "Don't see them today though."

"Here, paddle and I'll take a look around," Samuel said, absent-mindedly picking up his binoculars. "I bet they're nearby."

Moving farther from shore, the twins took turns, one paddling and the other scanning the water for manatees. Entering the Gulf of Mexico and the Ten Thousand Islands, brother and sister relaxed to enjoy the beauty around them, forgetting, for the moment, to mark their trail.

They traveled through clear water, speckled with emerald mangrove islands. Some of the tree-adorned islands had sandy beaches, while twisted, reddish mangrove roots edged others. As they cruised slowly by one island, Sumer and Samuel stopped to watch a great snowy egret and a flock of white ibis.

The long-necked egret, supported by tall ebony legs, teetered on a partially submerged mangrove root. Attempting a statue like appearance, the egret stared into the water and waited for crayfish or shiners to come within striking distance. Nearby, a flock of white ibis walked deftly through rusty red mangrove roots, prodding with their long, curved beaks for insects or worms.

The distant cry of an osprey caught the twins' attention. As they watched the fish hawk soar high above them, Samuel once again shoved off into deep water. It was nearly noon when Sumer took another turn with the paddle. She steered the canoe deeper into the Ten Thousand Islands as Samuel, looking through his binoculars, scanned the edges of the mangrove islands.

Instead of finding the manatees, however, he discovered a narrow waterway with its entrance covered by an enormous crooked limb. "Hey look! There's a hidden passageway going back into that big island. Funny, I don't remember seeing it before. In fact, I don't remember seeing this island before," Samuel said, looking around uneasily.

"Hidden passageway? Where? I don't see a hidden passageway," Sumer said as she dropped the paddle into the bottom of the boat and grabbed the binoculars from Samuel. "Furthermore, Samuel, now that you mention it, nothing around here looks familiar. Where are we, anyway?"

Samuel did not like the accusing tone in her voice. "We're not lost, so cool it," he said, trying hard to sound confident. He rescued the paddle from the bottom of the canoe and started maneuvering the canoe toward a large island, all the while watching for the gnarled limb and twisted mangrove roots he'd seen earlier. "Maybe I was seeing things," he said.

"Yeah, maybe," Sumer replied, still searching the face of the island with the binoculars. "Samuel, to your left, a great white heron."

"Where? I don't..."

"It's standing in front of that ... wait a minute ... I see your hidden channel!" Jumping up, she pointed wildly toward a large gnarled tree limb that drooped over the water.

"Sumer! Sit down! You're rocking the boat," Samuel said, fighting to steady the canoe. Sumer sat and Samuel looked in the direction her finger frantically pointed. "I see the white bird and maybe you're right about it being a great white heron. Let me see those."

Sumer handed the binoculars to her brother, who looked intently up and down the shoreline. "Hey, what do you know? It does look like a great white heron, and that's the channel I saw earlier directly behind it." Samuel grabbed the paddle and guided the canoe toward the partially concealed opening. "Let's go take a closer look."

The heron like bird flared and flew into the mangroves. The twins floated up to a large branch that had been twisted and scarred by wind, water and time. They peered under it. Beyond the crooked limb they saw a narrow tunnel zigzagging its way into the middle of the island.

"What do you think? Should we go in?" Sumer asked.

"Sure. Why not?" Samuel said, with more confidence than he felt. The twins scrunched down in the bottom of the canoe, slid the boat under the crooked limb then sat up to look around.

Samuel picked up the paddle from the bottom of the canoe and began twisting and turning the boat down a waterway shrouded in shadows. Interwoven mangrove branches made a thick canopy that blocked the sun's rays from air, heavy with insects, and water, black with tannin. The smell of wet, rotting wood was strong but not unpleasant. Samuel's muscles tightened as he pulled the paddle through still water — first one side, then the other. He and Sumer both strained to see through tangled branches to catch a glimpse of what was ahead.

Saltwater mosquitoes and the lack of any breeze made the journey painful and hot. The twins ventured deeper and deeper into the middle of the island. Sumer began swishing her hat wildly through the air in an attempt to keep the insects away. Her flailing arms did little to discourage them.

During one violent upward swoosh, her hand bumped something cold and scaly. She looked to see what her hand hit and came eye to beady eye with a black-yellow-and red- striped snake. "It's, it's a sn... sn... sn... snake," she stammered. The snake's multicolored body curled around a branch directly above the boat and its black-and yellow- striped head danced back and forth dangerously close to Sumer.

"Don't move!" Samuel warned.

"That's easy for you to say. I'm the one that ugly thing is drooling over."

Samuel stood up. As he did the canoe shifted, moving his sister's head even closer to the snake's bared fangs.

"AHHHHHHH!" Sumer's scream echoed through the trees.

"Don't move!" Samuel ordered. Aiming the canoe paddle at the snake's head, he swung tentatively and missed. He could tell by the look on Sumer's face that she was nanoseconds away from going ballistic. "Stay still," he whispered hoarsely. His palms grew clammy and sweat beaded on his forehead.

"No, I want outta here," she whimpered.

"Stay put. If you move it may strike. I'll get it this time, I promise." Samuel concentrated his eyes on the snake's head as if it were a baseball and the paddle a bat. He aimed and swung, this time clipping the reptile's head hard enough to daze it. The stunned snake uncoiled and dropped into the canoe. Sumer leaped backward. The boat dipped and bobbed, taking on water.

"I said, 'STAY STILL!'" Samuel spread his legs to steadying the bouncing boat. He carefully slipped the paddle under the dazed serpent and started to lift. The tubular body contorted, then fell at Sumer's feet.

"GET THAT THING OUTTA HERE OR I'M GOING OVERBOARD!" Sumer shrieked.

"I got it. I got it," Samuel said with forced calm. He again pushed the paddle under the snake's body, then, in one smooth motion, lifted and hurled the black-yellow-and red-banded serpent into the water.

Tears ran down Sumer's cheeks; her body, cold despite the hot day, trembled noticeably. She stared into the murky water where the snake had disappeared. She breathed deeply and tried to get a grip. "Thanks, I owe you," she said. "That looked like a coral snake. I thought they were land snakes."

"Yeah, I've seen them in the Everglades before. They're poisonous you know," Samuel said.

"No D-U-H," Sumer shuddered. "I wasn't freaking 'cause I thought it was going to invite me to a slumber party." She glanced around her. Everything appeared dark and sinister, and she became afraid. "Let's start back, Samuel; I think we're lost."

"No, we're not."

"Well, I don't care. The bugs, the snake and this whole place are getting on my last nerve. I want out of here," she said.

Samuel continued to silently paddle the canoe deeper into the gloomy mangrove forest.

"SAMUEL! Gram and Grandpa will be looking for us.

I want to go home. I know we're lost. Where's the compass? Did you at least bring the compass?"

Samuel grimaced; he had forgotten to get the compass from Grandpa Tom's pickup. Dismissing Sumer's complaints, he set his jaw in stubborn determination and continued to propel the canoe down the bug-infested waterway.

Anger replaced Sumer's fear. She stood up and made a grab for the paddle, but as she did, a low branch caught her in the middle of the back and knocked her off her feet. Her dignity damaged and her back stinging, she shot Samuel a killing look but had little time to brood as once again hordes of mosquitoes surrounded them.

Another 15 minutes into the trip, Samuel began to think maybe Sumer was right. Maybe going back was a good idea.

As if she sensed his weakening, Sumer again started to complain, "Samuel, this is really spooky. I want to go home!"

"Look," he whispered. "There's that great white bird again, and I think I see light shining through the trees ahead of us. Maybe it's a clearing."

Sumer, leaning forward, peered through the trees to look at the heron like bird and the spot of light behind it. When they approached it, the mosquitoes and low-hanging branches disappeared. The narrow channel widened into a lagoon. A lagoon like no other Samuel or Sumer had ever seen.

CHAPTER 10

Sumer and Samuel gaped in awe as the canoe slid from the bug-infested, mangrove-entangled channel into a lake of crystal blue water — deep water, clean water, water clear enough to see the bottom. The lagoon's floor, covered with white sand, supported mounds of rainbow coral. Around the intricate coral swam fish — long fish, short fish, round fish; purple fish, yellow fish, red fish.

Samuel looked around him, "I think we've stumbled into God's garden," he whispered.

"It feels quiet, like church." Sumer said.

White sand glittered like cut diamonds around the perimeter of the lake. Sumer picked up her glasses from the bottom of the boat and slid them onto her nose. Emerald green hibiscus bushes, heavy with large red, yellow and pink flowers, drooped around the edge of the beach. Butterflies, big as a small hand, floated then darted among the flowers. Sandpipers skittered along the water's edge, racing the waves in search of food.

On the twins' right, Norfolk pines spiked up behind the hibiscus bushes into the sky. Clumps of slash pines silhouetted the cloudless horizon to the left and stood sentinel over a grassy prairie. On the near side of the grasslands life-sustaining water gushed from underground springs and sent out a river of water. The water raced to the edge of a rock ledge; hopscotched and dodged its way around boulders, then cascaded down a waterfall into the lagoon.

Samuel, spellbound, picked up the paddle and steered the canoe toward the rock ledge. Allowing a gentle current to pull the boat, the twins floated through a rainbow of water crystals toward the waterfall. They shivered slightly as cool mist hit their hot skin. The canoe slid past a giant live oak tree with branches spread out to shade a large area of thick grass. Gray-green Spanish moss drooped from its branches. The moss swept back and forth in a gentle breeze that carried the scent of jasmine flowers across the water. A red cardinal, singing its cheer-whoit-whoit-whoit, called to the weary travelers to come and rest.

Sumer breathed in the sweet scent of jasmine and looked longingly at the tree's deep shade and its grass-carpeted roots. Samuel, however, pressed on feverishly, determined to explore all there was to see.

The grass ended at a sandy footpath. On both sides of the path, standing like tall fat soldiers, were citrus trees — green, leafy balls, heavy with orange and yellow fruit. In a reflex reaction to the ripe oranges, lemons and grapefruit, Sumer remembered that she had not eaten all day. "We'll come back," was Samuel's answer to the loud growl coming from his twins' stomach.

Beyond the orchard stretched a strawberry patch so thick with leaves and berries that a flock of blue birds found no place to land. The birds twittered in loud protest as they flew inches above the rich foliage. On the far side of the berry patch palms, loaded with large brown coconuts, and spear-leafed banana trees, bursting with bunches of yellow bananas, housed a cloud of yellow and green canaries.

"Let's land and get some food," Sumer said. She motioned toward the birds. "Lunch music, too. What more could we ask for?" But to her surprise and her stomach's dismay, Samuel continued to paddle around the lake's circumference.

They came to the border of a meadow where white string lilies waved above the grass and slash pines gathered to form giant shapes against the sky. The twins watched oversized, blue and green dragonflies helicopter above the swaying prairie. They caught sight of a herd of deer, their heads and antlers majestically lifted above tall spears of meadow grass. Samuel saw a flick of yellow wings and heard the trill-tee-dee of a southern meadowlark.

Kingdom Cove appeared surreal with its flawless beauty, amazing array of plant life and larger than life animals — but then the unbelievable took a turn to the far side of miraculous.

Sumer saw them first. They made up a very strange conglomerate and were gathered on shore and next to it.

Samuel, in a furor to get around the lake, didn't see them until Sumer kicked his shin and pointed. He opened his mouth to protest, but the complaint stalled in his throat when he saw the look on Sumer's face. He whipped around to gawk open mouthed at the gathering.

An extraordinary grouping of birds and animals were arranged in a semicircle. They faced the water and appeared to be in deep conversation. A roseate spoonbill stood in the middle on the grass with a loggerhead turtle on its left, a Florida panther in front and a brown pelican on the right. Two manatees floated on the waterside of the spoonbill.

"Pinch me!" Sumer said and continued in a whispery gush. "This must be a dream or the delusions of a sunstroke. It can't be real, places like this don't exist and animals don't talk to each other. Sure scientists study how animals communicate and they have come up with some amazing stuff, like with gorillas. Remember that special on TV last night? They were teaching sign language to gorillas, but this!"

She waved her arms to include the entire group of animals and chattered on, "This is carrying it way too far; manatees don't talk to turtles, pelicans certainly don't socialize with panthers. Where's my hat? I know I've been out in the sun too long." Then Sumer, slightly blue from lack of oxygen, took a deep breath and, suddenly dizzy, fell backward in the boat.

"Cut it out! This is not a dream and you're not having a sunstroke. Why do you have to be so melodramatic all the time? Hang on, we're going closer." As the canoe edged toward the animals, Sumer and Samuel heard diverse animal noises. The twins could not understand any of it but the atmosphere and posture of the animals was definitely that of serious discussion.

The two manatees, Sumer and Samuel recognized as Mindy and her mother, listened as they floated in shallow water. The roseate spoonbill, shaking its long, spatula-shaped bill first one way then the other, appeared to be lecturing the reddish-brown turtle. The golden-brown panther twitched the black tip of her tail from one side to the other as she rested in the grass. Her black-tipped ears stood at attention, listening intently. Next to the panther sat a brown pelican whose white-and yellow-feathered head rested on its breast. The pelican got up to waddle closer to the beach but sat down suddenly, favoring its left wing.

As Sumer and Samuel came close to the unlikely group, the animals, startled by the boat and humans, prepared to flee. Mindy turned to look at the twins. She quickly sent a grunty snort into the air. At her snort the panther, as well as the others, stood their ground. When the young manatee had given a short, but passion-filled, performance of snorts and grunts she turned and swam toward the canoe. She nudged the boat with her soft flat nostrils snorting and blowing water as if she wanted the twins to understand something.

Samuel reached down to pet the rough gray-brown hide. "What is it, Mindy? What do you want?" he asked, keeping one eye on the menagerie on shore.

Mindy dove deep into the lake then swam to the surface. She splashed wildly and slapped her fan-shaped tail on top of the water. Her strange actions baffled the twins. "What does she want?" Samuel asked Sumer.

"I think she wants us to come swimming with her," said Sumer. "And even if that's not what she wants, I'm hot, my head hurts and I'm going for a swim. After cooling down maybe, just maybe, I can make some sense of all this."

Standing up, Sumer dove into the cool, clear water. She and Mindy descended to the bottom of the pool. They darted here and there, exploring the underwater life. They were under the water for such a long time Samuel began to worry.

Finally, Sumer surfaced, took a deep breath and said. "Come on in the water's great." But to Samuel her words sounded like a series of chirps and snorts.

"What did you say?" Samuel asked.

"I said come swimming. Come see the fish and coral that's down here, they're unbelievable," she chirped.

Samuel started to get nervous. Sumer sounded more like a dolphin or bird than his sister. He could not understand anything she said. "Get out of that water. We're going home right now," Samuel ordered. "This is getting spooky!"

"I will do no such thing! You're just hot and grouchy. Dive in and cool off."

Samuel, by this time, was really getting freaked. He didn't understand a word Sumer was saying and not knowing what else to do, he paddled over to his sister intent on forcefully pulling her into the canoe.

Samuel grabbed Sumer's arm and Sumer, struggling to get free, upset the canoe. Samuel toppled into the water with an undignified splash. As soon as he hit the water, Mindy pushed the struggling boy down under the water then swam away.

Samuel labored toward the surface; his lungs ached for air. I'm not going to make it, I'm going to black out, he thought. His head finally shot above the water. "What are you trying to do, drown me?" He gasped between pants and ragged breaths.

"No, I was not trying to drown you, but I did have to push you under the water so you could receive the gift," Mindy snorted.

"GIFT! W-h-a-t... gift? Great, now I'm talking to a manatee," Samuel moaned. "I'm losing my mind, right? No, I'm dead. Yes, that's it. I drowned and now I'm dead. So young, too. I never even had a chance to get my driver's license."

"Now look who's being melodramatic," said Sumer. "I think we're both tired. The sun and heat have gotten to us. We're no longer thinking rationally. Pull the canoe over to the beach. I think you're right. It's time to go home."

"I know it must be confusing and frightening but you can talk to me and I to you. It's the gift of tongues," Mindy snorted. "Swim over with me to the others and I will explain."

"I guess we could follow her." Sumer remarked.

Looking at Sumer, Samuel said, "Hey, now I can understand you too."

"You couldn't before?"

"No! Why do you think I was getting so freaked?"

"Don't know; thought you were just being you, I guess," Sumer teased. "Come on, I want to show you something." And with that, she dove deep into the lake.

Samuel, close behind, let the cool clean water engulf and distract him from everything except the enchantment of the underwater world. He and Sumer swam through schools of gold- and blue-striped pork fish, green and red parrotfish, blue tang, red snapper, yellow and blue queen angelfish and large silver and black spadefish.

They chased small fish and large fish, first one way then the other. Giving wide berth to an enormous ray, they finally surfaced to find Mindy waiting for them. They still had no insight into their bizarre situation, so they swam to the beach and sat down on the warm sand.

"OK, let's hear it," they said in unison.

"Samuel, Sumer, this is Trina and her friend, Nigel," Mindy snorted, introducing the twins to the loggerhead turtle and brown pelican.

"I'm Rondolus," the roseate spoonbill added. His medium-sized heron-type body was covered with pink feathers — except at the shoulders, where bright red patches of feathers gave way to a white breast and neck. He was 3-feet tall with pink legs. His pink eyes watched Samuel and Sumer with a look of distrust.

"This is Zhora," the spoonbill added, pointing with his spatula-shaped bill toward the Florida panther. Zhora's black-tipped tail stopped twitching and she nodded her head slightly — a move that accentuated a darker stripe down each side of her golden-brown face.

"This lagoon that you have entered is called Kingdom Cove and serves as a sanctuary for wildlife. Birds and animals come here to seek help for themselves, their species or their habitat. God's spirit has given the water the gift of tongues. When an animal or a human dives into the pool, they are given the ability to understand and speak a language all can understand," Mindy snorted.

Rondolus gave them a cold stare. "Trina and Nigel have come all the way from Grand Island to ask for help," he croaked. "Nigel broke his wing colliding with an enormous structure some stupid humans are building directly on the beach." As he croaked the word "stupid," the spoonbill glared directly at Sumer and Samuel; then, looking away, he continued. "It's a beach where sea turtles have laid their eggs for centuries."

"Yes," Trina cut in, "Centuries." The loggerhead told them about the turtle nests that had been destroyed. She then described the building project being constructed on Grand Island's Beach.

Nigel told them he had been born in a London zoo then shipped to Australia. When the zoo in Sydney burned down, he escaped. He undertook the long and dangerous journey from Australia to the southernmost tip of Florida and continued up the coastline only to collide with the towering structure on Grand Island. He ended his story with a comical reenactment of his and Trina's bizarre trip to Kingdom Cove.

Zhora listened, keenly observing Rondolus who, as the story progressed, appeared to become more and more hostile toward Sumer and Samuel.

Burrowing Owl

Burrowing Owl

Burrowing Owl

CHAPTER 11

It was soon clear that Zhora had not imagined the hostility Rondolus felt toward the twins. Taking a threatening nose to beak stance, the spoonbill began to lecture Sumer and Samuel. "I never met a human I liked or could trust. They are noisy, destructive and leave litter everywhere they go. Their fast boats and fishing lines endanger everything in the water, and every year kill manatees, birds, turtles and others of us." He turned abruptly to Mindy and asked, "Why are you asking humans for help? They're the problem, not the solution."

"Excuse me, pinky. I resent that remark. Maybe some people cause problems, but not all of us do," Sumer said. She stood stiff-legged, one hand on her hip and the other wagging a finger in the spoonbill's face.

The spoonbill snapped its bill toward Sumer and would've made a spoon-shaped indention in her finger if she had not quickly retracted her appendage.

Samuel grabbed his sister's arm and pushed her into a sitting position. "Sumer, what's up with you? You're arguing with a bird!"

"He makes me so mad. Lots of people are working to save manatees. Laws have been passed and gadgets invented." she said.

"Oh yeah, like what?" Rondolus croaked, preening his feathers and feigning indifference.

"Like protective cages for propeller blades and sonar devices for boat bottoms. That's what!" Sumer said. She once more towered over the pink bird.

"From what I've seen, laws and gadgets aren't getting the job done, now are they?" Rondolus croaked as he nipped at Sumer's kneecap then resumed his grooming ritual.

Sumer stood her ground, telling herself she wasn't going to back down from a pink-feathered bag of gas. "Well what is your answer, to make the whole ocean a no wake zone?"

"Please, time is short and this is unproductive. Yes, some humans are thoughtless and cruel but others are not. Samuel and Sumer have been very kind to Mother and me. They saved my life last winter," Mindy snorted as she floated to the water's surface.

Zhora stood up, stretched her sleek body and began pacing back and forth. "It's apparent to all the animal kingdom that God made mankind the crown of his creation. He gave them something special that the rest of us don't have. He created them in His own image." The big cat stopped and sat down; she looked squarely at Sumer and Samuel. "God made you the crown of His creation. You and your kind were supposed to be good stewards of the earth. Your Adam and Eve weren't supposed to disobey and bring a curse that caused the entire earth to suffer." Zhora's tail twitched from left to right. "What great anguish sin has caused. Your kind really does owe us, you know."

The great cat once again stood up and began to pace back and forth on the beach. "Give us enough open space to roam free and raise our young. Is that too much to ask?" She looked again at Sumer and Samuel.

Rondolus began hopping up and down in agitation. "Yeah, how many golf courses, restaurants and malls do you guys need anyway?"

"I see greed and it saddens me. When is enough, enough?" Zhora once more rested in the grass, but the speed at which her black-tipped tail flopped back and forth belied her apparent calmness.

"The deuce, you say, I personally like the kiddies," Nigel croaked, waddling over to Samuel and sitting next to him. "The little mates are a great joy. I petition them for fish and do a bit of a jig. They laugh at bugger all, but then I can be quite a barmy fellow. Here watch me!" With that, the brown pelican got up and attempted a one-legged dance.

"Drat! I do wish I could settle my wing. It pains me so." He plopped down again on the sand and with a thoughtful look continued. "On the other hand, it does seem most adult chaps care little about the likes of us."

"That's not true." Sumer said, sitting down next to Nigel. "A lot of them do care. Gram and Grandpa do, and Mom and Dad did care."

"Did care? Why don't they now? They get bought off by the mighty dollar like all the others?" Rondolus jabbed.

"DO CARE! I MEAN DO!" Sumer jumped up screaming and wondering if she really meant did. She refused to give up hope for her parents' return. She decided her doubt was entirely the stupid bird's fault. She lunged at him and would have given his pink face a black eye if he had not deftly fluttered out of her reach and into a nearby tree.

Samuel hurried over to his sister and put his arm around her shoulders.

Seeing the pain in the twins' eyes, Rondolus congratulated himself. "Ha, hit close to home that time."

"Bad form, old man," Nigel commented, shaking his head with disapproval.

Sumer sat down with arms encircling her knees and the distance of time on her face. "Mom and Dad planned for years, wanted to travel to Africa, take pictures, put together a documentary. Somehow this project was going to help stop the destruction of animals like the African elephant and the black rhino. Nine months ago they went to Africa. Problem is..."

"They were attacked, taken hostage, dragged to a river. We don't know where they are now or if they..." Samuel gulped. He moved closer to Sumer as they both struggled back tears of hurt and anger.

Sumer jumped up to pace back and forth on the damp sand. She stopped and stared out over the grass and flowers that swayed in rhythm to a slight breeze.

"When Senator Gall returned Mom and Dad's things I took her journal." Sumer gave Samuel an apologetic look. "I read it under my covers at night with a flashlight. It helps me remember. I won't let myself forget them. I just can't!"

"Don't worry about it. I knew you had it. I didn't say anything because I can't bring myself to look at it yet. Still hurts too much."

"I learned a lot of things about Mom that I never knew before," Sumer said as she once more plopped down on the sand. "On one page she wrote, 'I listen to the trees creak in the wind and watch the soft fuzzy ears of a deer as it bounces up and down through tall grass. I smell dust as it puffs up from the feet of a burrowing owl and feel the loneliness of a pileated woodpecker drumming in the shadows of a tall cypress. All are a witness to the awesomeness of God's creative power, and I am humbled by my insignificance.'" Sumer looked across the clear blue water of the lagoon.

"'Then I remember God has the hairs of my head numbered, and I know I am greatly loved.'" Sumer screwed up her face to fight back tears. "'In the presence of God all hurt and anger disappear.'" Tears now flowed freely down Sumer's cheeks. She stopped talking and bent over to cover her feet with sand. "I love what it says, so I memorized it."

"Your mother seems nice." Mindy snorted. "What does she look like?"

Samuel's sad face and slouched shoulders sprang to life. "Her hair is not quite blond, more the color of wheat at the end of summer. It's long, hangs way down her back."

"Yeah, I like to braid it," Sumer said. "Her eyes are the color of spring leaves, and she's tall and thin. Not skinny, kind of willowy like."

"What about your Dad? What's he like?"

Sumer was now drawing circles in the sand with her big toe. "Dad's a big tease. He lets me and Samuel sit on his foot. Then drags us around the room, clinging to his leg. He calls our names, like he can't find us," she giggled.

"He loved baseball, loves baseball," Samuel corrected himself. He stretched out on the sand, right hand shading his eyes from the sun. "He coached my baseball team until ... until Africa."

Rondolus flew down from his branch to confront the twins. "I thought you said they didn't come back. They're dead, aren't they? You talk as if they're still alive!"

"They are alive!" Sumer rushed at the bird with fists clenched. "I know in my heart, they ARE ALIVE and will come home." Sumer stopped short of swinging at the pink bird, but her glare dared him to contradict her.

When he didn't say anything, she whirled around and struck an orator's pose — right hand jutting into the sky, her voice rang out like Abe Lincoln during the Gettysburg Address — "'All are a witness to the awesomeness of God's creative power, and I am humbled by my insignificance. Then I remember God has the hairs of my head numbered, and I know I am greatly loved.' They're not dead," Sumer said, looking into the eyes of the spoonbill. "I know it in here." Sumer tapped her midsection.

Samuel stood up. Sometimes he really admired his sister. Not very often because, after all, she was a girl. But sometimes ... sometimes he did.

Sumer sat on the sand and hugged her knees. She forgot those around her. She forgot where she was. For a few minutes she was once again a little girl, sitting with her mother in a big rocking chair. Back and forth, back and forth they moved, while her mother petted her brow and talked about God and His creation.

"God created a habitat for every living creature from the amoeba to the eagle. He built order and balance into the universe. He gave mankind the responsibility to maintain and protect that balance and order. Knowing and staying in the will of the Creator; quality of life preserved as God intended. Yep, pretty much sums it up," Mother Manatee snorted. She slapped her fan-shaped tail against the surface of the water as an exclamation mark to her statement.

"I still say some humans have a mean streak that runs way down deep, and a whole lot more of them just sit around like careless, indifferent toads," Rondolus croaked weakly and flew back to his perch in the tree.

The loggerhead headed for the water. Trina thought about the humans she saw rescuing turtle eggs from the Grand Island construction site. She thought about the redheaded woman who patrolled turtle nests and herded hatchlings into the ocean.

Immersing her large shell in the water, she grunted, "Only some humans are rotten."

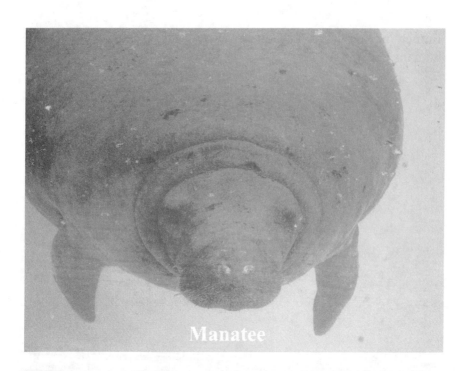

Manatee

Manatees

CHAPTER 12

Tired of deep conversations and sitting still, Samuel followed the loggerhead across the sand and dove into the water. Mindy and Mother Manatee floated to deeper water and went down like a submarine. Sumer ran to join her brother.

Samuel stood waist deep, raking his arm across the water's surface, sending wave after wave surging toward Sumer. She squealed and kicked water aimed at him.

The spoonbill watched their antics from his perch. "Hey! We still have a problem to solve!" He yelled. To Zhora, who lay resting at the foot of the tree, he added, "We're just wasting time anyway. No way are we ever going to convince humans to stop building on the beach. They don't care enough about us."

Still laughing and splashing, the twins swam back to shallow water. Mindy's nose and mouth surfaced under Sumer's armpit, sending Sumer into another fit of giggles.

"We need to get back to business," Mother Manatee snorted.

"Do your grandparents have influence among other humans? Will they help?" Mindy asked the twins.

Samuel returned to the beach and flopped on the warm sand. "Grandma Mariana is a wild life artist; she belongs to an environmentalist group that the church sponsors. Grandpa Tom still has connections at the county Sheriff's Office," he said. "I think between the two of them, they might be able to help if we can convince them that this," he spread his arms wide, "is all real."

"You don't have to. The construction site is right on the beach for all who care to see it," Trina grunted.

"Hey Samuel! Remember the stories Grandpa told us? The ones about Yatzu, the great white bird? I know this sounds dumb ... but do you think... this heron Max and Grandpa saw might help us? On the other hand, how do you find such a bird? Where would you even start looking?"

109

Sumer walked onto the beach and sauntered up to the tree where Rondolus roosted. Giving him a smug look, she climbed up and sat down on a large limb next to his.

Samuel laughed inwardly. His sister just couldn't seem to leave that bald, pink bird alone. "According to Grandpa you don't find Yatzu, he finds you."

"You k-n-o-w, there was a bird that looked like a great white heron, standing just beyond the crooked limb that guards the hidden channel. And we saw him again just before we entered Kingdom Cove," Sumer said. "You don't suppose...?"

"What does some bird named Yatzu have to do with the building project on Grand Island?" Rondolus asked, giving Sumer a hostile look as he floated back down to the ground. What did that girl think she was doing, infringing on his territory?

"Grandpa Tom and Old Max tell stories about a great white bird. They think it's a great white heron and Max thinks God sent it in answer to his prayers to help Florida's wildlife," Samuel said.

Sumer looked down at Samuel from her perch. "I asked Grandpa if he thought it was a guardian angel. He said no, he doesn't believe in guardian angels." She stood and reached for a higher limb. "Gram said he doesn't believe because then that would lead to questions about Mom and Dad. Gram said, right or wrong, sometimes people find it easier to not believe than to face the hard questions."

Trina, her large shell baking in the afternoon sun, once more sprawled on the beach. She recalled the great white bird and its flaming eyes as it stood under the mangrove tree on Grand Island's beach. She remembered the warm rain, washing over her, and the pelican; she remembered the great white bird, hovering above them. She felt the sensation again, as she felt it then, when its eyes met hers — like maybe it gave her the ability to communicate with and feel compassion for Nigel.

The magnificent bird then followed her and Nigel to Kingdom Cove, or did they follow it? Trina agreed with Sumer's grandfather, it was easier to ignore the hard questions than to search for the answers. On the other hand ... "I'll ask around. Can't hurt," the turtle grunted.

"A large white bird sent from God? The whole idea is absurd!" croaked the spoonbill as it paced in a huff under the tree where Sumer sat.

Trina, overcome by her predicament, lamented, "Something has to be done or where will I lay my eggs? I've been laying my eggs on Grand Island for years. In fact, it's the only place I've ever laid my eggs."

For the first time Samuel noticed how low the sun was hanging in the sky. "Sumer, come down from there! We need to get back. It's late; Gram and Grandpa will be worried."

"Don't be upset, Trina. Samuel and I will do everything we can," Sumer promised as she jumped from the tree, barely missing the fuming spoonbill.

Rondolus, startled by the girl's abrupt descent, flapped out of the way, but recovered quickly enough to nip at her knee as she hurried past.

"I wonder if we could find Yatzu? If he truly exists someone, somewhere must know something about him. I'll look into it," Trina grunted, dragging her large shell toward the water.

"Yeah, if, and I stress if, there is anything to those ridiculous stories," Rondolus grumbled.

"Sumer, Samuel, follow me. We know the quickest way home," Mindy snorted as she followed her mother into deeper water. "

"Most individuals lose the gift of tongues once they leave the lagoon, but once in a rare moon, especially with animals, it has lasted awhile longer. In any case, we'd better meet here again in a week," Mother Manatee snorted. "That will give us all time to work on a solution."

"Nigel, you want to come with us?" Samuel asked. We'll go to the vet tomorrow and have your wing looked at."

"Jolly good," the brown pelican answered, waddling toward the canoe. A meeting was set for the next week. Mother Manatee took the lead as canoe, with twins and Nigel riding inside, started down the channel toward open water.

Rondolus fluttered ahead of Zhora. They progressed toward the backside of the island, a route that afforded the panther a shorter swim to the mainland.

In their hurry to start home, none of them notice the great white bird that stood in the shade of the mangroves. Its long yellow legs sloshed quietly through shallow water as its blazing eyes focused purposefully on this team of oddly matched players.

Brown Pelican

Brown Pelican

Brown Pelican

CHAPTER 13

The sun was sinking quietly into the gulf waters as Sumer and Samuel rounded the last bend toward home. Tom stood on the lawn, holding his hat in his hands. He stared at the raffia palm as if it contained wisdom and understanding just out of his reach. Why was God putting him though all this? He looked up, scanning the waterway for the umpteenth time.

This time he saw a canoe with one kid paddling to beat the band and the other fussing with a large squatty bird. He slammed the wide-rimmed hat onto his head and started for the beach. His eyes, dark with displeasure, watched the twins pull the boat out of the water. "Where have you been all day? Your Grandmother and I have been frantic. You didn't tell us where you were going or even leave a note. NOT ONE WORD!"

"Grandpa, please calm down. We're really sorry. It was stupid, but we didn't mean to scare you. Time just got away," Samuel said, making a worried face at Sumer.

"We're really sorry. P-l-e-a-s-e, don't be mad. We have something awesome to tell you," Sumer said, torn between excitement over their adventure and guilt.

"Give us a chance to explain. It is totally unbelievable," Samuel said as he carefully took Nigel out of the canoe.

"What are you doing with that pelican?" Tom asked, squinting at the brown and white bird. "Be careful, he'll peck you!"

"Grandpa Tom, meet Nigel," Samuel said. "We think he has a broken wing and plan to have Dr. Matthews look at it first thing in the morning."

Mariana joined them when they reached the porch; her green eyes sparked with fury. The twins, seeing her anger, left Tom and Nigel on the lawn and hustled to find a large box for the pelican. Sumer also found remnants from the fish Mariana had trimmed and was cooking for dinner. They put the bird in the box, put the box on the porch, fed him fish heads and tails and hurried to wash up for supper.

"They won't believe us," Samuel worried.

"Yes they will. After all, Grandpa has seen Yatzu in action, and I'll bet that beach project is on the lot he told us about. The one Old Max sold to the Turtles And Me Educational Foundation."

"Yeah and they turned around a week later and sold it to a construction company."

"That's the one. We'd better hurry. Gram looked really mad and I'm starving. I saw apple pie for dessert."

After the twins were seated and the blessing said, Tom looked at Sumer and Samuel over his spectacles. Echoing the twins earlier command directed at Mindy, he said, "OK, let's hear it."

"So much happened, where should we start?" Sumer asked.

"At the beginning!" Mariana cut her fish with so much force that a piece of the tender fillet flew off her plate and landed in the butter. She looked around daring anyone to so much as grin.

The twins stifled their snickers and spilled their story with Samuel and Sumer quite often talking at the same time. When they finished, the twins took a deep breath and anxiously looked at each other, then at their grandparents. "The bottom line is, we need your help to fight this building project. Will you help us?" Samuel asked.

"You really don't expect us to believe all this?" Mariana put down her fork and looked at the twins in disbelief.

"I know you two always try to be truthful with your Grandmother and me, but the story you have just told us is preposterous!" Tom said.

"I know; it sounds ridiculous even to me but what we told you is true. Nigel's our proof." Samuel emphasized the finality of his statement by stuffing his mouth with an oversized forkful of potatoes.

"Your pelican friend seems tame but he doesn't talk," Mariana said, noticing Tom hadn't touched his food. She couldn't blame him; this conversation was completely unreal. She stared into her

116

cup of tea, hoping that any minute Sumer or Samuel would say, "Just kidding."

"We explained all that," Samuel said.

"It's doable you know," Sumer said, worrying the peas on her plate and eyeing the apple pie on the counter. "Science is learning more and more about the way animals communicate and if God was involved, well you've always told us all things are possible with God. Jesus told the Pharisees that God could make the very stones cry out. And what about Balaam's donkey? The Lord made it speak."

"I don't know what you saw or why you think you saw it, but staying out in the hot sun can do strange things to a person's head," Tom said pushing back from the table.

The day's worry had taken its toll on him and this discussion wasn't helping. Fatigue lined his face and his shoulders sagged.

"It's time for bed. Tomorrow we'll take the pelican to the vet, and talk more about this alleged building project on Grand Island," Mariana said.

"It's not an alleged building project. It's real!" Sumer said, putting her dishes into the dishwasher. Doing that simple task brought the improbability of the story into focus. If I were Gram I'd think we're blooming lunatics, she thought as the absurdity of it hit her full force. We took the word of a turtle and a bird.

Samuel got up from the table and handed his dishes to Sumer. "Can Nigel sleep with me?" He needed to believe in this day and felt that keeping Nigel close at hand would be reassuring.

"The porch will do nicely," Mariana said.

"Can I have a piece of pie?" Sumer asked.

"Mariana dismissed the twins with a wave of her hand. She looked closely at the ashen complexion of her husband, wondering if he had picked up the refill to his heart medication from the local pharmacy.

Samuel looked at Grandpa Tom's grayish complexion and also worried about the empty prescription bottle he'd seen laying on the counter that morning. "Grandpa did you remember...?"

Mariana cut him short with "the look" — neither man nor beast dared ignore Grandma's look. Without further comment, he and Sumer trudged disheartened toward the porch.

"Grandpa doesn't look so good, does he?" Sumer said. What if we made him worry for nothing? What if there is no building? What if he's right? It was just a sunstroke, a mirage, a figment of our imagination?" She closed her eyes, pushing fingers hard against both temples.

"You know everything we told them was true. We both saw it."

"We took the word of a stinking bird and turtle! Oh, sorry Nigel," she said looking at the squatty bird.

"We should never have worried them like that. I couldn't stand it if something we did caused Grandpa to have another ... "

"Don't say it! Don't even think it." With eyes full of unshed tears, Sumer looked harshly at Samuel. "I'm going to bed. I've got a headache." Patting Nigel apologetically on his feathery head, she walked into the house. Her hand reached back to catch the screen door just before it slammed.

"Goodnight, Nigel; you'll be OK out here, right?" Samuel rubbed his face with both hands. Should he have turned back this morning when Sumer wanted to? Would it be his fault if Grandpa Tom had another heart attack?

Blinking its eyes, the pelican snuggled down into the blanket that covered the bottom of his box. Samuel watched the bird for a few more minutes and with a deep sigh patted him. After turning off the porch light, he walked into the house.

Samuel lay on his bed and fretted about his grandfather. He thought about the day's events. Think positive. Grandpa is tough. He'll be fine. We'll call the county office tomorrow and find out the building is being constructed just like Trina and Nigel said. Then we can think of a plan, Samuel consoled himself, as sleep finally stole over him.

Cypress Tree with Spanish Moss

120

CHAPTER 14

Joe felt the DC-10 start its descent. Peering out his first-class window, he saw a million pin-dots of light spread out below. Tomorrow he was scheduled to visit Ghost Orchid Hotel's construction site on Grand Island. Out of the country for two weeks, he was anxious to find out how things were going with the project.

Duncan, Joe's construction manager, e-mailed Joe while he was in Saudi Arabia. The e-mail said several turtle nests on the hotel building site were accidentally destroyed. Duncan said environmentalists were causing a stink and were picketing in front of the project.

Joe chewed his drooping mustache. Surely the tree-huggers had gotten bored and gone home by now; after all, they were just eggs, and eggs sell in the grocery store for a buck fifty. He couldn't understand the fuss. Let the loggerheads find another beach where they can lay their eggs.

It was just one hotel. How could anyone lose sleep over building one hotel on the beach? Besides, the county approved an environmental variance, so the law was on his side for once. Having the only resort on the water's edge was going to make him a rich man. He'd show his old man he wasn't a good-for-nothing, a loser.

Joe's mouth turned up in a smirk. Rusty Ruskin was a pretty smart lawyer. He worked that railroad easement and those deed restrictions just right to find a loophole to the environmental setback laws on Grand Island. Joe knew his redhead lawyer had lied to the old man who sold him the property, but Joe didn't much care. Rusty bought the lot and obtained the variance and that was that.

The DC-10 jerked upward and Joe clenched his jaw. What was the pilot yammering about? They were to circle the airport for another 15 minutes until traffic on the runways cleared.

Joe bit his lip and forced himself to lean back against his seat and relax. Flying made him nervous. Sweat beaded up on his forehead; he wiped it with his sleeve. Think about something else, he told himself and managed to let his mind drift.

This was his second trip in four months to Jeddah, a principal seaport in the kingdom of Saudi Arabia. The first time he flew to Jeddah he delivered goods to a Saudi sheik that bought the hides of endangered animals. The second trip was to convince the oil-rich desert sheik to partner with him in building Ghost Orchid Hotel.

Joe sold everything he owned, plus delivered $200,000 worth of rare animal hides to the Saudi sheik in exchange for down-payment money for the land. He and Rusty scratched together enough to start pounding pilings and buy some steel crossbeams, but then their funds ran out. They needed a wealthy partner. Abdul Bahar Habib, with all his oil money, was just the man.

Joe bought new clothes and left Florida with barely enough money for a week at a hotel and food. He was now returning from Jeddah with a bank draft large enough to build the hotel exactly as he dreamed. The sheik was a full partner and had been quite clear about what happened to anyone who double-crossed him — a bomb placed strategically, poison that caused slow, painful death, a late-night visitor who found great pleasure in chopping off body parts one at a time.

Aw, heck, the guy was 10,000 miles away. How would he even know if Joe slowly squeezed him outta the action?

The DC-10 was losing altitude; Joe tightened his seat belt. Sweat once again broke out on his forehead. He chewed his mustache. I could have been killed, he thought as he remembered the twin engine's uncontrolled dive toward the desert of Northern Africa — the thousand-foot plunge; the light aircraft's unexpected recovery. The incident happened during a night flight across Northern Africa in a chartered plane. Joe chartered the private aircraft to smuggle hides to Sheik Abdul Bahar Habib on his first trip to Saudi Arabia.

The memory of his near-death experience sent a knee-jerk reaction through his body as the DC-10 descended into Southwest

Florida International Airport. The thud of Joe's heart tightened the knot in his stomach until it felt as if someone had kicked him.

The large aircraft's tires hit the runway; its jets went into reverse thrust then slowed it to a stop. Realizing he was holding his breath, Joe exhaled deeply. He listened as overhead compartments popped open and fellow passengers retrieved bags from under their seats. Several minutes passed before he was composed enough to collect his bags, but he stood ready when the plane's door opened. His head was pounding. Duncan better be here to meet me, he thought.

Duncan, Joe's construction manager, looked out over the heads of the crowd. He watched men, women and children move like an undulating river down the walkway that lead to American Airline's flight gates. His brown eyes scanned the passengers apprehensively as he watched for a small blond man with a bushy mustache and cold blue eyes.

Joe was not known for his mellow personality, and Duncan was rightly concerned he would see no humor in the fact that Sheriff Rainbird shut down construction on Ghost Orchid Hotel for a few days. Duncan put his reading glasses on top his head and contemplated the best way to break the news to Joe.

"A few days off will give things time to cool down," the sheriff had told Duncan.

Seeing his boss weave in and out of the throng of exiting passengers, Duncan called, "Joe! Over here!" After a momentary grip of hands, Duncan said, "Let me take your bags. How was your flight?"

"It didn't crash." Joe said, walking toward an airport coffeehouse with windows that looked out over the runway. "How'd construction go today? How many pilings are in place?"

"Your flight was late. What held you up?" Duncan asked, ignoring Joe's questions.

"Backed-up air traffic. How'd construction go today?" Joe repeated.

"Say, why don't you sit down, order some coffee and relax. Give me your claim tickets. I'll get your bags and meet you back up here in 30 minutes or so," Duncan hedged.

"I travel light these days," Joe answered, patting his carry-on luggage. "Duncan, what is it you're trying hard as the devil not to tell me? Something wrong at the site?"

"Just a little ruckus. Nothing anybody will even remember by next week," Duncan answered. He asked the waitress to bring two cups of black coffee.

"A ruckus? What kind of ruckus?"

"Red, the foreman, lost his temper and started shoving turtle-lovers around. Someone called the sheriff. Red and a few others are in the slammer for the night. The sheriff stopped construction until things cool down," Duncan explained reluctantly.

"Call that lawyer of mine, and get him down here," Joe said as he twisted his mustache so hard he winced. "Rusty can catch a red eye and be here tomorrow morning. Much as we've got at stake, it won't hurt him to miss a night's sleep."

The server set two mugs of coffee on the table, and Joe asked for cream. Sinking deep into his chair, Joe stared out the window and sipped the steaming liquid. He had a bad feeling about what Duncan told him.

Suddenly rallying, he pushed back from the table. Why should he care? He didn't have to deal with it, that was Rusty's job. "Let's get outta here." After flinging 10 bucks on the table, they left the coffee shop and walked through the terminal out into the damp, night air.

Duncan's long-legged stride led them to a new QuadTrax — candy-apple red, four-wheel drive and leather seats. A sports utility vehicle with a wide wheelbase, designed to prevent rollovers.

Looking around the vehicle, Joe let out a low whistle. This was some truck. It must have cost a bundle. Was he paying this guy too much or what? "I rented a condo for the next few months. Take me there. I'm beat. I want to inspect the construction site first thing in the morning, make a trip to the bank and then do some shopping," he told Duncan.

Immersing himself in the plush leather seat, Joe opened the window and took a long breath. Ahhh, the smell of Florida, he was glad to be back.

As they left the airport and headed for Interstate 75, Joe caught sight of a large bird wading in a shallow pool next to the road. The bird's snow-white feathers gleamed under the street lamp, and its eyes burned through the night air. They watched Joe as the QuadTrax drove past.

Joe shook his head. It couldn't be the same great white bird, and even if it was, nothing was going to stop him this time. This time, he was doing everything legal.

"Something wrong?" Duncan asked.

"No, just stop babying this fancy truck of yours and get me to my condo," Joe ordered.

Shark Valley Observation Tower

Everglades National Park

CHAPTER 15

Tom slept long and hard. When he woke, he was feeling better than the night before.

"The whole thing is crazy. I refuse to buy into that supernatural cove story." Tom hung up the phone and joined Mariana at the kitchen table. "They were right about the hotel. A large resort is being built not more than 50 feet from the water's edge on Grand Island.

"Setback laws require all manmade structures on the island to be built well behind the sea grass dunes. The county clerk said in this case, the land's use was restricted by railroad easements and deed restrictions. The easements and restriction barred the owner from building a resort of any magnitude anywhere except on the beach. The county made some special deal with the owner and gave him a variance on the setback. I'm sure the lot is the one Max sold. ...Turtles and Me Educational Foundation, my foot."

"Are you feeling all right this morning?" Mariana asked, handing Tom a cup of steaming, black coffee.

"I'm fine," he said. "Do you want to know the reason I'm sure it's the same lot? When I talked to one of the sheriff's deputies, he said there was trouble at the construction site yesterday. Environmentalist groups claim the project endangers rare turtle- and bird-nesting areas. They have been picketing the sight for a week. Yesterday afternoon, construction workers, angry because picketers slowed down construction, started shoving people around. Hot tempers on both sides exploded into a fight. A bunch of them spent the night in jail. The judge let them all out on bail this morning, but ordered them to appear in court next Friday. Construction was suspended until after the hearing." Tom stopped talking long enough to gulp his coffee.

"Craziest thing is the deputy said Joe Sorrow is the one building the hotel. You remember me talking about Joe, don't you? Young guy, been sent to prison twice for poaching. Got out of the state pen barely a year ago. I saw him last March when I was coming back from Flamingo City. He didn't look like a millionaire then." Tom said.

"He liked to play checkers. We played a few games while he was being held at the county jail. I wonder where he got the money to build a fancy hotel? He didn't win it playing checkers he was lousy at the game. Ghost Orchid Hotel, that's what he's calling it."

"I remember Joe, and as I recall he was young and hard-headed. Blond hair, cold blue eyes, kind of scrawny." Mariana said.

"Yeah, that's him."

"Now that we know Sumer and Samuel were right about the construction project, what's next? Are we going to help? But even if we wanted to, what can we do?" Mariana asked.

"Good questions, but an even better one is how the kids really found out about that hotel. The story they told us last night is a bunch of hooey." Tom said, tipping up his coffee cup.

Mariana poured Tom another cup of coffee and herself a cup of spicy tea. They sat at the kitchen table; the only sound came from Tom's cup clinking against the saucer. Mariana looked intently at a bright-yellow lemon wedge that floated suspended in her steaming teacup.

"I should call Max and tell him what a heck of a poor job his attorney did for him," Tom said, breaking the silence.

"Leave him alone. He'll just worry. Nothing he can do about it now. I better call the vet and see if we can bring that pelican in this morning," Mariana said.

"Can you and Sumer take the bird to the vet without me? I would really like to take Samuel, drive to Grand Island and do some snooping around."

"I suppose we can manage on the condition you get your heart medicine refilled."

"What did you say about snooping around?" asked Samuel, walking into the kitchen.

"Morning." Mariana said.

"Morning. What's up?" Samuel asked, glancing at his grandma then searching his grandfather's face for the fatigue that had been there the night before.

"I'm fine, Samuel, just don't go sailing off to some magical island again without telling me first, OK?" Tom said. "It's time to wake your sister. We have errands to run, and I want to get started."

"I already talked to her. She's got one of her headaches. She was up to get a cold washcloth for her head and went back to bed."

"Samuel, you and Grandpa get some breakfast. I'll go talk to Sumer. I can take the pelican to the vet myself."

"I don't think so, Gram. Nigel has never ridden in a car before. I'm afraid he'll get excited and cause an accident or something," Samuel said.

Just then Sumer staggered into the kitchen with a damp washcloth held against her forehead. Fumbling with closed eyes and outstretched hands, she reached for the kitchen light switch. "If Samuel can find our old dog carrier, we can put Nigel in there. I'll lay in the back seat with the pelican and keep him company. Then Grandpa, you and Samuel can go to Grand Island," she said.

Grasping the light switch, she flipped it to the off position and sighed deeply. "Sorry, but I can't stand all the brightness. I guess in the excitement yesterday, I forgot to keep on my hat and glasses." Even though her eye sockets ached and her head pounded, Sumer convinced her grandparents she was well enough to ride along to the vet's office.

Tom fixed cereal and cleaned a large bowl of ripe strawberries while Samuel found the dog carrier and carefully placed Nigel inside. After eating his fill of cereal and berries dusted with powder sugar, Samuel, dressed in clean shorts and shirt, placed the dog carrier on the back seat of Mariana's new red convertible and climbed into Old Blue to wait for Tom.

Samuel sat behind the steering wheel to get the feel of it. Maybe Grandpa Tom would let him drive to the main road today. Samuel was nuts about driving, and sometimes Tom let him drive on the back roads.

Slapping his trusty raffia hat firmly on his head, Tom locked up the house and joined Samuel in the blue pickup. In answer to Samuel's question about driving, Tom told his grandson, "Not today," and drove out of the driveway headed for the county sheriff's office.

Mariana and Sumer pulled out just in front of them and sped down the road headed for Banyan City's Veterinary Hospital. "I hope she doesn't get another speeding ticket today. You think buying her that red convertible was a mistake?" Tom asked Samuel.

"She'll be all right. And besides, she really likes that car."

"That she does," Tom chuckled. "That she does."

■ ■ ■

"The pelican's left wing is broken," said Dr. Jonathan Matthews, Banyan City's only veterinarian. He was a tall, gentle man. "Where again did you say you found this bird?" He quizzed Sumer.

"In the Ten Thousand Islands," she replied, avoiding eye contact.

The vet's blue eyes studied the expression on Sumer's face. He tried to figure out why a girl he normally couldn't get to shut up, was being so tight-lipped.

Taking advantage of the vet's preoccupation, Nigel jumped from the examination table to explore a counter filled with bottles and shiny instruments. The pelican pecked at one shiny tool and then turned to investigate a row of bottles. As he did, his rear tail feathers collided with a large bottle of alcohol and sent it crashing to the floor. Antiseptic fumes rose quickly and filled the air.

Dr. Matthews removed Nigel from the counter and, crunching through broken glass, set the pelican once again on the examination table. Sumer, gagging through clouds of vapor, ran to open a window. The vet twisted his torso; holding the bird with one hand, he reached for a syringe and needle with the other. He soon had Nigel sedated.

Mariana swept up broken glass while Sumer mopped up the watery liquid that settled in pools on the tile floor.

Dr. Matthews hunched over the pelican, oblivious to the goings-on around him, as he set and splinted Nigel's wing. When he was done, he gently placed the sleeping pelican back into the dog carrier.

While hauling bird and carrier to the car, the vet said, "You know, Sumer, there are laws against keeping protected species such as this brown pelican for a pet."

"I don't intend to keep Nigel. He came from Grand Island, and we'll take him back as soon as his wing heals."

"How do you know he came from Grand Island? I thought you said you found him in the Ten Thousand Islands." Dr. Matthews said.

"Grand Island is one of the Ten Thousand Islands." Sumer hedged, and she hastily climbed into the back seat of the car to avoid further questions.

In answer to his puzzled look, Mariana gave the vet a sly smile and waved as she put the convertible in gear and pulled away from the curb.

CHAPTER 16

The county building on Grand Island was two stories of white stone, surrounded by 100-year-old trees. As Tom and Samuel entered it's cool interior, they could see Joe with two other well-dressed men, standing alongside a large mahogany desk. One man with flame-red hair was talking to Sheriff Rainbird and his deputy.

"Well, as I live and breathe, if it's not Joe Sorrow," Tom said. The men stopped their discussion to stare at the newcomers.

"Well, if it isn't Tom DeLaluz. What're you doing here?" Joe asked. "I hear you left the Sheriff's department. Your idea or theirs?" Joe's look told Tom that he now understood why Tom hadn't searched the back of his pickup in the Big Cypress Preserve a few months back. "Who's the kid?"

"Found out you were in town, decided to drive over and see if you were in the mood for a game of checkers. This here is my grandson." Then, turning to Samuel, he continued, "Joe and I played checkers at the county jail a couple of years back while he was waiting arraignment on poaching charges. I beat him four games out of four."

"You beat me at checkers? You never beat me at anything, not even checkers. Besides, I don't have time for games. I got a hotel to build if the tree huggers'll leave me be."

Tom eyed Joe's new suit. "Looks like things have turned around for you," he said. "Or have they? Seems a rich man, like you, could surely find a place to build a hotel without cheating an old man out of his property and destroying prime turtle nesting grounds. Nasty business," Tom said, shaking his head.

"I don't know what you're talking about. Besides, what are you doing these days? Playing sheriff?" Joe said. "Looks like you and your hat have seen better days." His cold blue eyes shifted their gaze from Tom long enough to dust off his spotless lizard-skin boots.

133

"Gentlemen!" Sheriff Rainbird interrupted. "You all understand the injunction, right? No one's allowed on the disputed property until after the hearing on Friday. Tom, Samuel, see you in my office?"

"Sure, be right there," Tom said, glaring at the redhead with Joe.

Joe picked up his briefcase and stormed from the building with his associates parading close behind.

Tom and Samuel found their way down the hall to the sheriff's office and stood in the doorway, allowing their eyes to adjust to the dimness of the empty room. The window blinds were shut tight against midday heat; the only light came from a table lamp on the far side of the room. The lamp spilled its yellow light onto a polished table. A large chair relaxed against the wall. The chair, mostly dark blue, but lighter on the worn areas, beckoned to Tom. He crossed the room with a few quick strides and, placing his hat on the table, sat down. His hat didn't look that bad. The finely woven raffia palm drooped in a few places, but that just gave it character. What would Joe Sorrow know about character? True character. The kind that sticks with a man through good times and bad.

Samuel was enthralled with the sheriff's office. He slowly worked his way around the room learning about Grand Island's history from a series of pictures dating from the early 1900s.

Sheriff Cyril Rainbird entered the room, carrying a steaming cup of coffee. How's it going, Samuel? How are your grandmother and sister doing?

"Fine, sir," Samuel said.

"Tom, you want coffee?"

"Thanks, Cyril, but I had my two cups this morning. How are Ruth and the kids?"

Sheriff Rainbird put his coffee cup on the desk and switched on the desk lamp. He inspected unopened envelopes on top of his in-basket. "They're doing good. The girl graduates from high school next year," he said, handing Tom a picture of his daughter. "What brings you and Samuel to Grand Island today?"

134

"Nothing special, just needed to get out of the house. By the way, the suits with Joe, who were they?" Tom asked.

"The redhead was Rusty Ruskin, Sorrow's attorney, the other Duncan Farman, his construction manager. Tom, an old hound dog dressed in sheep's clothes is still an old hound dog. Why are you really on the island today?" the sheriff sat down, causing his wooden desk chair to creak in protest.

"Samuel needs material for a term paper about endangered species and the abuse of wildlife areas. Thought we could do some research in the county law library, see the destruction of sensitive wildlife habitat firsthand out at Sorrow's place, take some pictures. Most likely get the boy an A."

"Tom, we go back a long ways, but the judge's order still stands. Nobody goes on that site until after the hearing next Friday."

"You wouldn't like to give us a tour?"

"No tour."

"I hear Joe's building out on the beach side of the grass dunes. How'd he manage that?"

"That red-haired fellow got him a variance based on old deed restrictions and railroad easements. Joe also produced some archeologist that came up with a theory about Calusa Indian artifacts being buried along the railroad easement. The archeologist angle is a long stretch, but Rusty Ruskin harped on it long enough that it gave the county one more reason to abide by the original deed restrictions and give Sorrow his variance."

"An old guy named Max Thrusher, out of Everglades City, sold that property a few months back to an outfit called Turtles and Me Educational Foundation. They promised Max they'd establish a turtle-nesting reserve on the land. The old man sold it, thinking the property was protected from development." Tom studied a moth as it fluttered around the lampshade next to him.

"Max didn't read the contract carefully and his attorney, well let's just say he's 90 and has seen better days, didn't write a restriction clause into the paperwork like Max told him to. A week later the foundation sold the lot to Joe Sorrow."

"Sounds pretty underhanded," the sheriff said.

" Yeah, Joe's up to the top of his fancy new boots in old scum. For 10 years he's made a living at the expense of Florida's wildlife," Tom said.

"If he doesn't break the law, not much I can do about it, you know."

"That's not very encouraging."

"So, what do you want me to do?" Sheriff Rainbird asked.

"Keep an eye on him, don't let him get away with even the slightest of infractions. Are you sure you can't give Samuel and me a tour of Joe's property?"

"I'm sure."

"Guess I'll have to settle for looking at the county depositions and records. For Samuel's term paper and all."

"They're in the law library, but it's a mess in there; dust's an inch thick. You know how Nate is. Hasn't been in to clean for a couple of weeks; says he has the rheumatism," the sheriff said, eyeing Samuel's clean shirt and shorts.

"You needn't worry about the mess or the dust. We clean up easy, don't we, Samuel?" Samuel nodded, wondering what his grandfather was up to, telling the sheriff he had a term paper. Surely the sheriff knew it was summer break.

"Those documents are rather sensitive right now. It would be best to wait until after the hearing on Friday."

"Aren't they a matter of public record?"

"Oh, all right. For the sake of Samuel's education," the sheriff said with a wink.

Once inside the law library Samuel glanced at Tom inquisitively. "Grandpa, I don't have a research paper to write. It's summer vacation, remember?"

"Nothing like planning ahead — and what a perfect topic. It will work for English, history or social studies. Come on, let's get started."

Tom studied the documentation that was the basis for Joe's environmental variance. "This whole thing smells more and more like a mushroom farm on a hot July day," he said, standing up from a straight-back chair. "I think we need to go talk to Leonia at the county museum."

They left the coolness of the county building and walked two blocks in 95-degree heat to a second white stone building that housed the county's archives. Upon entering the museum, Tom asked to see Leonia Grenadier, the museum's curator.

"Leonia wrote her doctoral thesis on the ancient Calusa Indians. She's the best one to answer questions about the possibility of Calusa artifacts being buried on Joe's lot," he told Samuel.

"Good to see you Leonia," Tom said as they entered her office.

"Hi, Tom. Hey, Samuel. I remember seeing you and your sister at the museum a couple years back. You have certainly grown up. What are you, 18 or so by now?" she said and gave Tom a knowing smile.

"No," Samuel laughed with pride. "Almost 13."

"Tom, haven't seen you in months. Heard you had a heart attack. How are you doing?"

"Fine, just fine."

"And Mariana? She still painting? We could use some more of her work in the museum."

"She doesn't paint like she used to. Kids keep us both busy."

"I bet they do. Any word on your daughter?" She asked with a hesitant look at Samuel.

"Nothing new."

"Well, what can I do for you two today?"

"We're doing some research and we thought you could help. Did you attend the county hearings that resulted in Joe Sorrow receiving an environmental variance to build his resort directly on the beach?"

"As a matter of fact, I did attend part of it."

"Sheriff Rainbird told us there was an archeological angle. You know the scoop on that?"

"Yes, that's the reason I attended the hearings."

"You at liberty to give me your opinion?"

"Don't know why I couldn't. I know your ancestry is linked to the Calusa remnant in Cuba," Leonia said. "You're familiar, I'm sure, with their history, but with your permission I'd like to begin my story back a ways — to make it more meaningful."

"I've done a lot of reading but it won't hurt Samuel to hear it from an expert."

"Thanks," Leonia said, smiling. She was quiet for a moment, as if she needed time to respect the ancient Indians and their saga before she brought it forth in public.

"The Calusa Indians either had a settlement on Grand Island or used the island as a religious compound around the 12th century. Tradition has it that a cataclysmic hurricane swept across Southwest Florida at that time. When the Calusa found out this monumental storm was looming on their horizon, they evacuated the island leaving behind their belongings."

"Is this stuff part of the junk that was left?" Samuel asked, pointing to a nearby display case.

"You're moving ahead of me, OK?"

"Sure. Sorry."

"One thing we do know is that the Calusa left en mass and in a hurry."

"To get away from the hurricane?" Samuel said.

"Yes, probably to get away from the hurricane. Whether they simply didn't have time to take their belonging with them or whether they intentionally buried them for safekeeping, we can only guess, but we do know they left behind a large cache of artifacts."

"And what they left behind was buried," Tom added.

"Yes."

"The Calusa didn't have TV or radio — how'd they know a storm was coming?" Samuel asked as he dropped into a nearby chair.

"In the 1500s, when the Spaniards came to this area, they wrote about Calusa fishermen who traveled in great canoes as far out as 100 miles into the Gulf."

"A hundred miles out in the Gulf, in a canoe? No way. I'm not dumb enough to go that far in a canoe."

"Samuel, I'm losing my train of thought here," Leonia said with a frown.

"Oh, yeah, sorry."

"Where was I?"

"You had the Calusa Indians fishing in a canoe, 100 miles out in the Gulf with Hurricane Gertrude coming their way."

"Gertrude?"

"Well I figured the hurricane needed a name and I had a mean old teacher called Gertrude once. Figured it fit."

"Yes, well, let's see," Leonia said, smoothing her dress, adjusting her glasses and folding her hands so tight they turned red. "Hurricanes sometimes move slowly. The Indians in the village may have been warned about the storm a day or two in advance by fishermen who came back from one of these fishing trips. They may have buried the cache for safekeeping. On the other hand, they may not have had much warning. They may have left everything where it was and fled the island."

"And Gertrude buried it with mud and muck, right?"

Tom sensed Leonia's frustration with Samuel's interruptions and pulled up a chair for her.

"No thanks, I think better on my feet, but please, you take the chair."

Tom sat down and Leonia continued. "Either that particular tribe never came back to the island, or high water and wind dumped so much debris and changed the coastline to such an extent that when the Calusa did return, they were unable to find their possessions."

"Maybe all these masks and things were in a really big temple and Hurricane Gertrude blew over the temple and buried everything," Samuel said.

Leonia let out a long sigh. "Actually, that is pretty close to what happened, but your getting ahead of the story again." She twisted and untwisted her necklace, then abruptly dropped her hands and clasped them behind her back.

139

"Sorry."

Leonia smiled a smile that never reached her eyes. "When Frank Cushing and his expedition discovered the cache in the 1890s, they dug up the famous Calusa Key Marco Cat and those ceremonial masks," she said, pointing to the glass case, "They also found 70 crates of other things as well."

"Those aren't real masks, they're just pictures," Samuel said.

Tom gave Samuel a stern look.

"Well, they're not," Samuel shrugged.

"Leonia is kind enough to spend her time giving us this information; please save your questions and comments until the end."

The museum curator gave Tom a grateful smile and continued. "The original deer head mask," she said, pointing to one picture, "is in the University Museum in Philadelphia, but the rest of the masks were destroyed. All that remains of them are drawings and watercolors. When the wooden masks were dug from the mud and exposed to air, they started to decay and fall apart. One man on the expedition, an artist named Wells Sawyer, was foresighted enough to draw sketches and paint watercolors of the masks."

Samuel waved his arm frantically in the air. "Yes, Samuel."

"They found all that stuff on Grand Island?"

"Samuel, I though I told you to hold your questions," Tom said shifting uncomfortably in his chair.

"But she called on me."

"Yes, I guess I did. The artifacts were all buried on the north end of the island in a swampy area where the ground at that time consisted of mostly tannic muck. This historic find was preserved, in theory, by the tannic muck that surrounded it and kept air away from it."

"What's tannic muck?" Samuel asked then said, "Oops, sorry."

Leonia sighed. "Tannic muck is a rich subsoil that is made gooey by water mixed with tannic acid."

"You've seen that reddish stagnant water that sometimes stands at the base of mangrove trees," Tom said.

"Yeah."

"Tannic acid from the trees makes the water that color." Leonia explained.

"OK, so how does all this affect Joe Sorrow's lot?" Tom leaned forward in the chair.

"The archeologist that examined his property testified at the hearing that there is a small stand of buttonwood trees on Sorrow's property. He also stated that he found a swampy area in the middle of the property that consists of the same type of tannic muck that the Key Marco Cat and the rest of the wooden masks were buried. To add a little more interest, the cat was carved of buttonwood."

"Because of the buttonwood trees and this tannic muck, and without any actual excavation, they gave Sorrow the variance?" Tom looked at Leonia in disbelief.

Samuel stood up and stretched his way toward a large display case.

"Yes that's correct," Leonia said once more pulling at her necklace. "When Grand Island was originally developed in the 1960s, much of Calusa history was unknowingly bulldozed away by the developer. I guess the county commissioners didn't want to be responsible for destroying any Calusa artifacts that might still remain."

"Just a few buttonwood trees and a pool of tannic muck." Tom said.

"That red-headed attorney of Joe's is a very convincing fellow." Leonia became defensive. "He made it sound as if the county commissioners would single-handedly destroy the find of the century if they didn't grant the environmental variance."

"You know the archeologist who caused all this trouble?" Tom asked standing up and looking around the museum for Samuel.

"I don't know him. I've not heard of the organization he represents," Leonia face showed unmasked irritation. She indicated the interview was over by walking toward her office in the front of the museum.

"And you?" Tom asked, catching up to her. "What do you think?"

"I don't know!" She didn't slow her pace. "I haven't had a chance to go out there and look for myself."

"Thank you, Leonia. Nice of you to spend your time with us." Tom said. His disbelief had annoyed her, but he wasn't willing to apologize. How could people be so gullible? He wondered.

He looked around the museum for Samuel. "Now where did that kid get to? Excuse me for a minute," he said turning toward a large display case where he last saw Samuel. Tom was soon back, with Samuel in tow.

"Thank you, Miss Leonia," Samuel said. "I really like those masks, but I don't understand all the fuss about that little cat statue."

"Take my word for it, Samuel, the Key Marco Cat is a very valuable artifact. When you were here a few years ago, wasn't the original cat here on loan from the Smithsonian Institution?"

"I don't remember. I probably didn't think much of it then, either."

"I think it was," Tom said, frowning at Samuel. "Jade brought the kids to see it." Samuel started to speak, but Tom tightened his grip on Samuel's shoulder.

Tom and Samuel left the museum and headed back toward the sheriff's offices and law library.

"You were certainly a pain in there. What got into you?"

"I'm hungry. I was having a hard time concentrating 'cause my stomach was growling so loud," Samuel said as he ran to keep up with his grandfather.

"Yeah, right. Next time, behave yourself," Tom said. "You know where the vending machines are?"

"I'll find them."

"Go get something to hold you over." Tom said, handing Samuel a couple of dollar bills. I need to look at some case studies as long as we're here."

Samuel grabbed the money and ran down the hall toward a row of vending machines.

Tom decided to look for court cases where archeological digs endangered wildlife areas. After digging through litigation after litigation, he found one where the habitat of an endangered species was put at great risk by an archeological dig. In that case, the protection of the endangered species' habitat took precedence over the archeological site. In most cases, however, mankind's fascination with the past outweighed his concern over protecting wildlife areas. And big money, with mankind's frenzy to get rich, overshadowed them both.

In the deposition of the Sorrow hearing, Rusty Ruskin, Joe Sorrow's attorney, had argued that the wildlife habitat on Joe's beachfront property was not unique. He stated that turtles and birds could just as easily nest on neighboring beaches. Tom knew environmental history would not support that theory, because the curve of this particular shoreline gave the beach greater protection from wind and storms than other beaches in the area. He also knew that female turtles by instinct returned to the same beach year after year to lay eggs.

Tom scratched his chin. He didn't agree with the county commissioners' decision, yet whether he agreed or not didn't really matter. What mattered was finding a way to reverse the decision, and that task was going to be as difficult as giving sight to a blind man.

At that moment, Samuel reappeared with a candy bar and a can of soda. "What took you so long?" Tom asked.

"A dumb girl got her quarter stuck in the machine I wanted to use, and I had to help her before I could get my candy bar."

"You may think girls are dumb now but just wait a few years, and you'll be thrilled to help a damsel in distress. I'm ready to go, but I want to make one more stop. Then we'll have lunch ... if you're still hungry."

"Don't worry. I'll still be hungry. This detective stuff is hard work."

The one more stop proved to be Ted Rattowsky's office. He was counsel for an environmentalist group called the Endangered Species Foundation and would be representing the environmentalists who had been jailed the day before.

"There is no new evidence to present. All the pertinent issues were argued during the hearing with the county," Ted said, motioning for Tom and Samuel to sit down. "I'm just going to hammer on the turtle-nesting angle and ask for a moratorium on construction until November, when turtle-nesting season is over."

"Doesn't that just delay the inevitable?" Tom asked.

"Several associations have organized charitable events to raise money for the purchase of Joe Sorrow's property. The land, if purchased, would be set aside as an archaeological and environmentally protected area owned by the community. Our plan is to delay construction long enough, and to frustrate the owner often enough, that we can convince him to sell."

"Joe Sorrow is a greedy, hard-headed man and, from the sounds of it, this Rusty Ruskin got his morals in a back alley."

"Be that as it may, we're going to take a run at it."

"I hope for your success. Come on, Samuel," Tom said, standing up. "I think it's time for lunch. We'll get a sandwich and some cherry cobbler at the Purple Pelican."

After lunch, Tom and Samuel started back to Banyan City. Samuel fell asleep, leaving Tom to his thoughts. Tom cranked down the window and hummed along with the radio. He steered his old blue pickup as it twisted and turned down a narrow stretch of blacktop. The smell of hot tar drifted up from the road while strains of Simon and Garfunkel's *Sounds of Silence* filled the air. Tom, suddenly nostalgic, yearned for days gone by — a time when most of the area between Grand Island and Banyan City was wilderness and teemed with wildlife, a time when Jade was a young girl and lived at home. Tom shook his head. Change is not always good.

Samuel woke as the pickup bumped into the driveway and came to a stop. "What do we do now?" he asked.

"We wait until after the hearing on Friday and see what happens."

"I'm going to check on Nigel and wash up for dinner," Samuel said. When he reached the house, the boy took the porch steps two at a time and disappeared around the corner.

144

Tom climbed the steps one at a time. He took off his raffia hat and stared at it. What was Joe talking about? It was still in fine shape. Sure, it didn't look store-bought new anymore but that just meant it was finally broken-in. Tom placed it gently on a peg next to his old straw hat and went into the kitchen. He hoped Mariana didn't remember to ask him about his heart medication. He had forgotten to refill his prescription, again.

CHAPTER 17

The hearing on Friday did not go well for the Endangered Species Foundation; however, the construction project did not come away unscathed either. The judge upheld the county commissioners' decision but required Joe to build a turtle-proof fence around the construction site. He also gave the foundation two weeks to remove turtle eggs already located on the property. Construction was not to resume until the fence was finished and the turtle nests removed.

After the hearing Tom, Mariana, Sumer and Samuel sat in a large padded booth in the Purple Pelican, located across the street from the courthouse. They ordered lunch and listened to angry foundation members, who filled six other booths, as they discussed the judge's decision.

"Move the turtle nests? Who does that judge think he is kidding? Everyone knows disrupting a nest will kill some of the eggs," one large man sputtered.

"I guess the judge thinks it will kill less than a 5-gazillion pound bulldozer," Sumer said.

Mariana, surprised and embarrassed by Sumer's comment, cleared her throat and gave Sumer a severe look. Samuel stared at his hands and snickered. Tom's laughing eyes rendered his nudge of reproach totally ineffective.

"Build a turtle-proof fence? What a joke. Them turtles'll dig right under it," another member commented with disgust.

The big man took a bite of his sandwich. "I say get A.W. or the feds down here. They'll send Joe Sorrow packing," he said with half chewed food still in his mouth.

"We don't want outsiders coming in and telling us how to run our business. That's one sure way to lose control," said a middle-aged woman who scowled critically under a halo of golden-red hair. She absentmindedly smoothed the tablecloth with long red nails.

"We've worked hard to build and maintain a good relationship with local landowners. Don't forget our motto, 'We work with, not against, landowners to save our environment.'" Ted stared down at his untouched lunch. He didn't remember ordering the Caesar salad.

"Right! If we turn loose the big guns, all the businessmen and landowners will align against us," the red-haired woman said.

"We need them on our side if we plan to raise enough money to buy out Sorrow," Ted reminded the group.

"OK, so what now?"

"We have to comply with the judge's order to move the eggs, but be slow and methodical about it. Take the full two weeks." Ted poked at his salad.

"Then what?" The redheaded woman's carefully manicured hands flew into the air in frustration.

"Then we pray for a miracle," Mariana said, admiring the woman's passion. That seemed to be the final word on the subject and everyone settled down to finish his or her lunch.

The crowd dispersed after Ted gave instructions. First thing Monday morning they were to begin the search for turtle nests and to meticulously relocate any eggs that were found.

"What about the heron named Yatzu?" Sumer asked Tom later as they walked toward the car. "Do you think God sent him here to help us? Is it possible that a bird, even a great white heron, could do anything?"

"Sumer, it's just a heron, a bird, I tell you." But even as he said the words, Tom knew they weren't true. The great white bird was no ordinary heron. "Even if in some realm unknown to us, Yatzu, true to his name, was somehow sent by God to help protect manatees or a turtle that's slow as morning after a sleepless night, this is a huge building project, and Joe Sorrow has the law on his side. Granted it's a first, but this time they are on his side," Tom said.

"Well laws can sometimes be wrong!"

"That may be, Sumer, but it's still the law until we get it changed."

"God's bigger than any manmade law, and Jesus said everything is possible to those who believe." Sumer huffed.

Tom was chastised by the passion that his 12-year-old granddaughter had for God. Why is it that the very old and the very young possess such fervor for their faith? Tom wondered. While I, not so very old and definitely not so very young, stand here riddled with doubt?

"Tomorrow is the next meeting at Kingdom Cove," Samuel said. "The last time with Mindy and the others seems so unreal and far away. Sometimes I believe; then I decide it's a crock. After that, I figure that Sumer and I are probably both nuts, but I don't want to have that much in common with a girl."

Sumer, untrue to her normal nature, let that one pass. "Trina was right about the building project. And what about Nigel?" she said.

Florida Panther

Florida Panther

Florida Panther

CHAPTER 18

After the first Kingdom Cove meeting, Mindy and Mother Manatee guided Samuel and Sumer through the Ten Thousand Islands. When the twins got their bearings, the two manatees swam toward the mangrove channels in search of food. Trina, the loggerhead turtle, returned to the warm Gulf waters.

The roseate spoonbill doused himself liberally with lagoon water before following Zhora toward the back of the island – traveling that direction provided the shortest possible route to the Everglades mainland.

"You're dripping on me," the panther complained when Rondolus flew above her. "Why're you all wet?"

"I figured if I soaked myself good, maybe the gift of tongues would stick awhile longer. You should run back and take a final swim so we can understand each other after we're on the mainland."

"I don't need too. I'm getting a shower from you."

"It might prove helpful, you know, since we're friends now," Rondolus said.

"Sometimes communication is overrated." The walk and swim back to the mainland tired Zhora. When they reached the Everglades, she found a hardwood hammock populated with mahogany trees — Everglades hammocks are fertile areas higher than their surroundings and heavily wooded with hardwood trees — and she lay down.

"It feels like we've traveled a hundred miles today. I simply can't go any farther," Zhora yowled.

"See, it worked. I can still understand you," Rondolus croaked.

"Whoopee," was the panther's half-hearted reply. She flopped down under a large tree. "I have a horrendous pain in my side. I believe I may have started premature labor. I never should have agreed to this tedious journey with my cubs due in a few weeks."

"Premature labor? You're going to have cubs? Why didn't you tell me?" asked Rondolus.

"Well, it is a rather delicate subject to discuss in a mixed crowd," Zhora answered.

"What mixed crowd? I'm the only one here. I'm no mixed crowd. Besides, I thought we were friends. Why didn't you tell ME?" The spoonbill fumed.

"I assumed we'd go to the lagoon, afterward I'd return to the cypress forest and that would be the end of it. I would retire to the privacy of my den, birth my cubs and raise them in motherly bliss. This will be my first brood of offspring. I did communicate the fact that I was with cub to Mother Manatee, or rather, she guessed. Other mothers can tell these things, you know."

"Well, you'd better rest, I'll look around and see what I can scrounge for dinner," Rondolus croaked, still angry with Zhora for not taking him into her confidence.

During his search for food, Rondolus came upon an old snowy egret. They exchanged looks of distrust. Then the spoonbill flapped his pink wings and in doing so sprayed droplets of water on the egret. The spoonbill thought for a laugh he'd mention Yatzu, the great white bird. To his amazement the egret understood him and told him of an osprey that had witnessed some unusual acts by the great white bird. The egret pointed Rondolus to a nearby mangrove island where the osprey lived.

The spoonbill tightened his wings to preserve any water that still remained on them. Walking instead of flying took longer, but finally, the spoonbill arrived at the clearing. The osprey stood next to a tall tree and was tearing at a partially eaten fish with his sharp, hooked beak. The bird was dark brown on the back, but his forehead, cheeks, neck and breast shone white in the setting sun. Most impressive, however, were the fish hawk's feet, which firmly gripped its slippery prey. Each foot sported short spikes on its sole and four toes with sharp, curved claws.

Rondolus warily approached the clearing where the osprey ate. "Excuse me, sir," he said, "but I need to sprinkle you with water."

"Now why would you want to do that?" The osprey hissed.

Rondolus looked puzzled. "How is it you can understand me?"

"I've had the gift of gab for a few months now, ever since that white bird came around," the osprey hissed. "Now, get away from my dinner."

"Excuse me, but is your name Olli?" Rondolus croaked.

"Yes, who wants to know?" The osprey asked.

"I was told you could help me find a great white bird that is reputed to be a friend of animals in trouble."

"Nope, sorry, can't do that."

"You can't?"

"I saw him, though. I watched him save two Florida panthers from a man with one of those fire sticks. Then a few months later, I saw him again. The great white bird was in this very channel. He headed off a speed boat that, if left to its own devices, would have killed a half-dozen manatees."

"Let me get this straight. You know this great white bird, but you won't tell me where I can find him?"

"I didn't say that, exactly. To my knowledge, no one knows where he comes from or where he goes. You can't locate him or request help; he just seems to show up when he's needed."

"We could sure use his help now," Rondolus croaked.

"Why? What seems to be the problem?"

"Well, there's this Florida panther. She's not feeling well, says she's 'with cub'. She's afraid she's in labor, and if her litter is born prematurely, they'll die."

"She's just tired. Poor old thing. She'll be fine after she's rested a bit. Panthers are too nervous for my taste anyway."

"No, I think she's really sick. I need to find her something to eat."

"I'll get her a nice big redfish. After a good meal and a sound night's sleep, she'll be fit as a well strung violin," Olli reasoned.

"Hope you're right."

Sometime later, Olli with a large fish secured in his talons and Rondolus, carrying crayfish and shrimp in his bill, started toward the hammock where the spoonbill left Zhora.

"I'm sure this is the right place," Rondolus croaked spitting out the shrimp and crayfish.

"Maybe she went to hunt her own dinner."

"No, she was feeling real sick. I told her I'd bring back supper and I haven't been gone that long."

"We'd better look for her," Olli whistled.

Clearing the treetops, Olli saw a panther attempting to drink from a nearby pool, but a large alligator hindered her efforts. "Looks like your friend could use some help," Olli whistled as he, with claws outstretched, dived at the large reptile.

Hearing the cry of the osprey and seeing the sharp talons aimed at its eyes, the gator sank underwater and rippled away. Zhora jumped back to dodge the descending hawk but was grateful for his help when she found out he was friendly. Zhora watched the alligator slink away then returned to the pond's edge to drink deeply of the tepid water. Her thirst satisfied, the panther retreated to the safety of the trees.

"I desperately needed a drink of water, but I was too weak to fight that antagonistic gator. I'm sure it sensed my weakness and enjoyed taunting me," Zhora explained. She lay down under a large tree and gratefully chewed on the redfish provided by the osprey.

"Zhora meet Olli," Rondolus introduced the two.

Looking at Olli, Zhora saw a bird that some might mistake for a bald eagle. She recognized him as an osprey, however, by the broad, black cheek patches, brown bars on his tail and white under wings. His smaller size also distinguished him from a bald eagle. "Good evening, Olli," Zhora yowled, acknowledging the introduction.

"Olli has been telling me about a great white bird that helps endangered animals. It sounds like the one that girl was talking about. According to Olli, the heron is a drifter, and no one seems to knows where he lives or how to find him."

"I'm terribly sorry, but I can't concern myself with that at present. I am most anxious about the potential premature birth of my cubs," Zhora yowled.

She thanked Olli and Rondolus for the fish and shrimp they caught for her. "It was quite filling but I'm going to rest now. Hopefully, tomorrow, I'll be healthy enough to journey to my den in the Big Cypress National Preserve."

"Of course you're right; your cubs come first. You sleep. I'll stand guard," croaked Rondolus.

"I'll bring more fish in the morning," Olli offered.

"Thank you both for your kindness. Good night." The panther yawned and dropped off to sleep.

The following morning, just after dawn, Zhora woke to see Olli descend from the sky with a large mangrove snapper in his talons. The panther gratefully ate the fish and, somewhat strengthened, started for the watering hole.

"We'd better accompany you. Your alligator friend might still be lurking around the pond," croaked Rondolus.

Zhora's pain increased with each step. When the pregnant cat finally returned to the protection of the trees, she, barely able to stand, collapsed in the thick grass. "I know something is terribly wrong. If my cubs are born this early they will not survive. Oh! I should never have attempted this horrendous journey."

"Somehow we have to save her that walk to the pond," Rondolus fretted to Olli.

"I could fly to the beach and pick off a sand pail. Human's are always leaving them lying around. I can carry small amounts of water in one from the watering hole to the hammock."

"Do you think that'd work?" Rondolus asked.

"Sure," Olli whistled and set off for the closest beach. The fish hawk sailed high above the gulf water and after a time spotted a sand pail on a remote stretch of beach. The container was filled with seashells, and a round woman with curly gray hair sat beside it.

Olli circled, waiting for a chance to snatch the bucket away from the woman, but she continued to sit and sift through her treasures. He looked for something to distract her then dived toward a large conch shell that rolled in the surf. He retrieved the shell from the mildly undulating waves and dropped it within a few feet of the woman.

The woman, her attention diverted from the bucket, ambled toward the shell and, with water swirling around her ankles, stooped to pick it up.

Olli lost no time. He swooped down and knocked over the bucket. Shells clattered everywhere as they tumbled over each other and fell onto the sand. The noise caught the woman's attention, but she only stared in amazement as the osprey dumped the shells and, grasping the bucket handle with his claws, flew away.

The incredulous look on her face as she watched the bucket sail high above her head made Ollie speculated on the thoughts that most likely ran through the grandmotherly woman's brain: "An osprey that steals sand pails? My grandchildren will never believe this one."

Olli returned to find Zhora thirsty but claiming the pain had eased. He filled the bucket with as much water as he could carry and made several trips to the pond until the panther's thirst was quenched. He later brought her a nice-sized snook. After eating, Zhora slept while Rondolus and Olli sat in a tree directly above her.

This went on for several days, Olli bringing water and Rondolus and Olli supplying food. Even with plenty of food and water the panther became weaker each day.

"We have to do something. If she walks anywhere, she could lose the cubs, and I'm not sure how much longer we can keep her in food and water. That alligator hasn't found her yet, but he was much too close for comfort earlier today," worried Rondolus.

"We can continue the food and water. But protecting her against that alligator? I'm not sure, especially if it gets serious about doing her in," Olli added.

"It really sticks in my craw to ask humans for help, but I think that's our only hope," Rondolus decided. "That girl and her brother are meeting with the others at Kingdom Cove today. If you can take care of Zhora, I'll leave now and, with luck, arrive before they leave."

"I can handle it for a day, but I'll be leaving her alone while I fish, and if her condition worsens, there's not much I can do."

"Give it your best," Rondolus croaked. His pink wings spread, lifting him into the air. Olli watched with foreboding while the spoonbill soared into the sky.

161

CHAPTER 19

At dawn Sumer and Samuel put the brown pelican in the bow of the canoe and headed for Kingdom Cove. This time they told Tom and Mariana where they were going and even drew a primitive map with the approximate location of the miraculous lagoon. Sumer promised to wear her hat and glasses and they both agreed to be back before sundown.

After the twins left, Tom and Mariana stared at each other across the kitchen table. The crude map lay on the table between them. "I don't believe any of this. I'm going out to work in my workshop," Tom said.

■ ■ ■

Samuel paddled as far as Greentree's Store then docked the canoe. The twins ran up the steps and into the store. Rummaging through shelves and bins, they found mosquito repellent, snack food and drinks, which they placed on the counter alongside their money.

Mr. Greentree, a good friend of their grandparents, offered them a free soda and asked after Tom and Mariana. The storekeeper and twins chitchatted while the twins guzzled their sodas, then Samuel grabbed a grocery bag, filled with their purchases, and bolted for the canoe. "Hey, what's your hurry?" Mr. Greentree asked.

Sumer gave the elderly man a hug and said, "Gotta go."

According to Samuel's calculations by midmorning they should be close to their destination. Sumer and Samuel were not worried about finding the crooked limb, because, when they left the first time, they marked the channel's obscure entrance with a large orange scarf.

The journey took longer than planned. It was half past 10 before the twins and pelican rounded the northern tip of a large

162

mangrove island and saw the bright cloth. The wind blew the scarf straight out, then allowed it to fall, only to pick it up once more and flutter it wildly.

Sumer and Samuel bathed themselves in insect repellent and slid the canoe under the crooked limb that stood sentinel over the secret channel. The waterway was shrouded in shadows and covered with a canopy of mangrove branches. Samuel dipped and pulled the paddle through water, black with tannin. Silenced by the stillness, the twins peered around them. A strong odor of wet and decaying wood permeated the dark air. Sumer, for once, wasn't up for talking. Somehow the eerie waterway and nagging doubts about their destination didn't promote conversation.

Insects, warded off by the repellant, were, for the most part, ignored. The angry beauty around them was visually explored one leaf, one branch, one odd critter at a time. An hour later, the canoe and its occupants left the channel and entered Kingdom Cove. The wild and harsh voyage once again paled in comparison to the glory of the journey's destination.

The awe Sumer and Samuel felt the first time they entered the lagoon was not diminished by a second visit. Crystal water, abundant fruit, sweet flowers, musical birds, vibrant fish and butterflies the size of a child's hand all contributed to the atmosphere of miracles —even more so, than they remembered.

Sumer and Samuel, not seeing the loggerhead, the manatees, the spoonbill or the Florida panther, decided to go for a swim. Clear water beckoned to them, and, according to Mindy, a plunge into its depths was necessary to restore the gift of languages.

Setting Nigel into the water, Samuel, followed by Sumer, dived to the bottom of the pool. As before, they were spellbound by the beauty and bounty of the underwater life. Examining one amazing creature after another, they spotted a large school of fish and swam through the middle of the silvery shapes.

When they surfaced Nigel, alone, sunned himself on the white sand. Samuel glanced around anxiously. Worried last week's experience was a delusion brought on by the sun, and afraid he couldn't talk to animals, he swam with apprehension toward shallow water. Sloshing through ankle-high waves, he walked onto the beach and sat down next to Nigel. He screwed up his courage and, determined to find out once and for all if the gift of languages was real, asked, "How does your wing feel?"

No answer.

"Nigel, how does your wing feel?" he repeated, panic rising in his chest.

Nigel did not respond. The bird sat; he blinked; he looked at Samuel.

"Nigel! Can you understand me? I asked how your wing is doing!" The pelican moved from one foot to the other and settled down to watch Samuel with flickering eyes.

"I knew it! I JUST KNEW IT! It's all a big fat lie! Not true. Not any of it. The others aren't coming. None of it was real. Not one STINKING BIT OF IT!" Samuel kicked the sand and sent a white cloud into the air. He kicked a stick into the water and watched it splash, then stomped back to Sumer and, with tears threatening to spill, spluttered, "It's a lie. All of it."

"How can it be? Here's the lagoon. Nigel is real," Sumer walked over to the pelican and, bending over, looked him square in the face. Under her close scrutiny Nigel fidgeted and looked away. "If a bird could look guilty, I'd say this one is up to something."

"Yeah, right Sumer. Check the evidence. We're the only ones here and Nigel isn't talking. A bird looking guilty? I don't think so. As your friends'd say, 'Like D-A-H'."

"Well, u-m-m, OK, let's at least go exploring. Give the others time to show up. Maybe we're early."

"That'd be a first, especially for you." Samuel said.

"Funny. I want to look around. If the others don't shown up, we'll go home."

"OK, grab the bird. I'll get the canoe."

Sumer picked up the pelican and, "Tee-hee, tee-hee."

"He laughed!"

"Who laughed?"

"This bird just laughed."

"Get real. First he looks guilty, now he's laughing? Come on Sumer! Enough is enough!"

"Tee-hee, tee-hee," the pelican laughed. "Had you going, didn't I, mates? No worries, I can understand you. I couldn't resist pranking you. Such jolly fun."

"JOLLY FUN!" Samuel said, glaring at the bird.

"Nigel you little…" Sumer dropped the pelican onto the sand.

"I say, watch my wing," the bird croaked. "It's much improved, but, none the less, it's a bit tender. I do appreciate your assistance."

"Nice way to show your gratitude," Samuel said.

"Oh, bother. Where are the others?" Nigel said looking around. "Here comes, um-um …oh how my brain sticks sometimes…the turtle that's so bothersome about her age?"

"Trina?"

"Yes, that's the name, Trina. Here comes Trina." Nigel croaked, trying to redeem himself.

"I'm here. Let's get the show on the stage," the loggerhead sputtered as her leathery head popped out of the water. "Where are the rest, for pity sake? The sun is straight up."

"I see Mindy and Mamma Manatee. They just swam into the lagoon, but I don't see Rondolus or Zhora. What could be keeping them?" asked Sumer.

"As cranky as that spoonbill was last week, maybe he isn't coming," replied Samuel.

"Rondolus can certainly be surly, but he does want to help. So does Zhora," Mother Manatee snorted as her nose and mouth broke above the water. "Zhora agreed to this venture, in spite of the fact, that she is only weeks away from delivering cubs. All this travel can't be good for her."

"Zhora is having cubs? How exciting! When are they due? How many cubs will she have?" Sumer wandered from shallow water to flop on the warm sand.

"She's due in a few weeks. Being this is her first litter, there'll be one, two, three at the most," Mamma Manatee snorted.

"If they're coming, where are they?" Samuel asked.

"They'll be here soon." Mindy surfaced in shallow water next to the beach.

Trina dragged her large shell onto the sand. "Excuse me. Grand Island, remember?"

"All that court stuff didn't help much," Samuel said. "The judge didn't stop construction. He just put it off a couple weeks."

Samuel told everyone about the trip he and Grandpa Tom made to Grand Island, about their research and the hearing.

"The judge gave a group of environmentalists, named ESF, two weeks. Not much time." He looked around to gauge the reaction of the others.

"I hoped for better news," Mother Manatee snorted, blowing water from her nose.

"Mamma and I didn't find out anything about the white bird either," Mindy said.

Trina, resting her head on the sand, looked dejected. "The other loggerheads laughed at me. They wanted to know what a turtle needed with a bird-brained heron."

"Hey! Watch that bird-brain nonsense," Nigel said.

"Sorry."

"What could be keeping Rondolus and Zhora? Think they've met with foul play?" Samuel said looking at Nigel. "Foul play, get it?" He said.

"Very funny, mate, very funny," Nigel said.

"Patience. They'll be here. They're probably traveling slow because of Zhora's condition," snorted Mamma Manatee floating up, then submerging all but her eyes and nose.

"What are we going to do about that awful building project?" Trina grunted again. "Sumer and Samuel have come up empty. I've come up empty; you've come up empty. Everything hangs on Rondolus and Zhora, and they're not even here. My beautiful peaceful beach, what can be done to save it?" Trina wailed, losing her composure.

"My wing is healing nicely," Nigel croaked, walking over to the distraught turtle to show her his wing. "Sumer and Samuel will most likely be seeing me to Grand Island in a fortnight."

"It's getting late. We have to start home soon. What can be keeping Rondolus and Zhora?" Sumer, hands on hips and eyes searching the lagoon, paced up and down the beach.

"They'll be here; I'm sure they will. Give them a few more minutes," Mindy snorted.

"Meanwhile we must come up with a solution to the problem on Grand Island." Mamma Manatee dived under the water, she thought better underwater.

"The environmental group is raising money to buy the property and turn it into some kind of a safe zone, but they need time. Time to raise money. Time to muscle Joe Sorrow into moving Ghost Orchid Hotel to a better spot. I wonder where he came up with a name like Ghost Orchid Hotel?" Samuel said.

"The ghost orchid is a rare orchid, found in the Fakahatchee Strand of Florida. When it blooms the roots blend so perfectly with the orchid's host that the striking white flower appears to float in mid-air," Mother Manatee said, her large head once again breaking the water's surface.

"Oh, well, anyway, the guy needs to move his hotel to a better spot, a better spot for us that is." Samuel buried his toes in white sand and wondered about Mother Manatee.

"What about the great white bird Grandpa calls Yatzu?"

"Yeah, what about it?"

"Do you think those stories are true? Grandpa and Old Max say they are," Sumer said.

Mamma Manatee had gone under water to think and Mindy was bobbing up and down next to her. Sumer swam out to them.

Samuel followed. He walked until he reached waist deep water then he dived and disappeared. He surfaced behind Sumer and pushed her head under water. She came up sputtering and pounced on him. They both chased Mindy then Mindy chased them. Nigel remained on the beach and sunned himself.

"We need a solution," Trina wailed across the water.

Samuel looked at Trina then checked the position of the sun. "It's getting late. We've got to start home." He swam into shallow water then sloshed toward the canoe.

167

Sumer swam back to shore. "I guess you're right, but I'm worried about Rondolus and Zhora and we still don't have a clue how to save Trina's beach," Sumer said.

Samuel pushed the canoe close to where Sumer stood. "The judge gave ESF two weeks. Everyone think hard. We'll meet again in three days," Samuel said. "How do we get a message to Rondolus and Zhora?"

As if in answer to his question, a travel-weary Rondolus descended from the sky and skidded across the water to the beach. His feet barely touched the sand before questions came hurling toward him from all directions.

"Where've you been? Where's Zhora?"

"You're late. We thought you weren't going to show."

"What happened to you, old chap? You look like you've been dragged through a hedge backwards. Where's your mate?"

"Where's Zhora? What did you find out about Yatzu?"

Rondolus motioned for silence. "I need help from these two and their vet friend. We haven't a moment to lose. Zhora's sick. She's in terrible pain, thinks it's premature labor. The cubs aren't due for two or three weeks. If the cubs come this early they'll die. And the alligator will do her in if we don't get back."

"Alligator! What alligator?"

The pink bird flapped about in agitation. "I don't have time to explain. Hurry! Hurry! We must go!"

"Where? Where is Zhora?" Sumer asked.

"Everglades, in a large mahogany hammock. Olli's guarding her, but he can't hold out against the gator for long. Hurry, we must go. Now!"

"Who's Olli?" Samuel quizzed looking down on the spoonbill.

"Oh, for crying out loud, questions, will you never stop with the questions? Olli's an osprey, a friend. Let's go!"

The urgency of the situation finally dawned on the others. Sumer placed Nigel in the bow of the boat, and Rondolus hopped in beside the pelican. Samuel climbed into the canoe and grabbed the paddle, while Sumer pushed the canoe knee-deep into the water and belly-flopped into it.

Samuel paddled hard toward Banyan City, and for once Sumer wished there were two paddles. She wanted to help, but all she could do was fidget. Mindy, Mother Manatee and Trina, eager to help but not knowing what to do, followed close behind.

The twins arrived home in record time. When they rounded the last bend, Mariana stood in the middle of her flower garden. She heard Samuel's shout and looked up to see the strange parade. After calling for Tom, she rushed toward the water.

Tom heard the commotion and stepped from his workshop into the late afternoon sun. Seeing all the excitement, he followed Mariana down to the shoreline.

Samuel gave one last shove with the paddle and Sumer, jumping into the knee-deep water, pulled the canoe ashore. Tom helped his grandchildren beach the boat while Mariana, rapid-firing one question after another, picked up Nigel and placed him on the ground. The grandparents moved from disbelief to urgency as they made plans to rescue the endangered Florida panther.

"I'll grab the supplies we need. Mariana, you call Dr. Matthews. Have him meet us at the park's entrance. Put Nigel in his box. We've enough to worry about without concern over an injured pelican," Tom said as he and Samuel grabbed two long poles and a piece of canvas and threw them into Old Blue. Tom and Samuel, with Rondolus flying above, raced down the back road headed for Everglades National Park.

Mariana telephoned Dr. Matthews while Sumer gathered clean blankets, a first-aid kit and several gallon jugs filled with freshwater. Sumer piled the supplies into the red convertible then climbed inside. Mariana slammed the car door, pushed the gear stick into drive and flattened the accelerator. Tires spit broken shells in all directions as the car spun from the crushed shell driveway onto the road.

Alligators

Alligator

Alligator

171

CHAPTER 20

Olli watched Rondolus fly toward open water. He worried he couldn't properly care for the sick panther by himself. He dozed with one eye open throughout the morning, but he became fully alert when Zhora stirred beneath him.

"I'm going to the water hole," she yowled as she eased herself into a standing position. After a few short steps she collapsed onto the ground again. "Guess not, hurts too much."

"I'll get the bucket and have some fresh water in a jiff," Olli whistled. He grasped the handle in his talons and flew to the pond with bucket dangling comically beneath him.

A large gator, resembling a long black log, lay half submerged under water. He watched Olli fill the bucket and fly back to the hammock. His instincts told him the panther was growing weaker. When that feather-covered fishing pole went to hunt for food, he'd go see just how weak.

"I'm such a burden, Olli. I'm sorry. One more will be plenty. My appetite's a bit off. I don't require anything else, really."

Olli flew back to the pond. After two more trips an exhausted Olli and a somewhat refreshed Zhora settled in for a talk. "How long do you think it will take Rondolus to reach Kingdom Cove?"

"He'll be back by nightfall, sure as I'm a fish hawk."

"The meeting's at noon. Do you think Rondolus'll make it in time? I wonder if Samuel and Sumer will even help. Rondolus said some pretty nasty things to the humans."

"I'm sure they will," Olli answered. "I hate leaving you alone, but I'm hungry. If I don't go hunt some fish, we may both starve."

"I'm better now and not really hungry," Zhora lied. "Take you're time. I'll be fine."

"I won't be long." Olli promised and flew toward the bay.

Zhora needed to stay alert, but she was tired beyond description. She fought it by looking around her. A crow cawed from a distant tree. Her eyes drooped and she drifted into fuzzy sleep.

A twig snapped. Her eyes flew open. A 12-foot greenish-black alligator slithered into the clearing. It skulked toward her on four thick legs with its massive tail trailing behind it. Zhora felt its yellow eyes size her up. The gator opened its mouth. Its oral cavity was long and pointed, with rows of jagged teeth. The massive jaw slammed shut then opened and slammed shut again. Each time the jaws came together, they made a loud crunching sound.

Zhora growled, a low warning growl. The alligator moved closer. The panther stared at the reptile as questions streaked through her mind. Why was he bothering her? Did he know how weak she was? Under normal circumstances even the largest of gators wouldn't come near a Florida panther. Had he watched Olli bring her water?

She needed to escape. In her condition, neither climbing, nor walking, much less running was an option. Her only chance was to outsmart the alligator, to convince it she was still dangerous.

The gator inched closer. Zhora gave an ear-splitting yowl that ended in a deep warning growl.

The alligator stopped its forward progress. Its snout and eyes took on a smirking look. It advanced. Zhora forced another high pitched yowled. The gator moved into striking position. Snarling and growling, Zhora, with pain punctuating every movement, backed into the brush.

The reptile's eyes said, "No need to back away, you're sick and you're dying. I'm here to speed things up." Its mouth opened to show treacherous teeth. Its jaw shot forward; the teeth snapped shut.

Zhora jumped back, but not quickly enough. The gator's teeth ripped a gash across her right front leg. Crimson blood gushed from the leg. The life-giving fluid flowed onto white sandy soil, staining it bright red.

The sight of blood and the burning pain shot adrenaline through Zhora's system. Raw anger emanated from her throat. She bared her teeth, extended razor sharp claws and lunged at the

173

reptile. The gator threw her aside with one mighty flip of its head. Panther and alligator knew she was on the losing end of the match.

Zhora sought a tree and found a low-hanging branch that dipped toward the ground. Teeth clenched against the throb in her side, she gathered her strength and lunged toward the branch. The panther fell short. She lunged again. This time Zhora came close enough to grab the branch. She clawed and fought to hold on, to get a life saving grip. Searing fire shot through her belly. The big cat let go and crumpled to the ground. Winded and racked with pain, she struggled to stand but couldn't. Zhora closed her eyes and lay down, defeated. She waited for the alligator's crushing jaws to close around her. To drag her under the swamp's water.

Seconds turned into minutes. No painful blow came from the deadly jaws. Zhora opened her eyes a slit and saw white. She shook her head, "Am I dead?" She tried to move. A blaze of pain shot through her side. "No, I'm not dead. Dead couldn't hurt this much."

Forcing her eyes open, the panther saw a magnificent white bird standing between her and the murderous alligator. The gator advanced on the bird. Its jaws opened, snapped shut, opened and slammed shut again. Its long, pointed tail flipped to the right, to the left and back right. It postured, weighed its odds. The beast practiced the art of intimidation and intensified its glare.

The bird stood its ground. Its eyes blazed back a warning. Not a muscle cringed, not a feather flinched. The great white bird met the reptile's most ferocious efforts with the courage of one who has nothing to fear.

Confused by the bird's boldness, the alligator's resolve melted. Bigger and weightier than this feathered enemy, it believed it could wipe up the swamp with the haughty bird. But the daggerlike bill was a danger. During a fight, the gator might lose an eye. It liked its eyes the way they were. Well, it wasn't that hungry, but to be bested by a bird? The gator gave his most vicious glare. He once again flip his weighty tail from side to side, but in the end the sinister reptile backed out of the hammock and slithered into the swamp, its tail beating an unmistakable threat: Another day, panther, another day.

Zhora sighed deeply and closed her eyes. "Thank you, I really don't..." But the bird already soared high above the trees. She licked oozing blood from her leg and watched the bird's mighty wings carry it deep into the Everglades. Was that the heron they called Yatzu? She wanted Olli and Rondolus to come back. They would know.

Old habits die, hard. Zhora once more began to worry and fret. Would the alligator come back once it realized the white bird was gone? What was taking Olli so long? Had something happened to him? Hunger and thirst plagued her. How long could she survive without food and water? Where was Rondolus? He said they were friends. Some friend he turned out to be. He shouldn't have left her alone.

"Get a grip." Zhora mentally shook herself. She looked at the bucket once full of water, but now lying on its side. A wet spot on the sand was what remained of its precious fluid. She searched for a shrimp tail, a fish fin, anything abandoned earlier as insignificant. Nothing. Her stomach rumbled; her throat ached with dryness.

Despair and fear threatened to engulf her, until a sudden thought emerged. Why did the white bird protect her from the jaws of the alligator? Was she important to someone, someone of power? Hope strengthened her resolve. If Olli or Rondolus didn't return by nightfall, she would do whatever it took to drag herself to the pond. If the alligator was there, so be it. Peace came, and Zhora fell into a deep sleep.

When she woke, the sun was setting. Her black-tipped ears picked up a distant noise. It sounded like footsteps and human voices. She cocked her ears; there it was again. This time she was certain she heard humans approaching.

Fear once more enslaved her. Could they see her? Was she hidden good enough? What were they doing out here this time of day? Didn't the park close at sundown?

The footsteps stopped, and Zhora heard a different sound, the cry of an osprey. She glanced around and spotted her feathered friend, descending from the sky. A large fish hung from his talons. "Olli, Olli! Oh, Olli! How I missed you this afternoon. What kept you so long? I was never more glad to see a bird as I am to see you now."

"What happened?" Olli asked as he placed the fish in front of her.

"Be a dear and get me some water. My throat is dry as a desert."

"I want to know what happened." But, seeing how bedraggled she looked, he did as Zhora asked. He picked up the bucket, flew to the water hole, filled it and flew back to the ailing panther.

Zhora drank greedily and ate the fish with relish. Once again, however, she heard footsteps, coming closer. "Olli, someone is coming! Please go see who it is."

Olli, hearing the noise, lifted off the ground and flew toward it. When he returned he was not alone.

"Zhora! Zhora! What has happened to you? You look awful!" Rondolus exclaimed as he glided into the clearing with Olli.

"It was that hateful alligator. He almost killed me. I couldn't escape; the pain in my side crippled me. Look at this!" She said, holding up her right front leg. "His teeth did this!"

Rondolus looked at her leg. With dismay stamped across his greenish-pink face he said, "I'm so sorry."

"I gave myself up for dead, but a great white bird saved me. It defended me with such courage that the gator backed off. "I'm so glad to see you both," she said.

"Yatzu? You saw him?" Rondolus asked in disbelief.

"Yes. He was fearless. He saved me from that beast."

Somewhere in the distance a twig snapped and low voices rumbled. "Someone is coming down the trail. Quick, hide me!"

"I brought that girl and her brother. They brought their vet friend. I didn't know how else to help you."

"Oh, Rondolus! You didn't? They'll put me in a zoo or take my cubs away and put them in a zoo."

"Zhora, you need a doctor. Who else could I turn to? You and your cubs will die out here without help. Olli and I can't give you the kind of help you need. Look at what happened today! That girl is the most annoying creature I ever met, but I doubt she or her brother will allow anyone to put you or your cubs in a zoo."

When Sumer and Samuel approached the clearing, they saw osprey and roseate spoonbill standing protectively in front of a panther that as Nigel'd say, "looked like she'd been dragged through a hedge backwards." The sheen of the cat's golden coat was gone, her eyes were dull and her tail, once animated, now drooped flat along the ground. Fear and pain were evident in her large gold eyes.

The spoonbill made low grunting croaks but the osprey, eyes piercing through the dusk, watched in silence. Sumer and Samuel approached the panther. Rondolus and Olli flew to a branch directly above the panther.

Talking in low-soothingly tones, the twins cautiously approached Zhora. They told her they were taking her to a hospital where she and her cubs could get the best care. Did she understand them? They speculated she somehow knew they were there to help, because the fear in her eyes lessened as they moved forward.

Sumer and Samuel were kneeling next to Zhora and washing her leg with water and a mountain of white clothes when the vet and the grandparents joined them. Tom, Mariana and Dr. Matthews stopped, amazed by the scene. Zhora, fully awake and alert, was allowing Sumer and Samuel to tend her leg.

"I don't pretend to understand any of this," Dr. Matthews said. "Someone want to explain it to me?" He looked around expectantly, but no one answered. "Guess it'll have to wait."

The vet sedated the big cat, cleaned and wrapped her wound and, after performing a preliminary examination, said, "She's pregnant. I think I hear three heartbeats. It's hard to tell. Bring the sling. Sooner we get her back to the hospital, the better."

Tom and Samuel made a sling of two poles and a piece of canvas stretched between them. Soft blankets covered the canvas, and Zhora was placed in the middle of the blankets. The three males, one on each corner, and Mariana and Sumer on the fourth corner carried the sleeping panther down the trail.

Florida Panther

Florida Panther

Florida Panther

CHAPTER 21

Sumer pelted the vet with questions the minute he walked out of the examination room. "Is she pregnant? Are the cubs still alive? How many are there?"

"The ultrasound shows the panther is pregnant. Three heartbeats. Three cubs. She had a large ovarian cyst that burst. The bruises on her right side lead me to believe she took a pretty hard fall. An alligator most likely caused the gash on her leg.

"From the evidence, I'm assuming the panther had an altercation with an alligator, tried to get away and somehow fell. The cyst broke, probably because of the fall. It's draining now. I'll keep her quiet for a couple of weeks. The two largest cubs should survive."

"I thought you said there were three cubs. What about the third one?"

"The third cub is small, has a weak heart beat. It could have suffered damage in the fall."

"You have to save it, save them all," Sumer pleaded.

"I'll do my best. Can't promise more than that."

"Where is she? Can Samuel and I see her?"

"I put her in a cage in the largest operating room. She's sleeping off the sedative."

"Can we help take care of her?"

"I'm glad you asked. I already cleared it with your grandfather. He said you have to take turns, because one of you needs to care for Nigel. Is that the pelican with the broken wing?"

"Right," said Samuel. "I'll take the first shift. Sumer, you can relieve me in the morning." Sumer didn't relish sleeping in an animal hospital on a dingy old cot, so she readily agreed to the arrangement.

Dr. Matthews and Samuel carried a cot into the room where Zhora's cage was located. Blankets on the cot, a pillow for his head and Samuel was set for the night.

"Zhora should sleep until I make my morning rounds. If you need me, I'll be at home. Just dial eight on the hospital phone. It rings at my house. I can be here in five minutes."

At first Samuel thought it was cool to sleep on an army cot, but after watching distorted shadows skulk across the walls and listening to a barrage of freaky noises, he decided a more accurate description was cold and uncomfortable. The day had been exhausting, and as shadows blurred together and noises became routine, he fell into a deep sleep.

At midnight a silvery moon rose to shine through the room's high windows. A loud wail cut thought the moonlit room. Samuel sat up in bed. Another wail split the night followed by the bang of metal against concrete.

Zhora was awake, slamming her body against the metal bars of the cage. Her howl was the wail of one betrayed and frightened. "Zhora, calm down, you'll hurt yourself and your cubs." In response to the familiar voice, Zhora stopped banging, but she continued to yowl. Her eyes peered from the cage to accuse Samuel.

"Sorry about the cage. It wasn't my idea. Dr. Matthews said it was for your own good."

The panther continued to pace nervously and dig at the locked cage door. Samuel talked soothingly to the distraught animal. This calmed Zhora for a time, but soon she was again pacing and digging.

Samuel cautiously reached his hand inside the cage to stroke her silky fur. His fingers made contact, the cat jumped. Samuel jumped and smacked his hand on a metal bar. He pulled out his appendage and rubbed the skin that was turning blue. "See what you did," he told Zhora. She stared; he pouted. Finally he tried again, and this time, she quieted under his gentle touch. But the minute he retracted his hand, the digging and howling began again.

"Zhora, I can't let you out of the cage. Dr. Matthews will be furious if I do!"

Zhora looked at Samuel, blinking her eyes. He scratched her between her ears. "Can you understand me?" he asked her. Silence hung heavy for a moment, then the big cat once again began to dig, pace and yowl.

"Zhora! Quiet! You'll wake the whole town. I can't let you out!"

The panther stopped and again watched Samuel with blinking eyes.

"Those eyes, just like Nigel when I talk to him, it's almost as if you guys understand what I'm saying. You're going to get me in big trouble you know, h-u-g-e trouble."

Sitting on her haunches, Zhora studied Samuel as if she were taking in every word. "What I'm about to do is stupid, you know. Totally moronic." Samuel said to the panther.

Samuel checked to see that the heavy mesh door to the room was securely closed but not locked and the windows were shut but not latched. "You're still a wild animal," he explained to the panther. With sweaty palms and chest thudding, Samuel unlocked the cage door, and ran to stand next to the mesh exit door.

The cage door squeaked open. Zhora hesitantly stepped out. She looked as if she expected the pain in her side to return. When it didn't, she jumped up on Samuel's cot, but lay down quickly, favoring her right side. Samuel laughed with relief.

"No, Zhora, you can't sleep on my bed." With that, Samuel took blankets from a large supply closet and laid them on the far side of the room from the cot. He even retrieved an extra pillow. "This is your bed, now get off mine." Zhora, not budging, stared at him.

Samuel hesitantly pushed on her rump and she gingerly climbed down to settle herself on the blankets and pillow Samuel provided. Samuel moved his cot next to the exit. He rested with one eye open. Sometime in the night both eyes closed. Boy and cat slept.

At 6 a.m., Dr. Matthews arrived for morning rounds and saw Zhora and Samuel sleeping. "Well, I'll be. I wish I understood even a little of this." Afraid to cause a sudden change to their environment, he didn't disturb them. Instead he quietly walked into his office and called Samuel on the intercom.

Dr. Jonathan Matthews turned on classical music and played it into the intercom. "Samuel, Samuel, Samuel," he called. "Come to the phone please." He kept his voice low and soothing so as not to unnerve his patient.

The music wove its way into Samuel's dream. When he finally realized it was a real voice, Samuel sat up in bed. He looked at the white walls and high windows; he couldn't remember where he was.

"Samuel, Samuel, Samuel, it's Dr. Matthews," the voice said again. Samuel picked up the phone and heard the voice change from soothing to demanding. "Why'd you let Zhora out of her cage? She could have attacked you!"

Samuel, still half asleep, looked at the panther that was starting to stir. "She woke up and was tearing herself apart trying to get out of the cage. She hated being locked up," Samuel said. "She blamed me. Maybe she's claustrophobic or something. Once I let her out of the cage, she settled down and went to sleep."

"See if you can leave the room without disturbing her and come to my office. We have to talk!"

"She's already awake. She'd probably like some water and food, actually, so would I. You got anything to eat around here?"

Dr. Matthews brought Zhora a slab of meat and a bucket of water. She grabbed the meat as soon as it hit the floor then, guarding it, lapped water from the bucket.

As they walked back to his office, Dr. Matthews confronted Samuel. "Now what? I need that room for more than just a panther house, and what if she decides she doesn't like being shut up in that room, either?"

"She doesn't seem to mind the room but she despised the cage. Really hated it. I had to do something. I let you lock her up. She thought I betrayed her."

"And just how do you know that?"

"By the look in her eyes."

"She's probably claustrophobic," Sumer said as she entered Dr. Matthews' office, still out of breath from the two-mile bike ride from home to the animal hospital.

"Good morning to you, too, and what's with the all the claustrophobia diagnoses?" the young vet asked.

"We learned about it in social studies class," Sumer answered.

"OK, you win; I can't fight all three of you. She can have the whole room. It will curtail my practice some, but we certainly don't want her to lose the cubs."

"How is Zhora feeling this morning?" Sumer asked Samuel.

"Come see her; I think she's feeling much better."

Sumer and Samuel took turns staying with Zhora the next couple of days. Samuel, concerned how the cat would react if neither twin could be at the hospital, decided to bring Nigel to visit. He hoped the pelican would keep Zhora from being scared and lonely in his and Sumer's absence.

After some initial sniffing and posturing, panther and pelican got on like old mates. When Nigel was around, Zhora didn't seem to miss the twins.

The next morning, Samuel and Sumer fed and watered the two animals then raced home on their bikes. They told Grandma Mariana they were headed for Kingdom Cove. After jumping into the canoe, they propelled it through silky bay waters toward the Ten Thousand Islands.

The sun was high in the sky when the canoe left the bug-infested, winding trail and entered the serenity of crystal blue water surrounded by a miraculous degree of the extraordinary. Mindy, Trina, Rondolus and Mother Manatee waited for them. The others seemed nervous and anxious to get started, so Sumer and Samuel took a dip, gave a report on Zhora and Nigel's condition and got down to the business at hand.

"I've been thinking." Trina lifted her head as high off the ground as she could lift it. "Our human allies are stalling for time

185

to raise money. They are hoping to delay construction long enough for the owner to become frustrated and sell out, right?"

"Right," Samuel said, looking curiously at Trina.

"Well I think we might be able to help." The 200-pound turtle stretched her neck and head even higher off the sand and looked Sumer and Samuel in the eye.

"What can we do?" asked Rondolus.

"Hundreds of turtles live in the Gulf waters, and thousands of birds live in and around the Ten Thousand Islands. I say we all occupy the construction site about noon on Sunday. It will be a way to get much-needed attention for us animals and our cause. Plus the construction workers can't start work until we're all safely out of the way. If they try to remove us, as one turtle or bird is made to leave, another will take its place. We can keep that up for quite a long time, I should think."

"What a great idea," Sumer said and laughed. "I can see it all now. Big turtles, little turtles, tall birds, short birds, thousands of them covering the land from sea to dunes. It's not just a great idea, it's a stupendous idea!"

"How long will it take to gather up a couple hundred turtles?" Samuel asked.

"I already told you! We'll be there Sunday at noon. Rondolus, you and Olli round up the birds. Shame them; threaten them; do whatever it takes, but get them there. The more the merrier you know."

"Can I see Zhora first? I sure do miss her," Rondolus croaked to Sumer and Samuel. His earlier animosity toward the twins was fading.

"Sure, tell her to relax," responded Sumer. "Dr. Matthews has no intention of keeping her locked up once the cubs are born and big enough to survive in the wild."

"Nigel has been a big help, but I think he is ready to get out and test the strength of his mended wing. He wanted to come today. He hates being out of the action," said Samuel.

"But he loves the free fish even more," Sumer added.

"See you all on the construction site Sunday at noon," Trina called over her shoulder as she headed for the water.

"Sumer and I will alert newspapers, radio and TV stations. Somehow, we'll convince them to send news teams and photographers; publicity is essential for the fund-raising efforts," Samuel said.

188

CHAPTER 22

"Who does that judge think he is? Build a fence to keep turtles off a construction site? I hope those tree huggers are satisfied. This little fiasco is costing me plenty!" spouted Joe.

"What about that Rattowsky fellow? He had some nerve asking you to sell your property to the very people who are making your life miserable," added Rusty, Joe's lawyer. "Build the hotel somewhere else so the setback laws can be observed? Do those idiots have any idea how much time it took me, or how much money it cost you, to come up with a piece of ground that because of railroad easements, deed restrictions and the archeological angle allows an environmental variance? This whole thing was orchestrated so we could move the hotel onto the beach."

"Right! They aren't that naive." Joe said. He turned to Duncan and Red. "How long do you guys think it'll take to build the fence?"

"Two weeks if the supplies arrive on time. We'll have to pour a footing of concrete. Poles will be here Monday but the meshing won't be here for at least a week," Duncan answered. "It needed to be made of extra-fine wire with no sharp edges."

"We'll start with the poles and concrete on Monday," Red added.

" We can place them while we wait for the meshing," Duncan said. "At the end of the two-week period, it should all be in place."

"I know ESF is planning to take the full two weeks to dawdle around looking for turtle eggs," Rusty said. "I overheard that lawyer of theirs tell them to stall. They'll be turning over every piece of sand on the lot just to prove a point. And they're hoping to collect enough donations in the next two weeks to buy you out."

"Maybe you should consider what the Foundation comes up with for alternate property. If they're motivated enough, they might come up with a good deal," Duncan said.

"You going soft?" Joe asked.

"No, just thinking. A hotel this close to the water is not only a detriment to the turtles and birds, but it's also risky for the structure, and my reputation as a contractor. Anything built on the beach will be more vulnerable to storms than those behind the dunes. This is not a cheap fence they're requiring, either. It's going to cause cost overruns. And this won't be the end of it. Mark my words. There'll be more time delays, more trouble. The environmentalists won't give up this easy."

"Ghost Orchid Hotel stays where it is. Think about all them tourists. They'll love it, eating and sleeping next to the breaking surf. I can hear the dollars falling into the till now. Kaaching! Kaaching! Kaaching!"

"Well, I think it's a mistake," Duncan said. "Not much can be done until Monday. I'll make a few calls from my cell phone, arrange for concrete and poles. See you Monday," Duncan said and turned toward his truck. "I figure this is the last weekend I'll have, for awhile, to take my kids fishing."

"You're not going fishing tomorrow. It's only Thursday. I need you here tomorrow."

"What for Joe? Concrete and poles won't be here until Monday."

"You can measure, dig post holes, build the frame and get ready for the concrete."

"Thanks for reminding me. I better order lumber. I'll do the planning and order the materials from home."

"I pay you plenty. You're not taking off for three days. You made me agree to Sunday. Now you want Friday and Saturday? What you think I pay you all that dough for? So you can take those kids of yours fishing? No, no, no! Sunday, that's the agreement. Sunday is the only day of the week you're getting off until this project is done."

"Joe, I'm going home. I'll see you Monday." Duncan became stubborn.

"If you don't show up tomorrow you're fired."

"Right, Joe, and who will you hire to replace me? After that hearing last Friday, this project is hot. Nobody's going to want to touch it. You've got the whole island in an uproar.

"Red, you want my job? Rusty, maybe you want it?" He called over his shoulder.

Joe looked from Red to Rusty then back to Duncan. "Hey, lighten up. Can't you take a joke?" He said and forced a grin.

"Yeah, right, see you Monday." Duncan drove away, not knowing that Sunday would be anything but a day of rest.

Egrets

Osprey

Ibis

CHAPTER 23

Sunday morning the sun cut through a crack in the drapes and landed in Joe's face. Squirming to avoid the light, he threw a pillow over his head. The sun continued to heat his neck and ears until he found it hard to breathe. After hurling his pillow, sheets and comforter to the floor, he looked at his watch. It was still early, not even 10 a.m.

The bed bounced as he flopped back down. Rubbing his eyes, his mind clicked into gear. How was he ever going to make up for the two weeks of lost construction time?

There it was again, the dull ache in his stomach, a reminder of his doctor's recent warning: "Your blood pressure is too high, and you're probably getting an ulcer. Learn to handle stress better, and get some exercise."

"OK, Doc," he said, pulling on jogging shorts and shoes. "I'm going to the construction site, cut through to the beach and go for a nice long run."

A block from the property, his resolve to stay cool and not let things bother him ended. Angry red stripes crept up the sides of his face; blood vessels stood out in his neck. "You idiot! What're you doing on my property?" He yelled at a tall white bird that stood in front of the sign that read "Future Home of Ghost Orchid Hotel."

Bringing the pickup to an abrupt halt, Joe jumped out and slammed the door. He marched with determination toward the snow-white bird. Painful memories from an unhappy childhood flooded his brain and made him crazy with rage.

In front of him stood the great white bird, but into his mind flashed the grade-school image of Larry Cats saying, "Joey is a loser. Joey is a loser.

"Loser Joey," Larry's pudgy face mouthed. "He never wins nothing. He's such a loser, he don't even have bad luck. He's got no luck, no luck at all. No luck. No luck. Loser Joey! Loser Joey! Ha, ha, ha, ha..."

Joe lunged for the bird, seething with all the anger that had been bottled up inside him since childhood. "I'll show you who's a loser. You! I'm the one with the luck now. I've won, and there's nothing you can do about it. Now get off my land and don't come back." He raged at the bird.

"Is something wrong, young man?" an elderly man called from across the street.

Joe spun around, embarrassment flooding through him. "No, nothing. Can't stand big white birds, that's all. One bullied me when I was a kid. Hated them ever since," he said, trying to cover up his overreaction to the bird's presence.

What's wrong with you, man? He chastised himself. You're acting as if a scrawny old bird can somehow stop construction on Ghost Orchid Hotel. Man, you're losing it. Get yourself onto that beach and start running."

Joe started toward the beach. The great white bird stood in the middle of the lot. "You, featherbrain, are just a bird. You're not a threat to me," he said to the bird. "The doc is right. I'm not dealing well with stress these days. Exercise relieves stress," he reminded himself as he jogged toward the beach.

■ ■ ■

At 9:30 a.m., the early service ended. Sumer bounded out of the small white church, her stomach gurgling with hunger. "Come on, let's go."

"Are you sure you want to go all the way to Grand Island for breakfast? Your grandmother makes a mean pile of pancakes."

"You promised we could go to La Café De Paris for Sunday brunch," Samuel said.

"We haven't been on a family outing in much too long. Soon Sumer and Samuel will be off to college and you'll wish you had spent more time with them," Mariana agreed, walking toward the car.

"I thought you liked La Café's Sunday brunch. The piles of fruit, made-to-order omelets, waffles, pancakes...yum." Sumer rubbed her stomach.

"OK," Tom said and laughed. "You win. Last one to the car is, a ... a ... a, the last one to the car."

"Good one, Gramps," Sumer said and giggled.

"Well, when I got right down to it I couldn't think of anything," Tom said with embarrassment. "Senior moment, I guess."

The twins didn't say anything to their grandparents about the invasion planned by Trina, the loggerhead turtle. The scheme was too farfetched. They did, however, plan to request an outside table and keep one eye on the beach and the other one on Joe Sorrow's construction site. Even if nothing materialized, they could still enjoy all of their favorite foods under a canopy of palm and banana trees.

"It'll be a half-hour until we can have a table outside," Mariana announced after talking to the hostess. "I know how hungry you kids are. Would you like to sit inside?"

"OK, by me," Tom said.

"No, we can't sit inside!" Sumer blurted.

"It's just that we came here so we could see," Samuel added, scowling at Sumer.

"We'll sit by a window. You can see out of a window can't you?"

Sumer moved close to Samuel and whispered, "It's getting late; we can't wait a half-hour, and we can't eat inside. What're we going to do?"

"What's the problem? Did we come here to eat or talk?" Tom asked.

"P-l-e-a-s-e ask them one more time," Sumer begged. "Maybe there's a small table somewhere outside that they've overlooked."

Tom walked to the hostess station, then back. "There's one table, but it's in the smoking section and I ... "

"We'll take it," Samuel blurted then added, "If it's outside how much smoke can we inhale outside?"

197

"I guess we'll take the one outside in the smoking section," Tom told the maitre d', as he eyed the twins suspiciously.

The sun continued its climb to a straight-up position. Samuel filled and emptied his plate twice, but he kept a watchful eye on the surf and construction site the entire time. Sumer did little more than pick at her food; she was just too nervous. "It won't happen. It's too ridiculous to even think about," she chastised herself, yet she watched the beach anxiously.

Mariana and Tom, seemingly oblivious to the twins' vigilance, talked about the pastor's sermon, about Mariana's latest painting and about her upcoming art show. They discussed how disappointed they were with the judge's decision to allow Joe to continue building on the beach, about the neighbor who wanted Tom to build his wife a rocking chair, about Max having the flu and Tom's need to call and see how he was doing...

At the stroke of noon the serenity of Sunday afternoon was shattered. Sunbathers jumped up in astonishment. Shell gatherers stopped their frenzied hunt for the perfect shell. Young children shrieked with fear as older ones screamed in delight.

Everyone, young and old, stopped what he or she was doing and watched as a loggerhead dragged its large shell out of the gulf and onto the dry sand. Following close behind it was a green sea turtle, then another loggerhead and still another green sea turtle. Soon, another turtle appeared, then another and another came out of the water, all laboring toward Joe Sorrow's property.

"Hey! Look! Turtles, dozens of them, are coming ashore on the beach in front of the building project," Samuel said. "And the birds! Look at the BIRDS."

All at once the horizon began to shift as waves of white, brown, pink and tri-colored birds bore down on the island. Setting their wings, they prepared to land. Every protuberance of the partially constructed hotel held a pelican, an osprey or an anhinga. In, around and even on top of the turtles were sandpipers, herons, egrets, ibis and roseate spoonbills. Members of the endangered wood stork family, snail kites and frigate birds sailed overhead participating as airborne support.

"WA-HOO!" Sumer shouted. She jumped from her chair and stopped only long enough to make sure Samuel was coming. The twins raced toward the beach and, as they ran, they exhibited their delight as only almost 13-year-old can. They wrestled and laughed the whole way down to the water. After looking things over, they quickly headed back to get Tom and Mariana.

"What the?"

"I see it, but I don't believe it," Mariana said, standing with a spilled teacup dangling from her hand.

"Pay the bill. Let's go," Sumer wheezed as she sprinted off the boardwalk. She grabbed her side and came to a halt in front of their table.

"Quick! Call the newspapers and radio stations," Samuel said, coming up behind. "We need lots of publicity, remember?"

"Remember what?" Mariana asked setting her teacup on the table.

"Trina, you know, the loggerhead." Sumer panted as she bent over attempting to catch her breath. "She told us she could pull this off — puff, pant, puff — but we didn't believe her. If we didn't believe her — puff, pant — how could we expect to convince you? You — pant — already thought we were losing our marbles."

"Publicity is the most important thing. We want people to donate money so ESF can buy Joe's lot. I gotta go call the radio and TV stations."

"Don't forget the newspapers," Sumer added.

"I'll call the news media." Mariana said. "You two sit down and finish your orange juice. I don't want either of you saying things that will make them believe we've taken leave of all our senses."

Within minutes Tom, Mariana, Samuel and Sumer were headed toward the large crowd gathered around the turtles and birds. Mariana had to admit it was an awe-inspiring sight. Standing in and around the framework of Ghost Orchid Hotel, hundreds of turtles and thousands of birds covered the area between Gulf and grassy dunes.

"It's like an animal sit-in," said a middle-aged woman with golden-red hair curled loosely around her face. Long red nails and a ring on every finger adorned both hands. She wore a full-length red cover-up that floated as she walked.

"They're rebelling against that horrible little man with cold blue eyes and his monstrous building project," said her companion. In contrast this woman sported straight gray hair and a short blue-and-purple cover-up worn over a modest blue swimsuit.

"Let's join them. This could be fun, but watch where you sit!" Another woman said and giggled self-consciously as she followed the first two. Her small size, quick movements and vivid caftan brought to mind a bright, yellow canary.

Mariana watched the three women and wondered why she thought she knew them. Moving side by side, the red cover-up blended into the yellow caftan and the yellow caftan into the blue-and-purple sundress. They looked like a rainbow, floating down the beach.

The twins, laughing and punching each other, darted in and out of people, trying to get a better look. Tom stood off to the side; his smoky gray eyes glassy with tears.

He watched a great white bird slosh through the surf with water swirling between and around its yellow legs. The majestic bird made no attempt to join the animal sit-in.

Tom studied the bird then looked up into a clear blue sky. "Oh Lord! Why, when I see your miracles do I insist on calling them coincidences? What is wrong with me? Intellectually I know the drill, but my heart can't get hold of it. Your truth is so simple, yet I make it complex. Help me. Please!" Tom prayed.

Down the beach, Tom saw a thin man jogging from the south end of the island. The man's blond hair blew back from his forehead in sweaty clumps. His breath came out in heavy spurts from a scowling mouth topped by an unruly mustache. His rotating legs brought him closer and closer.

Tom, finally close enough to recognize the runner, saw the man's expression change from a concentrated frown to fury. It was too late for Tom to melt into the crowd. He had been standing apart from the others and his 6-foot-plus frame towered above most anyway. To make matters worse, the hat he wore made him quickly recognizable to all who knew him.

Joe, teeth clenched, eyes glaring, panted directly up to Tom. "You did this! You can't leave me alone, can you?"

"Joe, my family believes in proper management of wildlife and wildlife habitat, but I certainly can't take credit for this," Tom said flinging his arms wide to encompass the miracle of craziness around them. "I can't help but believe this time you're fighting against God himself."

"Somehow you did this, you and that stupid bird. You're both out to ruin me. You think you can play coy with me, but I saw him this morning. He stared at me with those eyes, just stared, always the stare of those eyes. I should have shot him, when I had the chance. I won't lose this time. You won't beat me — not this time!"

Joe clenched and unclenched his fists as he shook with rage. He took out his cell phone, paged Duncan, then called Rusty and Red. "Get down to the site NOW! We have a crisis on our hands."

Crews from three local television and radio stations already were setting up cameras and other equipment. One reporter, recognizing Joe from the environmental hearings, stuck a microphone in the future hotel owner's face. "Mr. Sorrow, do you think this is an omen that you should give up and move to another building location?"

"No! I do not!" snarled Joe. He shoved past the reporter and stomped back to his truck.

There was a flurry of activity as the reporters went from one group of people to another asking questions and taking pictures. Each group tried to make its answers more outrageous than the last to assure they appeared in newspaper stories and on television footage.

Radio and television crews covered every aspect of the wildlife demonstration. Pictures of sea turtles were taken from every angle. Pictures of the birds, close-ups and faraway shots were snapped in excess. The news crews interviewed anyone with an opinion about the feud between Joe Sorrow and the Endangered

Species Foundation. Mariana's "Rainbow Girls" turned out to be representatives from ESF. They were interviewed and allowed to request donations for ESF's land replacement plan.

When the sun positioned itself within inches of the Gulf's blue-green water, the demonstration ended as suddenly as it began. Birds returned to their rookeries. Turtles returned to the sea.

The media, photographers and bystanders watched the retreat then stayed long enough to observe the sun, now a brilliant orange ball, as it melted into the ocean. Sunbeams, bent at precise angles, turned cloud formations into a kaleidoscope of pink, purple and golden apricot.

Onlookers were awed by the blazing array of colors yet they lingered, hoping for more. They waited. They watched. Would they see the much talked about, though rarely seen, "green flash"?

The sun abandoned the sky, continuing its retreat into the ocean. Then, as the last point of light disappeared, a blaze of iridescent green light shot up from the blue water. The crowds stood mesmerized. It was real. They'd actually seen it.

The sun was down, and twilight settled in for a short time before darkness fell. Most turned to gather their belongings and start for home. Tom, however, watched the sky, and he alone saw the great white bird, with iridescent feathers and blazing eyes, rise and soar south across the horizon toward the Everglades.

203

Fresh Water Turtle

Fresh Water Turtle

CHAPTER 24

Monday morning, the concrete truck and the fence poles arrived on schedule. The construction crew started precisely at 8 a.m.

At 9, ESF volunteers arrived on site, joking and jostling one another. When they saw fence poles standing upright from the ground and heard the pound of heavy hammers against steel, the laughter caught in their throats. How could this happen after yesterday's apparent victory?

The volunteers began to work. Discouraged, they trudged over uneven ground to search for turtle and bird nests. The sun rose higher in the sky and beat down on all without mercy. The volunteers' frustration turned to anger then to despair as faces, arms and bodies dripped from the heat and humidity.

One man topped a slight incline in hopes of finding an ocean breeze and stood to look across still water. Soon he turned, running, shouting and waving, toward his fellow searchers. Despair turned to hope and hope to laughter as he talked and gestured excitedly.

The sun once again struck its noontime pose in the center of the sky, and once again hundreds of turtles and thousands of birds made their way to the building site. Construction and nest-removing efforts were abandoned as the animal sit-in launched into its second day.

Joe, determined, hired extra workers. The workers arrived at dawn and went home when the turtles and birds arrived each day at noon. This went on for five consecutive days. Pounding the fence poles was slow and tedious, but the workers made progress. Instead of two weeks it would probably take three, maybe four, but Joe was determined to complete the project.

Convinced that the great white bird and Tom were somehow behind all of his problems, he was doubly determined not to be beaten by a "bag of feathers" and "a has-been sheriff."

"I will win this time. I'll fight to finish this project as long as there's fight left in me," Joe said.

In the meantime, donations of $10, $20, even hundreds and thousands of dollars poured into ESF's headquarters from all over the world. The foundation hoped that before the fence was complete, enough money could be raised to make a deal with Joe Sorrow.

CHAPTER 25

A red sunrise announced the dawn of the sixth day. Strong winds blew from the southwest. An unusually high tide brought waves splashing within feet of the fence poles and concrete. Ominous black clouds scuttled eastward toward land. At noon, no sea turtles poked their leathery heads out of the water, and their feathered allies were noticeably absent.

The construction crews watched uneasily as waves broke closer and closer to their work areas. Mounds of brown-gray clouds bore down on the island. Duncan called the local storm center and was told a strong thunderstorm with damaging winds, heavy rain and dangerous lightning was headed toward Grand Island. "Thunderstorms such as this are not unusual during the rainy season," he told his crews. "Get lunch. Find shelter for an hour or two. We'll start again soon as the storm passes."

He and Red headed for Joe's condo to give him an update and wait out the storm. By the time they reached Joe's parking lot, the wind was rolling garbage cans across the road and unattended lawn furniture and toys were tumbling across yards. Fronds, atop tall palm trees, were facing eastward at a 90-degree angle. Lightning and ear-splitting thunder let go with a fury. Rain, driven by the wind, pelted the two men as they ran from Duncan's SUV and up two flights of stairs to the condo. Joe opened the entry door. It banged hard against the wall and closing it took all the strength he could muster.

In contrast to Joe's humble upbringing, this condominium was luxurious. The unit consisted of a spacious great-room, two bedrooms, two baths and a den. Duncan looked around the great-room at the stone tile leading onto thick, beige carpet. Queen Anne chairs stood across the room from a white-beige couch. A glass table with bronze base and four matching chairs dominated the dining area. Beyond were French doors that led to a lanai furnished in natural wicker with deep-green cushions. The lanai faced east and looked out over a large bay.

Joe walked down the hall and entered the den. He sat on a chocolate-brown leather couch with TV remote in hand. He switched from one channel to another and stared at the real-time portrait of storm damage that was changing an ordinary day into a day few would forget.

"I'm going to make a phone call. Tell Joe I'll be right back," Duncan told Red. He then called his wife to make sure she and the kids were safely at home. He told her about the storm and that he would be at Joe's condo.

Duncan joined the other two men and watched as local news channels displayed a waterspout that reached top to bottom on Joe's big-screened TV. The whirling funnel of gray-brown water swirled and sucked up helpless fish, sand and seaweed, clutching them all within its cylindrical grasp.

"This immense waterspout is five miles southwest of Grand Island. It's only one of many spawned by this tremendous storm," one weatherman reported, "and as you can see by the yellow and red dots on this weather map, lightning is a major player in this unexpectedly dangerous storm."

The words no sooner came from the weatherman's mouth than a bolt of lightning lit up the room, and on its heals, thunder shook the condo. Another strike cut through the dark then another.

As if they needed evidence the storm was moving toward them, each thunder boom came closer on the tail of the strikes. Suddenly everything went dark. The TV screen went blank; the lights went out. The ceiling fan slowed to a stop. Without the air conditioner's constant hum, silence settled down over the room. Lightning and its thunderous partner continued to rage outside; rain plunged past the windows in steady sheets of water.

"Electricity's out," Red said into the silent grayness.

Where'd I get such a brilliant foreman? Joe thought sarcastically as Red's words echoed in the stillness. "Everyone stay put. I got candles here someplace," he said aloud. Joe came back with a handful of waxy spires and a box of matches. The men lit the candles and turned on a battery-operated radio. Joe paced, Red stared into the candlelight and Doug, seeing a pack of playing cards on the coffee table said, "Cards anyone?"

The three men settled around the dining room table; Duncan shuffler and dealt the cards. The radio blared weather updates the men bet and passed cards.

"A full house, I beat you sorry losers!" Joe said.

"I see a checker set on the shelf. Anyone want to play checkers?" Red asked.

"That's a kids game. I'm on a roll. Deal them cards."

Duncan motioned for silence when the radio announcer's voice rose in decibels and became excited. "I'm standing just outside the radio station on the beach here on Grand Island and there are two kids in the water on surfboards. The sheriff's deputies are yelling at them to get out of the water, but they're not listening. One boy is riding the crest of the biggest wave I've seen since moving to southwest Florida. Those kids shouldn't be out there. They should be at home.

"Man, those waves are huge.

"Behind them, moving fast, are some ugly looking clouds; they're more brown than black. I'm headed inside to take cover." A door slammed and the roar in the background grew loud, so loud it hurt the ears.

"A giant water spout is headed for Grand Island's beach. Everyone on the beach take cover immediately! This is no game! Get out of the water," the announcer shouted.

"I can't see the kids anymore; they have been swallowed by the clouds. Oh, God help us, here it comes!"

Joe, Duncan, and Red jumped back from the radio as it spewed forth the reverberation of a tremendous crash, followed by sounds of plasterboard and cinder block collapsing, wood splintering and glass bursting into fragments. Eerie quiet followed the earsplitting wind, a silence complete except for air whistling past the microphone.

Joe stood up, lit a few more candles and paced nervously back and forth in front of the rain-drenched window. "That announcer was broadcasting from a resort next to my hotel site. I can't stand around any more, I'm going down and take a look around."

"I'll drive," Duncan offered. Boredom and cabin fever were getting the best of him. "The QuadTrax is our best bet for getting through to that area. You coming Red?"

Not many things unnerved Red, but storms had spooked him since he was a kid. "No, someone should stay here and keep an eye on things," he answered.

Duncan and Joe left the condo and made a dash for Duncan's SUV. Rain, driven by wind, pelted the two men and soaked through their clothes before they were halfway to the vehicle. Water dripped down Duncan's face and ran down his back. He jumped into the QuadTrax and slammed the door.

Moving onto the street, the truck drove through water that splashed window high. The wipers had trouble keeping the front window clear and every now and then a wind gust rocked them with such force Duncan fought to stay on the road.

The QuadTrax made it two blocks before a county deputy stopped them. "Road closed ahead. Trees down all over the place. Roadbed's under three feet of water. Power pole snapped in two. It's lying across the road just ahead. You'll have to turn around," the deputy told the two men.

Duncan, thinking he could skirt the problem area, turned the SUV east. Water on the roads continued to rise until the roadbed was totally flooded.

As Duncan and Joe entered one intersection, a wave-runner skimmed through in front of them. Duncan hit the breaks; the SUV started to fishtail. Turning the wheel into the skid, left then right, he gained enough control to head for a vacant lot. The wet, heavy sand stopped them, but it also trapped them. The QuadTrax sank deep into the wet ground.

Stunned, Duncan sat looking out the rain-drenched window. He had heard stories of wave-runners on the streets of Grand Island during bad storms, but this was the first time he had actually seen one.

"Are we stuck? Get us out of here; I want to see my hotel!" Joe's voice had the sharp edge of fear.

Duncan shoved the QuadTrax into reverse, hit the four-wheel-drive lever and slowly coaxed the vehicle back onto the rain-covered pavement. An emergency vehicle, parked in front of a large tree that stretched across the road, stopped all forward progress. Duncan backed up and headed down another street, only to find more emergency vehicles and more fallen trees. Finally, he stopped and asked one deputy if Naples, the mainland town where he lived, had been hit as hard as Grand Island.

"No, the worst of the storm veered straight east. Pretty much missed Naples," the Deputy reported.

Grateful that his family was safe, Duncan gave up and drove back to the condo. When he and Joe pushed through the door, letting in the wind and rain, Red was aimlessly moving checkers around on a black and red game board. "What'd you find out?"

"Not much. We couldn't get more than four or five blocks in any direction. I'm starved, haven't eaten since breakfast. OK if I make a sandwich or something?" Duncan asked Joe.

"I'm not stopping you. Fix me whatever you're having. Red, give me that flashlight. I need something outta the bedroom."

When Joe was out of earshot, Red asked, "How does it look for the hotel?"

"Not good, that's where the waterspout landed. I told him he was building too close to the beach. Maybe now he'll listen."

"I suppose the roads to Naples are all closed," Red said, wondering if he should start for home.

"Yep. Phone lines are down too. My cell phone keeps reading for emergency use only. Can't even call my wife," Duncan added.

"Stay here tonight, if you want," Joe grudgingly offered as he sat down to eat. "You'll have to flip a coin, see who gets the other bedroom. One can take the couch in the den. It folds out." Lapsing into silence, he ate his sandwich, then pushed back from the table and stood up. He opened his mouth to speak but turned instead and walked into the master bedroom, closing the door behind him.

Duncan lost the coin toss. He walked into the den and looked out the window. Total darkness. Electricity was off all over the island. Lightning, fingering its way across the sky, would occasionally light up the back yard enough for Duncan to see outside. Puddles were now small lakes, and the rain showed no sign of letting up. Wind gusts whipped palm fronds against the window and wailed through Australian pines farther back on the grounds. Duncan didn't pull out the couch; he let his feet dangle over the end. He listened to the rain, rolling thunder and moaning wind until he fell asleep.

Shell Wall

CHAPTER 26

Duncan felt cool air drift across his face and heard the air conditioner whir to life. It was dawn. They once again had electricity.

Duncan unwound his crinkled body from the couch and stretched his way into the bathroom. Later, making his way to the lanai, he watched the bright-yellow sun rise into a sapphire-blue sky. Palm trees and green plum bushes shimmered with diamond-shaped raindrops. Red cardinals and long-tailed gray and white mockingbirds trilled their songs into the cool humid air. Duncan took a deep breath. "Morning after a storm, there's nothing like it."

Wandering into the kitchen, he dumped heaping teaspoons of brown coffee into a stiff, white filter. Today could be stressful, Duncan thought. It's best if the coffee isn't so strong that it strips the enamel off our teeth. Joe doesn't need any extra reason to jump out of his skin.

A pungent aroma filled the kitchen as the coffee maker dripped its ebony liquid into a glass pot. Duncan breathed deeply; the smell reminded him of home. He picked up the phone and got a dial tone. He dialed his home number and told his wife he was safe and would try to get home early.

After scrambling eggs in a skillet, Duncan turned the burner to low and placed cinnamon rolls in the oven to warm. To his surprise, he heard the thud of a newspaper hitting the front steps. How had the delivery service gotten through the flooded streets? Opening the front door, he saw the *Island Press* neatly wrapped in plastic. He picked it up and walked to the lanai.

As Duncan settled into a soft-cushioned chair, Red came stumbling out of the bedroom. His eyes were half-closed and his red hair stuck straight up like a thistle.

"Out here!" Duncan called from the lanai. "Hot coffee's in the pot, and there's a cool breeze blowing in from the bay."

"Is Joe up yet?" Red asked.

"No, and don't wake him. Breakfast won't be ready for a few minutes," Duncan said, returning to his paper. "Listen to this! Can you believe it? The paper says those two kids, who were surfing during the storm, drowned. The police found their bodies late last night. What makes teenagers act so stupid? Thrills and fun, is that all boys think about these days?"

"That and girls and booze," Red said. "I did some pretty stupid things when I was a kid. I shudder to think about some of them."

"Yeah, I guess we all did," Duncan admitted. "But think of the pain their recklessness has caused family and friends."

"It's terrible. I'm glad I'm not in their folk's shoes right now."

"Yeah."

"Can I wake Sorrow now? I'm hungry."

"Sure, I'll set the grub on the table."

After eggs, fruit, rolls and coffee, the trio started toward Ghost Orchid Hotel. Because of downed trees, they were forced to walk the last four blocks to the building site. What the three men saw when they arrived made them wish they'd stayed at the condo.

Fence poles were ripped from the ground and strewn every which way across the sandy soil. The building's metal framework was twisted into corkscrews and the pilings had jagged holes where rebar had been ripped from the concrete. One or two concrete pilings leaned dangerously at an angle. Joe walked across the site kicking at fallen debris.

Duncan and Red decided it was best to leave him alone and set off to check on the construction machinery. Miraculously, it the equipment appeared to be in working order though fresh dents and scrapes covered its yellow paint.

"We start cleaning up as soon as the road is clear. Put the fence back up first then start on the pilings. This should only set us back a few months," Joe said after making a complete tour of the site. "Ghost Orchid Hotel will be ready by season after next."

"We're building behind the dunes this time, right?" said Duncan.

"Same as before. Nothing's changed. Storms come. Storms go. Only change we're going to make is to strengthen the framework this time. There'll be a run on building supplies; better phone in my order." With that, Joe turned and headed toward the QuadTrax.

Duncan shook his head and kicked the ground hard. "He's as big a fool as those two youngsters out surfing in the storm," he remarked. "What's it going to take to make him see the light?"

CHAPTER 27

The storm did not hit Banyan City as hard as it hit Grand Island, but fearing the thunder and lightning would unnerve Zhora, Sumer spent the night with her. The panther had regained most of her strength, and her right front leg was mostly healed. A large, three-sided wooden box now sat in the big cat's room with a yellow blanket covering its floor in readiness.

Every morning after examining Zhora, Dr. Matthews announced, "The cubs could be born any day now." He also warned Sumer and Samuel that when the cubs were born, the twins were not to touch them. "Zhora will not want the smell of humans on her cubs, and I don't want the cubs lulled into believing all humans are kind. They are better off completely wild."

■ ■ ■

It was 9 a.m. Tom sat at the kitchen table and listened to the news on the radio. The phone rang.

"Tom, this is Ted Rattowsky. Thought I'd call and give you an update about happenings here on Grand Island."

"I heard you guys got hit hard by the storm yesterday. Any real damage?" Tom asked as he walked to the stove to pour a cup of coffee.

"Yeah, a real mess. Two kids ignored barriers and the sheriff's deputies and went surfing in the Gulf. Guess the waves were just too much to ignore — they were the biggest this island's ever seen. Anyway the kids drowned. Their bodies were found late last night."

"Oh, no! Were they local kids?"

"I recognized the names, but didn't know either family personally."

"How awful," Tom said. "I can feel for their families."

Both ends of the phone line were silent.

"How about Ghost Orchid Hotel?" Tom finally asked.

220

"Hundreds of turtles and birds came to roost on the construction site everyday at noon for five days, but not one of them showed the day of the storm. It's almost as if they knew something was amiss."

"Yeah?" Tom turned down the radio so he could hear Ted better.

"The turtles and birds slowed down construction, but the storm brought it to a complete halt. A large waterspout turned tornado and came ashore. The funnel made a direct hit on Joe's construction site. The hotel was destroyed." Ted continued. "The fence —you should see the fence. It was ripped out and scattered all over the place."

Tom thought he heard a smile in Ted's voice and worried in a mind-dump of moral platitudes about counting your chickens before they hatch and shouting victory before the trumpet sounds. "Did he lose everything?" He finally asked.

"Actually no, by some miracle his machinery was spared. It was parked in the middle of some big trees. A few dents, less paint in a few areas, but nothing big."

"Have you talked to Joe?" Tom shifted the phone to his left ear and took a sip of coffee. "Blah!" It was cold.

"Sorry. What did you say?"

"Nothing, go on."

"What was the question?"

"Joe? Have you talked to him?" Tom repeated, pouring a fresh cup of coffee.

"No, no, I haven't. But I'm, that is ESF, is preparing a buy out offer as we speak. You wouldn't believe the mail and money we've received this past week. Actually that's one of the reasons I called. The committee would like you to attend the meeting between ESF and Joe. It'll be next Friday morning."

Tom sipped his coffee and thought it over. "I would like to, but Joe and I don't have good chemistry. He might see the offer as a victory for me and refuse it so, in his mind's eye, I don't win."

"I wish you would reconsider. You know Joe better than the rest of us."

221

"All I know about Joe is how to make him angry. You don't need that. Duncan, his foreman, seems to have a good head on his shoulders. Ask him to attend the meeting."

"OK, I'll keep in touch," Ted promised.

"Thanks," Tom said and hung up the phone. Staring at a fly as it buzzed around on the outside of the porch screen, Tom wondered if Joe would sell his property and move to another lot. Knowing Joe, he'll say no just to be ornery, Tom thought. Somewhere along the way, that guy decided the world is against him and that it is kosher to use any and all underhanded means to get even.

Tom continued to watch the fly buzz into the screen, fall dazed onto the step, get up and hit the screen twice more before taking off across the lawn. Ha! That fly has more sense than Joe. It wised up after only three hits on the head.

Samuel trudged up the steps and onto the porch. He let the screen door bang behind him. His casting net, fishing pole and metal bucket clattered to the porch floor. Samuel walked into the kitchen.

"I'm going down to the beach to net Nigel some fish. Want to come?" Samuel asked Tom.

"What? O-h, oh, yeah, sure. Be right with you," Tom answered.

Traveling side by side, grandfather and grandson were silent. Each wrapped in his own personal thoughts.

As they ambled toward the bay, neither took notice of the star-shaped, white jasmine flowers, sprinkled with diamond like raindrops or the large-veined leaves of the Zanadu, scrubbed clean by last night's storm. Pink and green bougainvillea vines that cascaded down one side of the garage were ignored, along with large sunflowers that raised their yellow and brown faces to the sun.

The damp grass under Samuel's naked feet made him shiver a bit. A brisk breeze, blowing in from the bay, caused them both to wrap their jackets tighter around their bodies, but neither said a word until they reached the water's edge.

"Grandpa, does it ever seem that life's like a bad roller-coaster ride, and you want to get off, but can't?"

"Life is painful, sometimes. What's bothering you, son?"

"Two boys drowned during the storm yesterday." Samuel, fighting back tears, looked at his grandfather.

"Yeah, I heard about that. Did you know them?"

"I knew one of them. His name was Cory Richter. He's a couple years older than me, but we hung out at the beach and messed around some. He was an amazing surfer. Wanted to go to Hawaii and take on the 'big ones'. Talked about how he was going to be famous someday. I know he shouldn't have been out in the Gulf during that storm, but I hear the waves were awesome. It's not fair. One mistake, one lousy, stinking mistake. Now he's dead. It's not fair!" Samuel brushed harshly at tears on his cheeks and looked away.

Tom put an arm around his grandson's shoulders. "Samuel, the sheriff's deputies tried to get those kids out of the water. The two boys knew the storm was coming. If they surf much they know about rip tides and undertows."

"Yeah, well, what about Mom and Dad? What'd they do wrong?" Samuel asked, shrugging away from his grandpa's grip. "Should they have stayed home and ignored that Africa's animals are being wiped out?"

"No, Samuel. Here, take a seat," Tom said, pointing to a large tree stump.

"Why does God let things like that happen to people?" Samuel asked as he slumped down next to Tom.

"Gram and I raised your mom with the belief that mankind is responsible to wisely manage the earth's natural resources. Because of this belief, your parents went to Africa to bring back photographs that would help make people aware of the plight of the African elephant, the black rhino and other endangered species." Turns out your dad may have had other reasons too, Tom thought to himself as he sat down next to Samuel.

Samuel stood up and faced his grandfather. "I know why they went. What I don't know is, why they didn't come back? I prayed

223

for them. I prayed for them every day they were gone. Fat lot of good that did."

Tom looked down at his hands. He clasped and unclasped them in his lap. "Life, if lived to the fullest, has risks. You can either do what you're called to do and accept the danger involved, or you can stay home in bed."

Samuel sat back down. "People die in bed too, Grandpa."

"You know what I mean."

"If they were following the will of God," the boy said, searching Tom's face, "why didn't He protect them?"

"What makes you think He didn't?"

"They're not here, are they?" Samuel said, holding out empty hands.

Tom's smoky, gray eyes became thoughtful. He took off his hat and raked large brown fingers through his dark hair, streaked with gray. "It's the age-old question of why bad things happen to Godly people. But remember, the Bible tells us God works all things together for our good if we love Him and are called according to His purpose. You can't see the whole picture unless you're looking at it through God's eyes."

"Grandpa, I only got one set of eyes," Samuel said. "And the way I see it, Cory's death and not knowing what happened to Mom and Dad are the worst of all bads." He emphasized this statement by kicking violently at a thick tuft of grass.

"Yeah, I know." Tom's shoulders drooped forward. "Questions about where they are and if they are OK tear at my heart every waking hour. I can't disagree that it's hard to imagine anything good coming out of the situation, but we can't see down through the ages like God does. We have to trust that He is good and knows what He's doing."

"Now you sound like Old Max. He's always spouting that kind of stuff." Samuel's eyes accused Tom.

Tom congratulated himself. He did sound like Old Max. "You think Jesus laughed when the crown of long, spiky thorns was pushed into His head? You think He enjoyed being nailed to that cross or having the sins of the world dumped on Him? He put up with a heap of pain and suffering for you and me. Can you even imagine how hard it was for Father God —to watch his own Son be treated like that? But where would we be if He hadn't? I'll tell you where. Dead. Living in sin with no hope."

"But Jesus came back to life," Samuel said.

"That's right. He was the first to be resurrected. That's our hope! All who believe in Him and His resurrection will live forever."

"But not always down here." Samuel stooped to pick up the bucket and net. "You think Mom and Dad are dead, don't you?"

"Because of their faith in Jesus they'll live forever."

"You know what I mean. Alive! Arms, legs, bodies walking around down here on earth." Samuel stomped up and down the shoreline to demonstrate.

"I don't know if they are alive, walking around down here like you and me. I hope, with all that's in me, they are. I want as much as you do for them to come through the back door of the house and call, 'We're home! Where is everyone?'"

"Do you really think that will happen?"

"I don't know, but I hope somehow, in God's infinite, mercy that someday it will."

Samuel started toward the water. "And in the meantime?"

Tom placed his arm around Samuel's shoulder and turned the boy to look him square in the eyes. "In the meantime, I cling with all my strength to the belief that God is good, and I trust that He will somehow bring good out of all this. I don't have the answers. But I won't stop praying! And I refuse to give up hope!"

Samuel searched Tom's eyes, then once again shrugged free of his grandfather's grasp.

After dropping the bucket, he unwound the rope from the casting net. He held the net's yoke in his left hand and pinched off sections of the lead-weighted skirt, flipping them over his shoulder. He held the final section tightly in his right hand. "Yeah, OK, whatever," he said and, turning away, spun the net clockwise high into the air.

The blue net opened like a parachute and floated down into the water. As it sank, the meshing surrounded a several silver shiners. Samuel, pulling the casting line, hauled up the net with 3-to 4-inch fish clinging to its webbing.

Tom helped his grandson pick baitfish out of the webbing and slosh them into a water-filled bucket. Tom nodded at the net. Samuel shrugged.

Tom stepped to one side, picked up the blue casting net and, with preparations similar to Samuel's, threw it high over the water. Being taller and stronger, he sent it farther than Samuel and hauled in even more shiners than before.

Relieved of his fishing duties, Samuel rolled up his pant legs and waded into the cool water. The soothing waves, the warm sun, the multitude of shells that beckoned to him from a narrow sand shelf, raised Samuel's spirits. "Look at all these shells the storm washed onto the beach. Sumer will just die when I show them to her."

"It's better than dying of old age, while I wait for my brother and grandfather to pick me up!" Sumer said.

"Oh, Sumer, sorry," Samuel laughed. "Did you walk all the way from the animal hospital?"

"Yes, I DID!" Sumer said.

Her grandfather looked sheepish, but continued to throw the casting net. "Sorry, Sumer, guess we took longer netting fish than we should've. Few more throws and we'll have enough."

"Yeah, sure!" Sumer said in annoyance. She could tell she wasn't going to get any more sympathy, so she waded into the shallow water to hunt for shells. Soon the bucket was full of silvery fish, and the twins' pockets bulged with knobbed whelk shells, creamy pink scallop shells, a conch shell or two and even a few sand dollars. They were careful to throw all the live shells back into the water, keeping only the ones without critters in them.

"I think we have enough. Let's go feed Nigel." Tom started toward the driveway. Water and fish splashed over the bucket's edge as he strolled toward the blue pickup.

Samuel lagged behind his grandfather. He picked up fish that flopped from the bucket and threw them back into the sloshing receptacle.

This time, the young man was keenly aware of the green grass, soft and damp beneath his bare feet, and the morning sun, as it warmed his neck and shoulders. He even stopped to watch a small lizard, dash-stop, dash-stop, across a low-hanging limb. The lizard exhibited a bright-orange throat fan. Its body color changed from green to brown to green as it proceeded from leaf to bark to leaf.

"Hey, look at this lizard. It's really cool," he called, but Sumer and Tom were already in the pickup. He looked again. The lizard was gone.

It's hard to tell what caused Samuel's thought process to jump from the pleasure of the moment back to feelings of pain and anger. It could have been the lizard's disappearance or the lack of someone to share his carefree moment. But, most likely, it was the turmoil caused by questions and answers that didn't seem to fit.

Whatever the motivation, Samuel's mood once more turned black. In desperation the boy turned his face skyward and asked, "Why'd Cory have to die, God? I know what he did was really stupid, but I do dumb things, too. Will I die the next time I pull some brainless stunt?

"Where are Mom and Dad? Did you protect them like Grandpa said? If you did, where are they?"

White Tail Deer

White Tail Deer

CHAPTER 28

When Tom, Sumer and Samuel arrived at the animal hospital, Zhora was showing signs that her time was near. "Great, just GREAT!" Samuel yelled, his sour mood very much in control of his emotions. "Zhora, you can't have your cubs today. We have to meet with Mindy and the rest of those guys at Kingdom Cove. You're going to have to wait until tomorrow!"

"I've never known a baby to wait for a convenient time to be born, Samuel. They come on their time schedule, not yours," Tom said.

"Well I certainly can't go to Kingdom Cove today," Sumer announced. "You'll have to go alone or take Nigel. I've never seen kittens born before, and Dr. Matthews said I could watch. Besides, Zhora and the cubs need me."

Samuel shot her a killing glare. "Too bad. You're coming!"

"How important is this trip to Kingdom Cove today? Can't it wait until tomorrow?" Tom asked.

"No, they're expecting us today and won't know to show up tomorrow," Samuel answered.

"How long does it take to get there?"

"The way Sumer and I travel, over three hours," Samuel said still glaring at Sumer. "But she's not much help."

"I do so help. You just don't appreciate my efforts," Sumer said, pursing her lips and squinting her eyes at Samuel.

"Yeah, right. There's not much effort to appreciate."

"Samuel, snapping at your sister isn't going to solve the problem," Tom reprimanded.

"It makes me feel better. If I have to go, so does SHE!" Samuel said, pointing at his twin.

"You just said yourself I slow you down. I certainly wouldn't want to do that." Sumer said, sticking out her tongue.

"Well you're going!" Samuel said, grabbing her arm and pulling her toward the door. "You're better than nothing, though not much."

"You're so kind, but I am not going! GET IT?" Summer said, digging in her heels.

"Samuel, with you and me paddling, how long will the trip take?" Tom removed Samuel's hand from Sumer's arm.

"We might make it in two hours, but it will be tough going, and we only have one paddle," Samuel said. He renewed his scowl at Sumer.

"We'll get another one. If it has to be done, it has to be done. Let's get going." Tom grabbed his hat and headed for the door.

"Zhora, you better wait until I get back!" Samuel ordered as he stomped out the door and gave it an extra-hard slam.

Tom and Samuel jumped into Old Blue and headed home. Mariana was waiting for them with a lunch-to-go and a large can of mosquito repellent. "Sumer called and said she felt bad about not going. It's really important to her that she stay with Zhora," Mariana explained, giving Samuel a shoulder hug. "Here's some power food and insect spray. I called Jim Greentree; he said you could use his canoe, the one with the flat back and motor if you like. I didn't explain what you're doing, just that you had an errand and needed to get back quickly."

"Good thinking, thank you. We'll leave the pickup at Greentree's store and go straight to the animal hospital from there. Are you going to the hospital now?"

"Sumer said she'd call when the panther's labor starts in earnest. I'll go then."

When Tom and Samuel arrived at Greentree's Store, Jim Greentree had his canoe in the water. "The motor's all gassed up and ready to go," he announced. "Just leave it here when you come back. I'll take care of putting it away. Better get going. Those cubs aren't going to wait all day."

"Thanks, Jim, I owe you one," Tom said as he and Samuel shoved off into the bay. The canoe, pushed by a 10-horse power motor, cut easily through the water. A slight breeze blew at their backs, seeming to wish them God's speed.

"It's low tide, so once we reach the channel, we'll have to paddle back into the lagoon. The water will be too shallow to run the motor," Samuel explained.

Neither talked much as the canoe sped toward the mangrove island that housed Kingdom Cove. As they approached the end of one large island, Samuel pointed toward shore, "There's the orange scarf."

Tom killed the motor and lifted the propeller out of the water. Lying down in the bottom of the canoe, they slid the boat under the crooked branch that guarded the entrance. "We're making good time so far," Samuel announced, looking at his watch. "But this is the tricky part."

Jim Greentree had placed two paddles in the bottom of the boat so both were able to paddle feverishly down the twists and turns of the channel. Ducking under one branch after another, they tried to ignore the mosquitoes and yellow flies that buzzed around their heads.

Halfway through the watery trail, they plunged around a sharp corner only to find a huge fallen tree blocking their path. "We're stuck! Now what? That tree wasn't here before!" said Samuel, looking at his watch.

"The storm most likely brought it down," Tom said as he pulled the canoe up to the fallen tree. Taking off his sweat-soiled hat, he raked callused fingers through his hair and looked at the massive trunk. They couldn't go around it. They couldn't go under it. The only possibility was to go over, and Tom was not sure they could manage that either. After taking the motor off the canoe, he climbed onto the fallen tree and up another one. He wedged the motor between two high branches. Tom told Samuel to climb out of the canoe and onto the felled tree trunk. He then proceeded to descend into the water.

"I'm not sure you want to do that, Grandpa. There are snakes in that water."

231

"Well that sounds like a real good reason to hurry. You pull the canoe over the tree and I'll push."

Tom lifted and pushed the back of the canoe while Samuel pulled and tugged from the front. "This tree is slippery. I'm having a tough t-i-i-m-m-e-e," SPLASH! "Holding on," Samuel finished as he slid into the water. He climbed back onto the tree and again tried to pull the canoe over it. Again he fell into the water. On the third try, Samuel braced his feet against two branches. Samuel pulling while Tom shoved, they were able to get the canoe up and over the tree and into water on the other side. "What about the motor?" Samuel asked.

"Is there another way out of this Kingdom Cove?"

"Not that I know of."

"Then we'll leave the motor here and pick it up on the way back," Tom said as he once again began propelling the canoe down the dimly lit channel.

When the water deepened, Samuel said, "There's Mindy and her Mother. I just saw them swim under the boat. How'd they get under that tree?"

"There must be another way into this cove. How close are we, anyway?"

"Five minutes or less."

"We've been gone over two hours. Better pour it on," Tom said, paddling more fiercely than before.

Soon Tom saw the narrow, bug-infested waterway widen into a large lake. The majesty of the lagoon breathed a miracle into his heart.

Samuel saw the expression on his grandfather's face. "Thought Sumer and I made it all up, didn't you?"

A low whistle escaped Tom lips as he looked speechlessly around the lagoon. The crystal clear lake. Life-giving water that bubbled from underground springs to race over rocks and plunged down a waterfall. Flowers, larger than life. Butterflies the size of a small hand. Row upon row of trees overwhelmed with yellow, orange, red and green fruit. Fish of every size and color. Songbirds that sang just to celebrate the joy of life — a joy that permeated the very air.

Tom experienced an overwhelming sense of God's presence. How extraordinary, he thought, to be able to walk through a garden like this with the Creator. To sit under that large live oak tree and ask questions at the feet of Jesus.

Samuel could see Rondolus as he paced on the beach and Trina's leathery neck and head craned to look their way. Mindy and her mother floated in the middle of the lake, and Olli sat in a tree, carefully observing the fish that swam below him. "Come on, Grandpa, we need to dive to the bottom of the pool so we can talk to Mindy and the others," Samuel explained.

"You go ahead, I'll wait here," Tom said, still basking in the beauty that surrounded him. Samuel plunged to the bottom of the pool then quickly resurfaced. As his head popped out of the water he chirped and squeaked at Tom. "I can't understand a word you're saying, Samuel. This is just too much for an old man like me to take in. Go on without me."

With one last unintelligible plea, Samuel swam to shore, sat down on the sand and began giving the animals an update. When he was finished, Trina grunted, "We've done all we can. I hope it's enough. If Joe Sorrow doesn't change his mind and accept the foundation's offer, I don't know where I'll lay my eggs." The loggerhead began dragging her large shell toward the water.

"I hope this Joe fellow is a reasonable man," Mother Manatee communicated. "I'm afraid it's out of our hands now, whatever the outcome."

"Zhora was acting weird this morning, and Dr. Matthews said she is going to have her cubs today." Samuel said. "I need to get back."

"Why didn't you say so? Let's go!" Rondolus said.

"Can we meet at the cove again later? Sumer wanted to stay with Zhora today, but I'm sure she'll come the next time." Samuel said, walking out to pat Mindy's rough gray hide.

"We met for one specific reason, and have done everything we know to do. That's the way Kingdom Cove works. We meet. We

233

do what we are able. Then we leave the rest in the hands of the Almighty. Faith and trust in him is our mission from here on out," Mother Manatee said.

"We'll still see each other in the bay," Mindy comforted, nuzzling his hand with her nose.

"That tickles," Samuel laughed then quickly sobered. "But it won't be the same, will it?"

"I'm afraid not. Thanks for your help. You've been a good friend," Mindy snorted.

"I just know all our hard work will make a difference," Mamma Manatee added.

"Let's get going!" Rondolus croaked as he and Olli headed toward Banyan City."

"I'd better go too," Samuel said. He patted Trina and gave Mindy a quick scratch between her ears.

He dove reluctantly into the lake, and as he swam through the cool clean water, his mind whirled. Surely there was some reason for returning to Kingdom Cove. The world's always suffering from one environmental crisis or another. He, Sumer and the animals of Kingdom Cove could help with any one of them. Now, however, he needed to find his grandfather and start back.

■ ■ ■

Tom paddled slowly though the water. The lagoon rocked him gently in the arms of its beauty, and Tom's soul, for the first time in almost a year, was at peace.

He beached the canoe and stepped onto the white sand. Warmth from the sun-drenched sand soaked into his feet. He turned to look out over the lagoon. Its crystal-clear water beckoned. He dived into its depths. The miraculous water surrounded him, cleansed him, renewed him and only when his lungs burned from lack of oxygen did he start toward the surface.

His head popped above the water at the same time a great snow-white bird swooped low over the canoe and landed in shallow water. Tongues of fire blazed from his eyes, breathing life into Tom's soul. "Thank you for all this," Tom spread his arms wide. "Thank you for ... just thank you."

The bird stared, warmth radiating from his eyes. Tom stared back then swam to shore. He walked into the coolness of grass, shaded by a giant live oak. He sat, he considered and he allowed the breath of life to permeate his very being.

He ambled between rows of trees, heavy with fruit, and in answer to his grumbling stomach, picked some oranges. A bright-orange sphere bulged from each pocket while Tom juggled three more. He wandered back down the sandy trail, which led to the giant oak. Gray-green Spanish moss swept downward from the tree's massive branches and swayed in rhythm to a soft breeze.

Tom sat again in the tree's shade. He leaned against its rough bark and listened to the warble of a bird that sat on a branch high above him. He closed his eyes, but his stomach growled in protest. Three oranges lay invitingly on the grass. After he poked, smelled and squeezed each one, he chose the plumpest and dug his nails into its firm rind. The smell of bitter orange oil, reminiscent of Christmas morning, rose from the fruit. His hands, sticky with dripping, squirting juice, pulled apart one section after another and popped them into his mouth.

■ ■ ■

Samuel swam to the middle of the lake where he had left Tom and the canoe. They were no longer in sight. The boy's arms and legs treaded water in a slow circle while his eyes searched the shoreline. He looked as far as the large oak tree then began with smooth strong strokes to swim toward land.

Samuel waded ashore, grabbed his towel from the back of the canoe and dried himself. Still mulling over the possibilities of more Kingdom Cove adventures, he sat down next to his grandfather. Tom's large, sun-tanned hand offered the boy a peeled orange. They ate in silence with juice dripping down their chins.

Tom took out a wet white handkerchief and, wiping his mouth on one side, offered Samuel the other. "Have you eaten any of

235

those strawberries?" He motioned down a sandy pathway toward a colorful strawberry patch. "They're huge, bright red. I can smell their earthy fragrance from here."

Without a word Samuel was up and started down the trail. "Come on, slowpoke," he laughed over his shoulder.

"Hey, I actually understood you that time," Tom said.

"You been in the water?"

"Took a quick dip's all."

"That's all it takes. I'll race you," Samuel said sprinting down the sandy path.

Not showing much speed, Tom arrived at the edge of the patch in time to see his grandson force a 3-inch strawberry into his mouth. The two picked as many red orbs as could be carried and returned to the shady oak. They sat, they ate, and they drank frosty water from a nearby spring.

"We'd better start home." Tom said. He looked around longingly then walked slowly toward the canoe. After hoisting the boat into the water, they climbed in, picked up the paddles and veed the bow of the canoe through the water.

Tom looked back at the soft green grass, the deep shade, the life-giving water that splashed up from underground springs. "This is the way God intended life to be. Too bad Adam and Eve ... and the rest of us," he reluctantly added," had to go and screw it up."

Tom and Samuel paddled to the mouth of the narrow passage. They stopped for a last look. Tears of yearning swelled up in Tom's eyes as he prayed, "God, this boy has finally come home; don't let me get lost again."

"What'd you say?"

"Just telling the Lord what a joy it is to meet Him again."

"We better get a move on," Samuel said, pointing to his watch. He then put his back into pushing and dragging the paddle through the water.

Egret

Sandpiper

CHAPTER 29

They left the lagoon and were immediately engrossed in twisting and turning the canoe back down the bug-infested trail. When they came to the fallen tree, Tom slipped out of the canoe and into the water.

The tide was incoming now, and the water hit him chest high. He lifted and pushed the canoe over the fallen trunk while Samuel, anchoring his feet between two branches, pulled and tugged. This time, partly because the water was deeper and partly because Samuel knew what he was doing, the canoe went up and over with much less trouble. Once the canoe was on the other side of the tree blockade, Samuel climbed into the canoe and grabbed hold of a branch to steady it.

Tom climbed up the tree, retrieved the motor and stretched down with it. "Can you grab this, Samuel?"

Tying off the canoe, Samuel once again climbed onto the tree. He stretched his body up to meet the dangling motor and grasped the propeller casing. He called up to Tom. "I got it!" and lowered the motor to the fallen tree.

Tom climbed up the tree to take a last look out over the water. "Good news is the water is deep enough to use the motor the rest of the way." He called from his lofty perch. "The bad news is the wind is picking up and getting across the Gulf is going to be murder."

He and Samuel reattached the motor and were soon weaving their way toward the mouth of the channel and the crooked limb that guarded it. When the canoe cleared both, Tom and Samuel were confronted with 4- to 6-foot waves. Gale-force winds burst from the south, inflicting their full fury upon the Gulf water and whipping it into valleys and peaks of whitish froth.

"HANG ON! This is not going to be pretty!" Tom shouted.

As if to prove his point, a blast of wind hurled his raffia hat from his head, and with a malicious twist, dumped it into the churning Gulf. Tom grabbed at the wide-rim hat, but as he did, a rogue wave slammed into the side of the canoe. Samuel was knocked to the floor of the canoe and Tom was thrown off balance. "GET TO THE BACK AND LEAN ON THE LEFT SIDE!" Tom yelled as he leaped for the right side. By reacting quickly they were able to stabilize the canoe before it capsized.

Samuel fought to keep the boat steady and to restart the motor, while Tom, with arms and paddle stretched to the maximum, lunged for his hat. The canoe was pushed west; the waves bobbed and dipped his hat east. Tom paddled against hostile water to close the gap between boat and hat, but the hat never had a chance. It was thrown to the top of one wave just to be crashed on by another. It fought its way to the water's surface only to be quickly slammed down again. The hat was pushed farther and farther away. Finally, the raffia palm hat with its brown leather band gave up the fight and sank out of sight.

Tom looked at the swirling gray water in anguish. His daughter, Jade, gave him that hat. The raffia hat's watery death and Tom's inability to save it brought back the helplessness and emptiness he felt when Jade disappeared.

"Why do you take away everything I love?" He yelled into the sky as the wind howled.

Loss once again pierced Tom's soul and pain imprisoned him as he catapulted from his mountaintop experience at Kingdom Cove into the all to familiar valley of despair. Oblivious to Samuel's calls for help and unable to cope with the angry water that encircled them, he lost sight of all hope.

Waves crashed against the side of the canoe and threatened to sink them. All Tom wanted was for the darkness to come, for the agony to stop.

He heard Samuel call as if from a dream. He looked up and saw the boy struggling, fighting alone against the vast Gulf of Mexico. Tom sat in the canoe, frozen with grief.

A voice began to rise up from the depths of Tom's soul, "Anyone who loves his father or mother more than me is not worthy of me; anyone who loves his son or daughter more than me is not worthy of me; and anyone who does not take his cross and follow me is not worthy of me. Whoever finds his life will lose it, and whoever loses his life for my sake will find it. My grace is sufficient for you, for my power is made perfect in weakness."

The reminder of God's grace brought tears to Tom's eyes. The words of Jesus steeled his spine. He fought for focus and struggled to pull himself together. Samuel's survival depended on his getting a grip. Tom needed to head the boat into the waves and move it quickly toward shore.

Samuel, finally able to start the small motor, was making painfully slow progress against the angry water. Tom took over steering. Samuel grabbed the paddle and feverishly pulled it through the water to help move the canoe forward, keeping its nose headed into the wind.

Time after time the boat rose to the crest of a swell just to be slammed down into a trough. Each time the boat bottomed out, the jolt made Samuel's head and neck ache. The boat rose up; the boat dropped down. It twisted; it turned and Samuel's stomach churned with each movement. If he allowed himself to dwell on it, he'd be seasick. He forced his concentration to the boat, on keeping the bow pointed toward shore, on moving toward safety.

Samuel's shoulders ached with fatigue. When the wind suddenly went slack, he didn't question the apparent blessing. He placed the paddle on the canoe bottom and, with hands gripping the muscles on his shoulders, kneaded out the soreness. His body was wet; the air felt cold. He found a semi-dry T-shirt and pulled it over his head. Still shivering, he forced one foot into a wet tennis shoe and grabbed the other. He turned to give his grandfather a jubilant thumbs-up for their apparent success, but the gesture froze in the salt air.

Samuel saw rather than heard the words, "WATCH OUT!" as a 5-foot surge of water crashed against the side of the canoe. White foam and gray salt water swirled into the boat and out again, taking Samuel's beach towel and the second tennis shoe with it.

The life jackets tried to follow, but Samuel flung himself across the boat and grabbed at them. His right hand clutched the white strap of the closest jacket and his left clawed at the second as it swirled out into the water, then floated back again. He grabbed it, catching the strap with his finger, and tossed it to Grandpa Tom. Samuel wrapped the other one around himself as the canoe began to sink.

On hands and knees Samuel groped through belly-deep water, searching frantically for a bait bucket or anything suitable to bail water. The canoe tipped front-end up, and a bait bucket sloshed between his legs and arms. He clasped the handle and began to frantically pitch water from the boat.

Samuel forgot how wet and cold he was. He forgot how much his neck and head ached from the jolting motion of the heaving boat. He was determined to keep the canoe afloat. Shoulders searing with pain, the young man, like a robot on high speed, dumped one bucket of water after another over the side.

He prayed for the first time since Cory's death and hoped that God was not too mad at him to listen. He and his grandfather were in the Almighty's hands, and somehow that acknowledgment gave Samuel strength. He became determined to throw out more water than the angry sea could pour in.

The influx of water killed the motor, but Tom, able to restart it, skillfully moved the canoe, now half-filled with water, forward. He pointed its bow into the wind that was once again howling around them. After the water in the canoe was reduced to ankle-deep, Samuel dropped down on the seat to take a break. He glanced up, and Greentree's Store was less than 50 yards in front of them. A long slow breath in, a long slow breath out, and he resumed baling until the front tip of the canoe hit dry sand.

Jim Greentree was pacing in front of his store, and when the boat came near the beach, he waded out to help drag the canoe ashore. "Mariana phoned a few minutes ago!" he shouted into the wind. "If you want to watch that panther give birth, you better hurry!" Tom climbed out of the canoe and slumped onto a bench. What's wrong, man? You don't look so good!" Jim said.

"It's nothing. Just tired. Samuel, go get the truck," Tom said, tossing the keys in the boy's direction.

Samuel caught the keys and ran to Old Blue. A look of sheer determination froze on his face as he, grinding gears, lurched the truck forward. He brought it to an ungraceful halt in front of his grandfather. Leaning on Jim Greentree, Tom climbed inside.

Samuel put in the clutch, shifted into first and lurched forward; this time the truck's engine died. "Feel the clutch, son, f-e-e-l the clutch," Tom coached.

Samuel turned the key and the motor came to life. Determined to do as his grandfather said, he let the clutch out slowly and fed the truck gas. Lighter on the clutch, heavier on the gas, left foot up, right foot down. He was driving. Maybe not smoothly, but at least steadily, they moved down the road.

"Want me to drive you to the doctor?" Samuel asked, but Tom stubbornly refused, insisting he was just tired.

Samuel drove victoriously into the parking lot of the animal hospital. He helped his grandfather into the building, where they joined Mariana and Sumer at the birthing room's, observation window. Sumer and Samuel paced back and forth in front of the window; Mariana and Tom sat on a bench as they waited for the panther to give birth. Dr. Matthews, deciding the panther could handle the delivery on her own, joined Tom, Mariana, Samuel and Sumer to watch for signs of trouble from the window.

The panther lay down then got up, dragging her hind legs. She half-walked half-dragged herself around the room once. She lay down in the blanket-covered box. Her eyes glazed with pain, but soon a look of concentration replaced the look of agony.

Tension in Zhora's hindquarters increased; she was now pushing in earnest. One small wet blob slipped out and it seemed to give relief to her tortured body.

Mother panther started to lick the afterbirth from the first cub, but before it was clean pain again filled her eyes. This time, the intense concentration came quicker, but the tightening of the hindquarters lasted longer. Finally a second, larger cub was born.

Dr. Matthews had been holding his breath. Now, he coached the big cat from outside the window. "Come on, Zhora, you can do it. Just one more, just one more," he whispered.

The panther proceeded to clean the two cubs as if she were finished. "I know there's one more; if she doesn't expel it soon, I'll have to interfere. Meanwhile I think we can take a break, give her a half-hour. Man, you don't look so good." Dr. Matthews said, looking at Tom. Seeing the goose bumps on Samuel's arms, he added, "I think you two could used a hot cup of something."

" Hot chocolate?" Samuel asked.

"I'll take a cup of hot coffee if you've got it," Tom said.

When they walked back from the vet's office, a third cub was next to the other two. "It looks so small and lifeless. Is it breathing?" Sumer asked.

The big cat stood over the cubs licking them. Dr. Matthews decided the little family needed some privacy and attempted to send everyone home. "Time will tell if they all survive. Cruel as it may seem, we must let nature take its course. If we interfere, Zhora may refuse to accept any of them."

Sumer's face clouded over, and tears trickled down her cheeks. "Please, Dr. Matthews, go see if the tiny one is OK," she begged.

"If it were dead, Zhora wouldn't be cleaning it," the vet hedged. He was determined to keep the cubs away from all human contact so they would have a better chance of surviving in the wild. Sumer didn't let it drop until Dr. Matthews agreed to keep an eye on the tiny one.

Tom, even after the coffee, looked pasty. Mariana handed him two aspirins and made him sit down while the twins named the cubs.

It was hard to tell what the small panthers looked like, because they were still wet and mostly hidden by Zhora. Sumer and Samuel moved from one end of the window to the other, as they tried to get a better view. They could see only three little lumps snuggling in the blanket. They saw that one was larger than the others and assumed it was a boy cub. They named him Bud. The smaller two, they decided, were probably girls, so they christened them Sasha and Tiny.

Sumer, earlier in the afternoon, sneaked Nigel, Olli and Rondolus into the hospital to watch the birth process from a remote window. The three were so quiet, she completely forgot about them until after the birthing when Rondolus started flapping around with so much excitement that Dr. Matthews ordered them all out.

Olli, a true gentleman, retreated without a fuss, and Nigel waddled out under his own power. Rondolus, however, led the twins on a merry chase up and down the corridors. He ran down one hallway then, flapping over their heads, flew down another. Grandma Mariana watched with amusement until the excited bird collided with a mop, protruding from a pail of soapy water. White foam, water, mop and pink feathers all flew in different directions. Sumer and Samuel slipped and skidded into a jumble on the floor.

"All right, things have gotten completely out of control, enough of this foolishness." Giving the stunned bird her sternest look, Mariana pointed toward the open door at the end of the hallway, and Rondolus had enough sense to march himself to the end of the lighted hallway and fly out into the dusk.

Mariana mopped up water and soapsuds while Sumer and Samuel took a last look at Zhora and the three cubs. Samuel and Tom, still in damp clothes and Samuel with only one shoe, followed Mariana and Sumer into the parking lot. The wind was now still.

"Where's your hat?" Mariana asked Tom.

"The wind blew it off." Samuel said, moving closer to his grandfather as if to protect him. "Grandpa tried real hard to get it back, but he couldn't. It's swimming with the fishes."

"It is?" Mariana asked as she peered into Tom's face.

"Mom's hat?" Sumer gasped. "Why couldn't you save it?"

"The wind was unbelievable out there. We tried, didn't we, Grandpa?" Samuel linked arms in solidarity with his grandfather.

"Yes, son, we tried. We really tried. I'll miss it. Just got it broken in." Tears sparkled in his eyes. He was tired and pain shot through the middle of his chest. With great effort he put one foot in front of the other.

From the all-consuming joy of Kingdom Cove, to the raging sea and the words that sprang forth when he had lost all hope and now this satisfaction at the cubs' birth. How was he to think about all this?

Was there a reason he never remembered to refill his heart medication? Maybe Max was right, Tom thought. Maybe I really do have a death wish.

The words Savior and Lord sprang to mind, and Tom realized that though he had once made an alter call, he had never allowed Jesus to be Lord of his life.

"I've always reserved that job for myself. Turns out I'm not so hot at it. You want the job. You got it," he said in silent prayer. "I'm hard-headed and not easy to lead, but if you want me, here I am. Time to start being the man you called me to be."

Mariana walked close to his right side. Her skin felt soft against his arm; her mixed scent of hand soap, shampoo and lilac oil delighted his nose. He watched Samuel and Sumer as they raced ahead. He was the most blessed of men.

Tom put his arm around Mariana and hugged her close to his side. The chest pains, he was quite certain, were heartburn from too many oranges and strawberries. But, be that as it may, on the way home he was going to stop and refill his heart medication. Maybe tomorrow he'd even stop at Greentree's store to look for a new hat.

Florida Panther

Florida Panther

Florida Panther

CHAPTER 30

It was midnight when Dr. Matthews came back to check on Zhora and her cubs. He found Tiny, the smallest cub, lying several feet away from the rest of the cubs. She was not moving, and the young vet could not tell if she was breathing. The other two cubs, blindly feeling for their mother's warm milk, wobbled around the large box while Zhora paced back and forth. His every instinct urged the young vet to rush into the room and see if anything could be done to save Tiny. Yet he feared Zhora would become even more upset if he interfered.

How could he keep Zhora's smell on the cub, eradicate any human smell and still take the cub from the room to treat her? Inspiration struck. "THE BLANKET!"

Hoping his idea would ensure Zhora's later acceptance of the cub, the vet put on surgical attire and grabbed a pair of sterile scissors.

He waited until the mother cat was busy with Bud and Sasha, then he entered the room and slithered along the wall. After reaching the birthing box, he bent behind it and slowly pulled on a corner of the tattered yellow blanket. The young vet moved with extreme caution and speed to cut away a large piece of the blanket, grab Tiny and bolt for the exit. He felt Zhora's hot breath coming close behind him as he raced though and slammed the door. The kidnapping of her cub left the big cat howling with anger.

Dr. Matthews could feel Tiny's weak attempts to breathe as he rushed the cub to an examination room. Being mindful not to touch the cub with anything but the blanket, he gave her an injection to ward off pneumonia. He forced several drops of warm soybean milk into the cub's miniature mouth with an eyedropper and placed her, completely surrounded by the blanket, into an incubator.

He walked back to the birthing room and, resting his forehead against the cool mesh of the door, looked at Zhora. Mother panther yowled angrily at him, then paced feverishly from one end of the room to the other. Jonathan stood and watched.

"You're angry with me aren't you? For good reason, too, I took your cub. She was dying, Zhora. I tried not to interfere, but I'm a doctor. I couldn't let her die. I'll give her back as soon as I'm sure she'll live." Fatigue dripped from his voice. "I'll give her back."

The panther looked at the young vet then continued pacing. A few minutes later, however, she settled down to allow Bud and Sasha to nurse. Somewhat relieved, Jonathan wandered wearily back to the examination room. He fed Tiny a few more drops of warm soymilk, set an alarm to go off in an hour and dropped onto an old army cot to sleep.

He slept soundly until the alarm jolted him awake. So progressed the night. He fed Tiny, checked on Zhora, then collapsed for another hour's sleep.

As a golden glow lit up the eastern sky, the young vet slipped, a much revived, blanket-wrapped, Tiny back into the panther's room and closed the door. Zhora approached the wiggling, blanket lump and cautiously smelled it. She looked at Dr. Matthews, twitched her tail haughtily and walked back to the other two cubs. Seconds later she again came close, smelled the blanket-covered cub and ambled away.

The young vet opened the door ready to retrieve the cub. "If you don't want Tiny, I'll just have to raise her myself," he said frustration surging from his voice.

Zhora watched as Dr. Matthews opened the door and, kneeling down, reached for the nearest corned of the blanket that still covered Tiny. Without even a warning growl the panther leaped to stand over her smallest cub. Vet and mother panther locked eyes in a stare-down until Dr. Matthews removed his arm from the room and closed the door.

Zhora came close, sniffed the blanket bundle one more time. She looked at the vet then gently picked Tiny up by the nape of her neck and carried the small cub to where Bud and Sasha were hungrily waiting. All three cubs were soon nursing greedily.

Weak with relief yet elated beyond description, Dr. Matthews did something he hadn't done for years. He fell to his knees and thanked God. The young vet was wise enough to understand something truly good had happened and to know that the night's successful outcome was not his to claim. Unshaven, exhausted and clad in sleep-wrinkled clothes, Jonathan Matthews crawled back onto the army cot and slept without dreaming.

Gopher Tortoise

Gopher Tortoise

Gopher Tortoise

CHAPTER 31

"Mariana, does anything need to be done with Jade and Alan's house? I think I'm going to D.C. to check things out at the end of the week."

"Why the sudden interest in the house?"

"I decided it was about time."

"Mrs. Smith, their neighbor, called yesterday to report a sprinkler head was broken on the irrigation system. Her husband turned off the water because it was shooting 15 feet into the air. Why are you really going to D.C.?"

"I'm going to see Senator Gall, find out if there's been any word from his two agents in Kenya. It's time I take a more active role in finding our daughter and son-in-law," Tom said.

"When are you going?"

"Friday afternoon. Senator Gall can see me Saturday. I'll get the sprinkler fixed Monday and be home sometime Tuesday."

The rest of the week was cooler than normal and rainy. Mariana spent her time painting, and the kids spent all their free time helping with Zhora and the cubs.

Tom drove himself to the airport after lunch on Friday. The flight to D.C. was bumpy and nerve-racking, so he was glad when the Boeing 737 put down at Dulles International Airport. He took a cab to the hotel, checked in and went to bed.

Saturday morning he called room service and ordered breakfast for two. He read the *Washington Post* as he waited for Senator Gall to arrive.

Tom heard a knock on the door. Minutes later Senator Mike Gall sat across the table from Tom and stabbed at a watermelon ball with his fork. "It all depends on how you look at it whether or not we're making progress. Bill, one of the agents in Kenya, e-mailed me early this week. He and the other agent found information on several fronts. No clothing, jewelry or other articles attributable to Jade, Alan or their abductors were discovered at the time or since, either downstream or at the place where the five sets of footprints entered the Mara River."

"You are using this information as proof they were not killed and eaten by crocodiles?"

"It's not proof, but since crocodiles are not real fastidious, it does point in that direction."

"They also searched the river banks for evidence to substantiate that a boat was tied up and left waiting for them. Rope scars on trees, broken brush. It's been nine months, things heal quickly in Africa; they didn't find anything conclusive." Mike Gall helped himself to a second cup of coffee.

"Didn't they look for evidence of a boat right after it happened?"

"I went all through the written report. I hate to say it, but the initial investigation was pretty sloppy," the senator admitted.

"So basically we're back to square one."

"Ed said they questioned some villagers downriver. A boy remembered a boat with Bwana, Memsaab and Masai. The boy said he saw the boat the same day as his sister's wedding festival. As far as Ed could determine, the couple was married in late October, early November."

Tom ran a hand across his unshaved square jaw. "That sounds like it could have been them. How do we find out more? What can we do to hurry this up?"

"We can't do anything, just yet. Don't have enough evidence to demand the FBI reopen the investigation.

"Bill and Ed have been reassigned and will leave Kenya in a few weeks, but Bill is determined to make a full-out effort in what time he has left. He said something about knowing Jade and Alan from D.C. Said Jade was some lady."

Tom looked hard at the Senator. "I'm glad he's so dedicated. Now maybe we'll get some action. What do we do in the meantime?"

"We wait."

Tom poured a cup of coffee; he studied the ebony liquid in his cup. "I'm getting real sick of that answer."

"I know, but it's the only one I've got." The senator drank pulpy orange juice from a stemmed crystal glass and stood to go. " My son has a baseball game. How long you going to be in town?"

"I fly out Tuesday morning. I have work to do on Jade and Alan's house."

"You'll be here until then?"

"Yeah."

"If Bill or Ed find solid information, enough to open up an official investigation, I'll send you a telegram. How about the code words 'Hope springs eternal' if they find any hard evidence, and 'Let the dead bury their dead' if they leave Kenya without finding anything more."

"Sure, fine," Tom said. His eyes followed Mike Gall as the senator let himself out of the hotel room.

Tom walked to the bathroom, turned on steaming hot water and lathered his face. He didn't know what he had expected to find when he got to D.C. The Senator's report was actually encouraging, but Tom was sick and tired of not knowing. This waiting stuff was, as Sumer would say, "getting on his last nerve." I should just get on a plane and go over there, he thought.

"Hope springs eternal?" "Let the dead bury their dead"? Senator Gall was sure getting into this espionage stuff.

CHAPTER 32

Sumer and Samuel visited the panther nursery daily. After the cubs' 2-week birthday, the twins arrived at the hospital early one morning. The door was locked and Dr. Matthews did not answer when they knocked. They used a hidden key to unlock the door and let themselves into the hospital.

"I know Dr. Matthews doesn't want us going into the room with Zhora and her cubs, but what can it possibly hurt?" Sumer asked.

"The idea is to preserve wild things in the wild, not make pets out of them," answered Samuel.

"Yeah, I know, but I just can't help it. I want to pick those cuddly little fur balls up and hug them to pieces."

Samuel looked at the three small cubs. They had soft, golden-brown fur with dark-brown spots and a black semi-colon above each eye. Their sky-blue eyes were alert and full of mischief. They chewed on and tumbled over their mother. Zhora lay proudly and patiently enduring all the roughhousing as she twitched her black-tipped tail from side to side — an act that encouraged the cubs' antics. "Yeah, they're cute," he said but quickly added, "I think on this issue, we knuckle under to Dr. Matthew's rule."

"Well, I'm not! I'm going to play with the cubs. Zhora won't care." Sumer carefully unlatched the mesh door and started to ease herself inside. As she cleared the doorway, Zhora stood up, a move that sent Bud, Tiny and Sasha cartwheeling. A deep warning growl came from the mother panther's throat.

"On the other hand, maybe today is not such a good day to play with the cubs." Sumer backed out and closed the door.

As the door closed, Dr. Matthews came around the corner. "You two are up early. Want to feed Zhora?" He asked. "But remember, no touching the cubs."

"Remember, no touching the cubs," Sumer sing-songed, with sarcasm after the vet left to get the panther's food.

The twins placed bowls of food and water just inside the door and watched as Zhora meandered over to her breakfast with the cubs tumbling after her. Dr. Matthews saw the longing in Sumer's eyes. "I know it's tough not being able to play with the cubs, but it's for the best. Trust me, it is."

Sumer hated being told, "it's for the best," and she really despised the phrase, "trust me." She gave the vet a sour look, turned on her heel and stomped out the main door. After giving her kickstand a not so gentle kick, she climbed onto her bike and rode it toward the bay.

Peddling hard against the wind, she attempted to justify her anger at Dr. Matthews and his stupid rules. No matter how hard she tried, however, she couldn't squelch a persistent voice that bubbled up from within her. "You've been blessed to be involved in saving Zhora and her cubs. Don't discredit your work by disobeying Dr. Matthews and endangering the cubs' ability to survive in the wild. The reason you became involved in the first place was to help save endangered species," the voice admonished.

"OK! OK!" she finally conceded. "But I still don't have to like it." Continuing to push the bike pedals feverishly, she rode to the edge of town and into Everglades National Park.

Traveling down a dirt trail, she was soon surrounded by waving fields of saw grass dotted with water ponds and hardwood hammocks.

A great blue heron waded in a pond on one side of the narrow road. The black mask of a baby raccoon peeked out from under a tangle of bushes on the other side. Down the trail a ways was a large alligator, sunning itself. Sumer could feel her anger dissipate as she watched the blue heron jabbing its long beak at shiners in the pond. She tiptoed closer to the bushes to see the raccoon. It blinked at her, then chattered noisily and scrambled away. After giving the gator plenty of room, she continued down the narrow trail.

She laughed at the antics of a blue jay and stuck her nose in the middle of a bright yellow wildflower. She decided Dr. Matthews was right and steered her bike back toward the animal hospital.

I'll do what's best for the cubs, she thought. And I'll help instead of hinder the Doc. He's got a big job if he wants those panthers back in the wild by the time the cubs are 7-weeks old.

Great Blue Heron

Brown Pelicans

Egret

CHAPTER 33

For two weeks Duncan, Red and the construction crew cleaned up the damage inflicted on Ghost Orchid Hotel by the tornado — crumbling concrete, twisted metal, splintered lumber and fallen tree limbs. New building materials were ordered, but as Joe predicted, supplies were scarce. First priority for building materials had been given to emergency facilities, second to existing homes and third to existing churches and businesses. New construction came in line as a distant fourth.

"Well that's it," announced Red as he and his crewmembers threw the last scraps of debris into a large construction dumpster. "We are finally back to ground zero. Are you going with Joe to meet with Ted Rattowsky and ESF representatives tomorrow?"

"If Joe goes," Duncan answered. "Last I heard he wasn't even planning to show up. I guess I can understand his excitement about having the only hotel with a restaurant just feet away from the pounding surf, but is it worth rebuilding after every storm?"

"We won't have fence poles or mesh until Monday," Red said. "If it's OK with you, I'm going to tell the crew to take off until then. They've been putting in long hours since the storm."

"Sure. Maybe I can do some fishing with my children this weekend. Guess I'll go over to Joe's and tell him we're done with the cleanup and see if he's meeting with ESF and their lawyer in the morning. Want to come along?" Duncan asked.

"Thanks, but I'm meeting some of the guys for dinner. Gotta go home and clean up. See you first thing Monday," answered Red.

"You're not going to the meeting?"

"Hadn't planned on it. Let me know if Joe wants me there. See you." Red gave a two-finger salute and headed for his battered, green pickup.

Duncan ambled toward his red QuadTrax. He racked his brain for a creative argument to motivate Joe's attendance at the ESF meeting the following morning. Unable to think of any novel approach, he decided he should go whether Joe did or not. Then at least someone would know what the group had or hadn't come up with. Knowing the facts, in Duncan's mind, was always better than being ignorant.

As he pulled out his keypad to unlock the QuadTrax's door, he caught a flash of white to his left. He turned just as the great white bird floated to the ground several feet in front of him. It stood there, observing Duncan in a serene, authoritative manner.

"You must be Joe's white nemesis," Duncan said to the bird. "Can you tell me how to get him to that meeting tomorrow? Our reasons may be different, but you and I both want Ghost Orchid Hotel moved behind the sea-grass dunes. I can only guess at your reason," Duncan said and climbed into his truck. "Me? I'm strictly interested in my reputation as a contractor. Being prime contractor on a project that gets washed away by one storm after another is not good for my standing in the building community."

When Duncan emerged from the sand parking lot onto the main road, he called Joe from his cell phone and was glad to learn all his scheming was unnecessary. Joe already had decided to attend the meeting. "Just for the pleasure of telling Ted Rattowsky and his tree hugging bunch that no matter what they come up with, the answer is still no." Joe said.

He continued to blather on about how the animal sit-in and storm had caused delays, but he was certain all his misfortune was now behind him. He told Duncan he planned to be more stubborn than the bad luck that was following him. "The debris is cleared; the fence is going up Monday," he said. "I feel good! My luck is definitely changing and I haven't seen that witless white bird since the storm."

To tell Joe that his "witless white bird" had been on the construction site not more than 10 minutes ago would be cruel so Duncan let it pass.

The next morning, Ted and the foundation's representatives sat around a massive wooden table discussing the fine points of the proposal. They were into their second cup of coffee by the time the hotel owner and his lead contractor opened carved French doors and entered the large conference room.

"Glad you came," Ted greeted them, standing with his right hand outstretched toward Joe. "Would you like a cup of coffee or a Danish?"

Joe allowed Ted's outstretched hand to dangle unmet. "No! I already had breakfast and I have a hotel to build, so get to the point. You said you had an offer I couldn't refuse. Let's hear it, so I can refuse it and get on with my work."

"No need to be hostile," Ted replied. "We want to work out a solution that is good for you and the environment. ESF's goal is for the businessmen in this community to prosper and, at the same time, to protect our wildlife. We can work together and not be at one another's throats all the time. Would you care to sit down?"

"No, I'm a busy man. Let's just get on with it," Joe snapped.

"The Endangered Species Foundation has been the recipient of some very generous donations. The money was donated to help us protect the turtle and bird nesting areas that Ghost Orchid Hotel endangers. Because of these donations we are in a position to deliver a generous buyout package to you," Ted said, looking directly at Joe.

"Yeah, and just what do you consider to be, as you call it, generous?" Joe's cold blue eyes glared at Ted.

"We know you paid $2 million for your current property. We are prepared to offer you $2.5 million. Plus we are willing to negotiate a deal for you with Mr. Owens. He has a piece of beachfront property for sale that is larger and would fit your needs better than your current location," Ted continued. The attorney sat down to leaf through some papers on the table.

Holding up several sheets of legal-size paper, he continued. "I have a copy of the offer you made on Mr. Owens' property six months before you bought the property you now own. He was not interested in selling at that time, but has changed his mind. I think

266

we can negotiate a price of less than $3 million for you. I'm sure you know Mr. Owens' land parcel is a third larger than yours." He looked up from the papers in his hand. "Purchasing his beachfront property would allow you to put your current building design on the land behind the sea-grass sand dunes and retain the goodwill of the community."

"What you people don't seem to understand is that I don't stay up nights worrying about the goodwill of the community," Joe said, taking a hostile stance. "When Ghost Orchid Hotel is finished, it will have the only restaurant that is just feet from the waves and water. It will be the most popular place on the island. Your sea-grass dunes be hanged."

A woman with curly red hair and nails painted bright red threw up her hands in disgust. "You're one of the most bull-headed men I've ever met. Hasn't it occurred to you that being that close to the waves and water is what caused all the damage you're now cleaning up?"

"We're done. The lot's cleaned up, back to ground zero." Joe looked at Duncan for confirmation. At Duncan's nod he continued. "That storm was a fluke, a fluke, I tell you. Odds are another tornado won't hit that area for a hundred years, and I don't plan to live another hundred years." He gave the woman a smug, satisfied look.

Another member of the Rainbow Girls stood to be recognized. Her small stature and yellow dress made her look like a canary, yet her voice was bold and forceful. "You know what the Scriptures say about the foolish man who built his house upon the sand? The rain descended, the floods came and the winds blew. They all beat upon his house until it fell, and great was its fall."

"Foolish man? Ha! I'll be the richest man in this town in a few years," Joe said. Under his breath he added, "No one's ever going to call me a loser again." With that he turned and marched out of the room, slamming the door behind him.

Duncan made a feeble attempt to apologize for his employer's bad manners by saying, "I'll try to talk some sense into him, but he has been very hard-headed about Ghost Orchid Hotel remaining at

267

its current location. Furthermore, he's convinced that his bad luck is changing." Duncan's eyes swept the faces of the committee; he shrugged and followed Joe out the door.

"See you about 10 on Monday," Joe said, as Duncan dropped him at the condo. Joe shut the QuadTrax's door, whistling as he walked up the steps.

"Poor dolt, he really believes this thing is over and that he's won," Duncan muttered and shook his head.

269

270

CHAPTER 34

Duncan arrived on the construction site early Monday morning. The eastern sky announced the rising sun with shouts of color. Pink and purple stratus clouds streaked across the sapphire sky as a blazing semicircle of gold ascended from the horizon.

In the western sky a full moon, shining from a backdrop of blue velvet, stood sentry over the Gulf of Mexico. A salt air breeze blew inland. Duncan sat on a tree stump, coffee mug in hand, drinking in the beauty of the morning.

He brought the coffee cup to his lips and smelled its steam. He marveled at his surroundings.

Minutes later a whining motor broke the silence. Duncan turned to watch as a dusty maroon truck, loaded with metal fence poles, struggled to get through soft sand on the construction site. Its progress was slow.

He stood, straightened his shoulders and headed in the direction of the parking lot. Halfway between stump and truck, he felt a warm wind that sent shivers across his back and down the length of his spine.

Duncan looked up to see the great white bird. It soared like an enormous kite from one end of the lot to the other. The soft flow of air created by the bird's wide-reaching wings brought to mind a murmur that, as Duncan stood in the middle, sounded like a whisper. He struggled to hear the quiet words that floated on the breeze. But in the end, Duncan's heart wavered.

Distracted by a foreign voice that spoke loudly into his face, Duncan found himself doomed to the fate of the rest

"Yaha per kiss if Hukumut Hay? Ye Samaan Kaha Utarna Hay?" The truck driver asked.

"Y-a-t-il encore quelqu'un qui parle anglais?" Duncan, frustrated by an increasing number of non-English speaking tradesmen, looked at the trucker and signaled for him to unload the fence poles on the far side of the lot.

The driver backed his truck in the direction Duncan's finger pointed. Duncan heard the plink, plink, plink of metal fence poles as the man dropped them in a pile. Before the plinking stopped, he also heard car doors slam, alerting him to the fact that his construction workers had arrived.

"*Bonjour, Red. Le nettoyage is termine. Nous commencons a reconstruire ce matin.*" Duncan said in greeting to Red.

"*Warum Sprichst Du frazosisch? Versuchst Du Lustig Zu sein?*" Red replied, thinking this was no time for practical jokes.

"*Oi stratagos amie heyki. Pou arokomai?* " The new crew chief said and looked around confused.

"*Quel est votre probleme ce matin? Y-a-t-il encore quelqu'un qui parle anglais?*" Duncan said in disgust and motioned for everyone to get to work.

Several crewmembers stood in a circle with hands creating excited pantomimes. Their voices grew louder and louder. They weren't speaking English, and from the anger and frustration in their voices Duncan concluded none of them were even speaking the same language.

"*Dicunt non agnitio alienus verbus deligum,*" a young man whined in annoyance. He'd been told he didn't need foreign language experience for this job.

"*Amar zahar yanaf.*" A man of Hispanic descent said and pointed toward the great white bird.

Duncan walked into the middle of a group of workers. "*Quel est votre probleme, ce matin? Y-a-t-il encore quelqu'un qui parle anglais?*" His questions were answered with angry looks and raised voices, each speaking in a different tongue — none that he understood.

"*Ce est pire que de Tour de Babil.*" Duncan moved between two men, who were posturing with fists raised. "*Tout le monde sortir de ici! S'en aller! S'en aller!*" He waved wildly and yelled for everyone to clear out.

The baffled and irate workers heard Duncan's angry words and saw Duncan's violent gestures. Concluding he wanted them to leave, they hurled their hard hats into the dirt and stomped en mass back to parked cars and trucks.

Joe arrived on the construction site at 10 a.m. and found Duncan collapsed onto a stump. His face, streaked with dirt, was cradled in his hands; his hard hat had been pitched into a pile of brush.

"Que esta pasando aqui? Donde esta todo el mundo?" Joe asked, looking around for the construction workers.

"Quel est votre probleme ce matin? Y-a-t-il encore quelqu'un qui parle anglais?" Duncan said for the umpteenth time.

"Por que estas hablando frances? Yo quiero saber donde estan los obreros y porque no estan trabajando?" Joe asked, confusion and anger mounting.

Duncan stomped off toward his SUV.

A hint of panic rose in Joe's voice, as he followed Duncan and pelted his back with questions. Joe needed to understand where his crews had gone.

"Ils disent calchace mais je ne crois pas en la chance. C'est le grand oiseau blanc. Au revoir." Duncan spun around. He thrust his finger into the sky and pointed toward the great white bird. Without a word he climbed into his truck, slammed the door and gunned his motor. His tires dug into the ground and spewed sand in all directions as he drove away.

Dumbfounded, Joe returned to the job site. He approached Duncan's stump. He searched the distant beach and Gulf water for answers. Where were his crews? His foremen? And what was wrong with Duncan?

Joe remembered a little French from high school. He understood some of what Duncan said, especially the part about bad luck and the great white bird. But why was Duncan speaking French?

Scanning the horizon, Joe's eyes focused with uneasiness on a large white bird that floated to the ground in front of him. Yatzu's eyes burned like fire. His snow-white wings stretched wide to shield the nesting area from the hotel builder.

"DON'T YOU EVER GIVE UP?" Joe's shouted. "I wish I'd shot you when you were in that cypress tree!" Joe, blind with furry, ran to his pickup.

He screeched from his lot onto the roadway and raced from one coffee shop to another. When he saw Duncan's QuadTrax and Red's pickup next to the Purple Pelican, he abandoned his vehicle and stormed into the diner.

"Anyone want to tell me what happened at the construction site this morning?" Joe demanded, marching up to a booth filled with his employees.

"One minute, I'm sitting on a stump finishing my coffee; the next, I'm surrounded by people who don't speak English," Duncan answered.

"You weren't speaking English, either," Red piped up.

"What a bunch of crap! Talk sense and tell me what happened?" Joe demanded.

"It's the great white bird. He's bad luck to us," answered a Hispanic worker.

"White bird?"

"You know, your great white bird friend. He was there this morning. The big bugger flew so low I could of grabbed it," Duncan said, looking up from his steaming black coffee. "It drifted over me and I felt a warm wind that sent a chill from neck to belly. I could swear I heard a real quiet voice, coming out of the wind. Tried to understand the words, but they seemed to be just out of reach." Duncan shook his head sadly and with lowered eyes stared into his steaming cup.

"That white bird is not my friend!" Joe said, his voice low and menacing. "Red, Duncan is hearing voices and has obviously lost his mind. Can you tell me what happened?"

"It wasn't just Duncan. Nobody was speaking English. It was weird. I couldn't understand a word anyone said!" Red answered. "Reminded me of when I was a kid and my old man made me go to Sunday school. There was this Bible story…"

"I don't have time for Bible stories." Joe paced in front of the table – his hands clenched in front of him, his face turning red.

"I think you better take time." Red was uncharacteristically bold. "Like I was saying, there's this Bible story where these people, after the great flood, were supposed to spread out and fill the earth. They ignored God and all hung out in the same old place. One day they decided to build a tower to reach up to heaven, and God screwed up their plans real good."

"I know I'm going to regret this, but I'll bite. How did God screw up their plans?" Joe asked.

"That's what I'm trying to tell you," Red said. "He did it by messing with their language. The tower was never finished because no one understood what anyone else was saying. That tower was called the Tower of Babel. This morning was a Tower of Babel kind of morning!"

"You're either an idiot or a fool! That story doesn't have a white heron in it!" Joe said.

"Admit it, Joe! There's something strange going on here," Duncan said.

Joe suddenly recalled the Sunday he'd gone for a run on the beach and found his construction site littered with turtles and birds. What had Tom, that nosy has-been sheriff, told him? Something like, "I can't help but believe this time you're fighting against God himself."

Joe looked from Red to Duncan and back to Red. He spun around to face the whole group. "Did anyone else see this white bird?"

A tall lanky construction worker look down at Joe, then stared at his boots. "Looked like a great white heron, except for them eyes. Big honker. Eyes like fire. Just like Duncan here said, it meandered back and forth across the lot. Weren't no shadow but the wind from its wings got us all," he said.

Abdul Bahar Habib, Joe's Saudi Arabian financial partner, was demanding progress. The sheik didn't care about excuses. If he didn't get satisfaction soon, he'd send one of his goons to visit Joe. Maybe he'd even liberate a few of Joe's body parts. To make matters worse, the sheik was a superstitious man. If he heard reports that God was fighting against this project he'd demand his money back and Joe didn't have the money to give back.

Sweat beaded up and ran down Joe's forehead as he wrestled against the inevitable. In the end, the great white bird, the animal sit-in, the tornado and now this Tower of Babel thing, were too much for him to ignore.

"That cussed bird has won this round. I'll have to sell Abdul on the idea of a bigger site and tell him we need more money. I may have to retreat, but I won't go away. DO YOU HEAR ME? I WON'T GO AWAY!

"I should have killed that bugger six months ago when I had the chance!" He said, venom hissing from his voice. He took his cell phone from his breast pocket and demanded, "Duncan, you got Rattowsky's phone number?"

"Yeah, I've got his business card somewhere," Duncan said, digging into his wallet.

Joe, fighting to get his emotions under control, listened to the phone ring once, then twice, then a third time. "Ted? Joe Sorrow, here. Hey, sorry about my rudeness the other day," Joe lied. "I thought it over. Decided goodwill might be important after all. Offer on my land still good?"

"Sure."

"Three mil' is high for Owens' property, but I'd give him same as I get for my property."

"Mr. Owens is asking three million but I'll see what I can do. Mind telling me what changed your mind?"

"*C'est le grand oiseau blanc,*" Joe said, fighting to keep sarcasm out of his voice.

"What?"

"Let me know what Owens says."

"Sure thing, talk to you later." Ted hung up the phone.

"*C'est le grand oiseau blanc?*" Ted thought. He picked up the phone again and dialed Tom's number. "Hey, Tom, this is Ted Rattowsky. You speak a little French don't you?"

"Some. Why?"

"What does, *c'est le grand oiseau blanc,* mean?"

"It's the great white bird."

"What's the great white bird?" asked Ted, more confused than ever.

"That's how you translate *c'est le grand oiseau blanc*. It's the great white bird," repeated Tom.

"What did Joe mean by that?"

"What are you talking about, Ted?

"Joe Sorrow has finally agreed to sell his land. When I asked what changed his mind he said, '*C'est le grand oiseau blanc.*' Does that make sense to you?"

"Yes, I am ashamed to admit it does."

"What?"

"Nothing, it's just hard on my ego to realize my 12-year-old granddaughter has more faith than I do. Congratulations, Ted. Maybe they'll elect you mayor or something."

"Yeah, right. Talk to you later. I have to call Mr. Owens and negotiate a buy on that other beachfront property I promised Joe."

Tom clicked the receiver then dialed another number. "Max, guess what? It looks like the ESF finally convinced Joe Sorrow to move to another lot."

"It suspect it were the Lord, not that ESF outfit," Max said. "Never doubted God for a minute."

"No, I don't suppose you did," Tom said and hung up the phone.

Great White Heron

278

Great White Heron

CHAPTER 35

The early morning was dark and so thick with fog you could feel its clammy weight. With no moon, the blackness appeared complete except for three columns of yellow that spilled from a door and two windows of the animal hospital. Five shadowy figures moved in and out of this filmy light as they carried supplies to the vet's white cargo van. The last and heaviest item, a metal cage containing Zhora and her cubs, took the strength of all five to lug it. The panther cubs were 7 weeks old, and the cat family was being returned to its wilderness habitat.

Dr. Matthews wanted to reach the Big Cypress National Preserve by daybreak. He climbed into the driver's seat. Mariana and Tom hurried in beside him, and Sumer and Samuel scrambled in through the cargo door to settle on a bench seat in the back. The window defogger whirred to life as the young vet steered the vehicle down a two-lane, blacktop road headed for the reserve.

Samuel, not able to see past the fog, soon fell asleep. Sumer, blocking out the drone of adult conversation, mulled over the events of the past three months.

Once Nigel's wing completely healed the pelican flew into the Ten Thousand Islands and Sumer hadn't seen him since. She did see a pink spoonbill that may or may not have been Rondolus. Ospreys were common in the Everglades, and it was hard to tell which one, if any, was Olli. Sumer assumed that by now Trina had laid her eggs and returned to her normal life out in the Gulf of Mexico. She and Samuel had seen Mindy and Mother Manatee in their usual feeding places.

The Endangered Species Foundation completed its purchase of Sorrow's property and immediately began restoration. Sea-grass plantings covered the dunes on the lot. Behind that, newly planted trees, bushes and native groundcover battled the summer heat for survival. One wooden walkway, designed to allow limited observation of nesting areas, ran from the parking lot, past where an archæological team had set up camp, and all the way to the beach.

Archaeologists, down on hands and knees, sifted and dug with small hand tools through tannic muck and debris uncovered by the tornado. They hoped to find Calusa Indian artifacts, maybe even another Key Marco Cat.

Joe Sorrow was tearing down unwanted trees and clearing brush from his new lot. This time Ghost Orchid Hotel would be constructed behind the sea-grass sand dunes with wooden walkways the only means of getting over the dunes and onto the beach.

The white van left the main highway shortly before sun up. After that, the vehicle and its occupants bounced down one primitive road after another. Zhora yowled — jostling in the small cage made her crazy. Sumer stared out the window. In the distance, fog lay heavy across the cypress forest. Lighter wisps steamed up from water ponds and grasslands near the road. The van did a 90-degree turn and headed south on not much more than a dirt path. The human passengers as well as the caged panther family were thrown up, down and from side to side as the young vet tried his best to dodge ruts and dry water holes.

Samuel was no longer asleep, and even the cubs were complaining at a deafening roar. The road at last ended. "I guess Zhora and her cubs will have to make it on their own from here," Dr. Matthews said as he brought the cargo van to a bumpy halt.

"I'm sure they'd prefer it," Sumer commented more to herself than anyone else.

Muted streaks of sunlight began to penetrate holes in the distant forest. Tom, Mariana, Sumer and Samuel gladly tumbled out of the van. They listened to the vet's instructions.

"OK, everybody. Unload the cage, then back in the van before I release the cats."

"Why the fuss? Just turn them loose," Samuel said.

"She's a wild animal with cubs. I'm not taking any chances. OK?"

"I'm going up on top of the van's roof. Any problem with that?" Sumer asked. "Samuel you want to come? We can see better from up there."

"Help with the cage first." Tom said.

Sumer and Mariana took one corner of the cage while Dr. Matthews, Samuel and Tom took the other three. Four nervous panthers scuffled and yowled inside, making process difficult, but at last the cage sank securely to the ground. Sumer and Samuel scrambled to the van's roof while the three adults climbed inside.

Dr. Matthews pushed a remote button. The latch released and the cage door lurched open.

Zhora quit howling and poked her nose, followed by her ears and full head, out of the cage. She sniffed the wind and inhaled the cool damp air of freedom. Excited by their new environment, the cubs scrambled out and away from the cage. Sasha tumbled after a butterfly, Bud pursued a lizard into the brush and Tiny sat in the middle of the so-called road, marveling at her new world.

Zhora, biting gently at the nape of her cub's neck, deposited Sasha next to Tiny. She then yowled Bud back into the fold. Before they got a second chance to scatter, mother cat urged her fuzzy golden balls of energy to the far side of the road and aimed them toward the forest.

The twins sat on the roof. Tom, Mariana and Dr. Matthews got back out of the van and stood next to it. All five watched the mother cat prod and chase her cubs toward the distant cypress trees.

Where the heavy grass ended and the dense woods began, Zhora stopped. She sent a piercing yowl into the morning air as a final salute to her human friends, then gave her head a powerful shake and walked into the forest. The twins strained for a last glimpse of the panthers, but mother and cubs seemed to be swallowed up by the heavy fog and thick foliage.

A blanket of loneliness settled around Sumer and Samuel. As they sat silhouetted in the early morning light, a chill clung to them like the dampness that covered the forest. Sumer wrapped herself tightly in a too large sweater. "If this is so right, why do I feel so awful?" she asked her brother.

In the midst of this gloom, something beautiful suddenly landed in a nearby pond. Its feathers, white as snow, and eyes, like flames of fire, burned through the fog. It's arrival brought comfort and warmth to the humans and their warring emotions.

With the rising of the sun, enlightenment also dawned. The truth of the summer's adventure finally penetrated Samuel's heart. He, Sumer, Grandma Mariana, Grandpa Tom and Dr. Matthews had been an integral part of something much larger than themselves. They may never see Zhora and her cubs again but the panthers were alive and free. He and the others helped win at least one battle in the war against extinction. They had been a part of God's great tapestry of hope for his creation.

Unable to control the excitement in his voice, Samuel jumped down from the van and ran to Tom. "Grandpa, do you remember telling me, the day after Cory died, that even when life is hard, God is always good? I didn't believe you, but you were right." He jammed his fists deep into his pants pockets and thrust out his chest. After inhaling deeply of the bright morning air, he continued. "You were right; somehow and through it all, God is good."

Tom remembered that morning after the storm. He remembered Samuel sitting on the tree stump, and he remembered pouring out his heart to his grandson. A lump rose in Tom's throat. He nodded and laid a large sun-tanned arm across Samuel's shoulder.

"Everyone in the van," Dr. Matthews interrupted. "I've got surgery at 10 this morning." Sumer, Samuel, Mariana and Tom slowly hoisted the cage and themselves onto their seats and slammed the doors. The vet, after settling himself behind the wheel, deftly steered the vehicle toward Banyan City. Conversation, sparse at first, lapsed into silence until they reached the edge of town.

"Sumer, you and I still need to talk about where you found that pelican and why the panther let you and Samuel get so close to her. I don't have time just now, though." He rounded the last corner to their house and slowed the van to a stop. Sumer, Samuel, Mariana and Tom climbed out at the bottom of the driveway.

"We'll get together soon and have that discussion," the young vet said as he waved and sped down the road.

"Not if I can help it," Sumer said under her breath and raced with Samuel toward the house.

Tom and Mariana followed their grandchildren at a much slower pace. When they reached the porch steps, Sumer and Samuel came dashing toward them. "We need to go shopping for school clothes! Tuesday is the first day of school and I've nothing to wear," Sumer said breathlessly.

"Yeah, and I lost one of my good tennis shoes that day in the storm. My old ones are disgusting; they're too dirty for even you to get clean," Samuel said.

"We should probably go this afternoon. Come to think of it, shopping might be a good diversion for us all. How about it Tom, want to go to the mall?"

"No, thanks, I'd rather have a root canal." Tom's sarcasm was obvious. "Besides, I promised a certain young lady," he said winking at Sumer, "that I'd get started on her cedar chest this afternoon."

"Let him stay home," Sumer begged. "When we take him shopping, he's always in a hurry and nags us to buy the first thing we see, no matter how ugly it is."

She grabbed Tom's new straw hat, slammed it down on her head and imitated her grandfather's deep voice. "That looks good. Just get it so we can go home. Are we going to spend all day here? We've been here 15 minutes already. I'm getting sick. Is this place hot or what?" Everyone, including Tom, laughed at her flawless impersonation.

"OK. You win," Mariana conceded. "We'll let him stay home."

Before noon Mariana, Sumer and Samuel were driving down Highway 41 toward the mall. The twins' spirits were high at the prospect of starting the school year with new jeans, new shirts and new shoes. Mariana, determined not to let their purchases get out of hand, was nonetheless enjoying the animated chatter that drifted in ebbs and swells from the back seat.

Tom eager to start his new project made a list of supplies and steered Old Blue toward the lumber store. He purchased cedar, hardware and a new saw blade, needed for the chest then, whistling loudly, traveled down a back road toward home. He piled the wood inside his workshop and walked toward the back door of the house.

Nearing the west side of the house, he saw Sheriff Rainbird's car parked in the front driveway. Gongs of alarm rang through his head. "That blasted red convertible; I never should have gotten Mariana that car, she drives it like a manic!" he chastised himself as he ran up the steps.

The sheriff, with his hat pulled down over his face, rocked on the porch swing. "A-hem," Tom cleared his throat.

"Oh, sorry, had a late one last night," the sheriff sat up, blinking at Tom.

"What's up Cyril? You got a reason for your visit or you just needed a quiet place to take a nap?" Tom said, relaxing.

"I have a reason, but if you're going to get smart about it I'll go back to town," the sheriff said and dug into his pocket. "Got a telegram for you somewhere."

Tom turned white under his brown skin and Sheriff Rainbird, seeing his reaction to the yellow piece of paper, asked, "You want to sit down?"

"Guess I'd better." Tom sat down on the swing. The sheriff handed him the Western Union telegram.

Tom took out his pocketknife and opened the blade. His hands shook as he broke the seal on the envelope. He hesitated, took a deep breath, unfolded the telegram.

After reading the words on the yellowish paper he said. "It's from Senator Gall. It says 'Hope Springs Eternal.'"

The sheriff looked expectantly at Tom. "Want to tell me about it?"

Tom walked outside and sat on the porch step. "Thanks, Cyril, for bringing this out to the house. But I can't just yet. I'm not even sure I know what it means myself."

"We've been friends a long time. When the time is right you'll tell me. Anything I can do in the meantime?"

"No, but thanks."

Sheriff Rainbird walked to his car, slammed the door and was gone.

Tom sat on the steps. He stared at the spreading green lawn that dipped into the water of the Gulf of Mexico. He looked at everything and saw nothing. He had read books about Africa and its green coffee fields, its high mountains and vast brown plains, its lazy rivers that became angry and fast during the rainy season.

What information, buried deep inside the wilds of Africa, did Senator Gall's agent friends find that triggered this telegram?

Tom caught a white flash out of the corner of his right eye and turned. The great white bird landed in front of him, its sword like beak grasped a well-worn raffia palm hat with a brown leather band circling the crown. Yatzu placed the hat at Tom's feet.

Tom searched the bird's eyes. Light burned in them with such passion and power that he comprehended it only in part. Yet one thing Tom saw clearly as he stared into their depths, Jade and Alan were coming home.

Tears filled Tom's smoky-gray eyes. Not bothering to brush them away, he jumped up and, with arms held high, swayed to an inaudible song. He waved the raffia palm hat. He laughed. He whirled. He danced across the yard.

*"But they that wait upon the Lord
shall renew their strength; they shall
mount up with wings as eagles;
they shall run, and not be weary; and
they shall walk, and not faint."*
Isaiah 40:31 (KJV)

The Grace of our Lord Jesus Christ be with you all.

Photo Acknowledgements

Pictures for Beyond the Crooked Limb were taken with permission from the following:

Caribbean Gardens, The Zoo in Naples, FL

Joanie's Blue Crab Café, Ochopee, FL

Miami Sea Aquarium, Miami, FL

Port of the Islands Resort, Naples, FL

Smallwood Trading Post, Chokoloskee, FL

St. Mark's Episcopal Church, Marco Island, FL

Wooten's Everglades Airboat Tours, Everglades City, FL